FIRESTORM

Ann

FIRESTORM
An Ellora's Cave Publication, December 2004

Ellora's Cave Publishing, Inc.
1337 Commerce Drive
Stow, Ohio 44224

ISBN #1419951467
Other available formats: ISBN MS Reader (LIT), Adobe (PDF),
Rocketbook (RB), Mobipocket (PRC) & HTML

Cover art by: *Syneca*

Warning:

The following material contains graphic sexual content meant for mature readers. Firestorm has been rated *S-ensuous* by a minimum of three independent reviewers.

Ellora's Cave Publishing offers three levels of Romantica™ reading entertainment: S (S-ensuous), E (E-rotic), and X (X-treme).

S-ensuous love scenes are explicit and leave nothing to the imagination.

E-rotic love scenes are explicit, leave nothing to the imagination, and are high in volume per the overall word count. In addition, some E-rated titles might contain fantasy material that some readers find objectionable, such as bondage, submission, same sex encounters, forced seductions, etc. E-rated titles are the most graphic titles we carry; it is common, for instance, for an author to use words such as "fucking", "cock", "pussy", etc., within their work of literature.

X-treme titles differ from E-rated titles only in plot premise and storyline execution. Unlike E-rated titles, stories designated with the letter X tend to contain controversial subject matter not for the faint of heart.

Also by Author:

FIRESTORM

Ann Jacobs

Chapter One

Three deafening booms resounded, shattering the lazy silence of a sunny July day. The wooden floor shuddered beneath Kate Black's feet as she sprinted to the porch.

Except for blue-orange flames shooting obscenely from the drilling site at the bottom of the hill, an acrid wall of darkness obscured the source of the noise.

Coughing, she went back inside and stared out a window at the flaming sky. What was going on down at the derrick?

Looking away from the conflagration, she rooted through a drawer. Finally. She found the business card the drilling company man had left with her and reached for the phone.

* * * * *

Jake Green slammed on the brakes and sprang out of his car. Braced to find broken bodies in the aftermath of the explosion, he let out his breath when he saw Skip Ward and the rest of the drilling crew pumping foam on a burning generator.

"What the hell happened?" he yelled over the hissing of the pumps.

Skip let go of the hose he'd been steadying and mopped a filthy palm across his brow. "Jake. You picked a hell of a time to get here. Generator decided to blow up. Looks like we'll get the fire under control before it spreads to the fuel tanks, though."

"How can I help?" The fierce heat from the fire, on top of a temperature already climbing toward triple digits, had sweat dripping off Jake's brow.

"Go call the sheriff. This was no accident. That damn generator was less than a year old." Skip cast a disgusted look at the twisted heap of steel still smoldering under a blanket of fire extinguishing foam.

"All right."

As soon as he stepped inside the battered trailer, Jake heard the phone ring.

"Ward Drilling," he snapped, annoyed that he'd have to deal with this call before contacting the sheriff.

The woman on the other end of the line sounded damn near hysterical. Her name was Kate Black, which was about all he managed to decipher between her sobs. Who the hell? Then Jake remembered. She was the woman who owned this southeast Mississippi land.

He tried to calm her. "No, no one was hurt. No, ma'am, the fire's not going to spread to your house."

"Will you keep on drilling?"

Typical woman, fretting about where her next season's wardrobe was coming from. "Nothing's going to stop us from drilling this well. Look, Ms. Black, would you mind getting off the phone so I can call the sheriff?"

"You're certain it's safe to stay here?" Her voice sounded calmer now. "Should I come down to your office?"

"Don't be an idiot. Calm down and stay where you are. It isn't as though we have an oil well fire down here. All that's burning is a generator, and the fire's under control." He hung up none too gently and dialed nine-one-one.

* * * * *

"It's sabotage. No doubt about it."

Jake pried off his boots and rested his feet on a cluttered table. "This is the fourth incident at our oilfields in less than a month."

Skip glanced up from the sink, his hair dripping wet but his face no longer coated with blackened grease. "Who's doing this to y'all, and why?"

"Obviously someone who wants to drive GreenTex straight into bankruptcy."

"Another independent oil company?"

"Could be. The bastards haven't left us a hell of a lot of clues." Jake met Skip's sober gaze. "Dale Larson died last week in the explosion at our field outside Lubbock. Three of our most productive wells there are out of commission for God only knows how long. Now your generator blows up."

"Yeah."

"It's almost as if the bastards knew the security team wouldn't get here until tomorrow."

Skip shrugged. "Hell, it's almost as though they knew exactly when you'd be driving onto the scene so they could greet you with a big bang."

"Can the graveyard humor," Jake snapped. But he mentally replayed his friend's offhand comment.

Had Skip just hit onto something important? "Who knew I was coming?" he asked.

"No one here, except me. What about at GreenTex?"

"Dad. Scott. Probably their secretaries and a handful of others. The security chief."

No one Jake didn't trust implicitly.

But then he'd trusted Alice, only to have come home from a quick trip to the company's Venezuelan fields to learn she'd destroyed his child and betrayed him with a long-time business rival.

"You back to stay?"

Jake shrugged. In the week since he'd flown halfway around the world to see firsthand the damage some madman was doing to GreenTex Petroleum's domestic oilfields, he hadn't had time to think about the state of his own self-imposed exile. "I'll be around until whoever's doing this is behind bars. You mind me barging in here?"

"We can always use another pair of eyes, not to mention a good strong back." Skip's grin gave Jake a stronger feeling of welcome than his words. "Hell of a thing about Dale," he said, his expression sobering.

"Best foreman I ever worked with." Good-hearted, dirty talking Dale Larson, dead at forty-five because some son-of-a-bitch wanted GreenTex Petroleum out of business.

Jake would never get used to Dale not being there, yelling orders and making things happen in the GreenTex oil fields where he'd lived and died. "Who, damn it? Who has it in for us?"

"I don't know, Jake. I'm gonna bring this well in for you, though. Soon. You certain no one else knew exactly when you would be getting here?"

"Hell, *no one* knew exactly when I was going to get here. Not even me. I'd planned to leave Houston about the time the explosion happened. I couldn't sleep, though, so I took off about two in the morning and drove straight through. Only times I stopped were for gas—and breakfast, at a little café about fifty miles south of here."

"You didn't call anybody from your car?"

Jake shook his head. "Didn't even pick up the cell phone."

Spending eighteen months at remote oilfields in the Saudi Arabian desert had cured him of the habit of talking while he drove. He'd damn near jumped out of his skin a week ago when the car phone had beeped while he drove his Porsche out of the GreenTex hangar at Houston's Hobby Airport. "You don't suppose someone at the café—"

"You saw somebody?"

"No one I knew." But Jake remembered the creepy feeling he'd had, that somebody had been watching him while he ate. He'd wondered why, because he didn't look all that different from the other men in the dilapidated café.

Sure, his jeans and pearl-snapped chambray shirt had seen less wear than some. And his olive skin, baked from spending months under the blistering desert sun, was dark enough to make the locals stop and stare, take notice there was a stranger among them. But he didn't think he'd drawn much attention from the rest of the customers.

Hell, he hadn't even been the only high roller in the place. Jake pictured a pot-bellied, ruddy man who'd lumbered out of a mud-spattered, brand-new Lincoln, his Tony Lama boots caked with damp red clay.

"I didn't talk to anybody. Wait, I told the waitress I was coming here when she asked where I was headed."

"Doubt some waitress in a country café would be tied up with these bastards. Don't worry. They'll slip up. And when they do, you'll catch them." Skip scratched his chest through a filthy, oil-soaked T-shirt. "I need a shower."

"Go on, clean up. I'm going outside for a while."

Stopping at the base of the derrick, Jake gave his thoughts free rein. He would find the saboteurs—and he wouldn't go back and hide in GreenTex's Saudi oilfields when this was over.

This was home. He hadn't run from the smell of fresh air and raw petroleum, or from the American countryside with its piney woods and mesquite forests. And he didn't want to miss the rush he always got when the drillers brought in another GreenTex gusher.

What he had run from was betrayal. And since there was no way in hell he'd give another woman the power to hurt him the way Alice had done, he had no need to hide and lick his wounds.

"Goddamn you," he muttered, both to whoever was trying to destroy GreenTex and to his faithless ex-wife.

* * * * *

From the top of the hill, Kate stared down at the piece of ground where the drillers were so certain they would find oil.

The hour before nightfall was Kate's favorite time of day. She liked watching the skeletal derrick sparkling eerily, its fluorescent lights mingling with reflected rays from the setting sun.

A man strode out of the trailer and stood alone at the base of the derrick. A stranger, she decided, knowing that she'd remember if she'd ever seen him before. He made her pulse race, her breathing turn ragged.

The man looked like a modern Adonis, one with the tensile strength and eerie beauty of the drilling rig beside him. The waning sun highlighted his wavy dark hair and emphasized the power of long lean legs encased in worn denim and dusty leather. Shadows obscured his face and blurred her view of his torso.

From a distance, he epitomized tough, muscled masculinity. The macho kind of man who had always put her off and sent her running to the safety of Pop's arms—or David's, until he'd made her choose between him and taking care of her father.

Angry with herself, Kate choked back her tears.

She had no reason to cry. No reason at all.

She listened to the roar of the huge drilling engine and the pounding of metal deep down in the rocky earth. She pictured herself alone but for that oil well, her loneliness appeased by staring at rough, hard men like him. Imagined her emptiness filled by fantasizing that he was ramming into her the way that drill was pounding the moist clay soil of her homeland.

A shudder wracked her body. Moisture pooled between her legs, tears shed for want of —

Him?

Until he looked up and saw her, she couldn't stop staring at him. Even then, it took her a minute to turn and look toward the distant woods.

The sexual energy that suffused her body when she first saw him stayed as darkness began to settle, bringing with it a cooling breeze. Vivid in her mind was a picture of the man, as intimidating as the massive machines he had mastered, as magnificent as the land from which he would coax the magic stuff called oil.

Deep inside, she sensed that if she touched him, sparks would fly.

Chapter Two

"Ms. Black?"

The voice was deep, seductive, with just a touch of a Texas twang. A cultured voice, not the harsh drawl she'd expected to hear from an oil rig roughneck. A voice tinged with sarcasm, not unlike the voice that had rudely dismissed her fears when she called down to the rig this morning after the explosion.

That voice made Kate's breasts tingle and fueled the hunger deep inside her. A tiny rivulet of moisture made its way down her thigh, the tear a silent plea to free the sensual woman buried inside.

"Yes."

Suddenly she was afraid to face the stranger who had obviously watched her staring at him. He surely would see the need in her eyes, the heat that scalded her cheeks.

But Kate had to face him. "I was looking to see if the men had gone back to drilling," she said. With luck he'd believe she had been staring at the well, not him.

"They have." His sensual lips curled into what could have been a hint of a grin or a mocking smile.

Kate guessed it was the latter. "My first name is Kate," she said, covering her discomfort with the cloak of polite conversation.

"Jake Green. GreenTex Petroleum. I talked to you when you called down to the rig this morning. Look, Ms. Black, we're as anxious as you to bring in a gusher down there. And Skip Ward's the best driller around. You don't need to worry, and you don't need to look over our shoulders. There's oil under that piece of ground, and we'll find it."

"Why are you here?" Mr. Ward had said GreenTex hired his company to drill the well. He'd also told her GreenTex, the large independent oil company that owned the leases on her land, wouldn't be directly involved with the wildcatting operation until the well came in.

"Because someone's trying to sabotage this operation."

"Sabotage?" The word conjured up visions of shadowy men from warring third world countries, political intrigue, and senseless death and destruction. Things like that didn't happen in rural Mississippi, or so Kate thought.

"Yeah, sabotage. As in exploding generators and broken drills," Jake said, his lips curling in a half-smile that didn't reach eyes almost black but for intriguing glints of gold. "As in delays we can't afford. Delays that might make you wait a little while to reap the rewards from that well."

There it was again, that implication that he considered her interest in the well to be singularly self-serving. "You said something like that this morning. What makes you think I can hardly wait to become rich?"

"Honey, you're a woman." He looked her over from head to toe, very slowly, apparently taking in every feminine curve.

It felt to Kate as if he were stripping her naked with his dark, brooding eyes.

"And you're a chauvinist." Kate shouldn't care, but she didn't like this man seeing her as some grasping woman on a quest for wealth. For that matter, she didn't care much for getting wetter between her legs just because he'd seared her with his gaze.

"Sorry, I've got too much on my plate right now to bother with polite subterfuge. You want royalties. I want money gushing in to GreenTex coffers from this well, not pouring out to the drillers and the security people who'll be arriving tomorrow. No need in prettying up facts. Do you have any idea who might be causing us this trouble?"

"No."

Jake ran a hand through sable-colored hair that looked as though it could use a trim. How would the different textures, soft on top where it was longer and crisp around the ears and against the tanned skin of his neck, feel against her fingers?

She itched to find out, to smooth back the wayward strands the hot wind had blown onto his sweaty brow. But she shook off that urge. Jake Green apparently had a chip on his shoulder so big it would knock her for a loop if she tried to slip beneath his prickly defenses.

"There have been other incidents at GreenTex wells. One man is dead. I have no reason to believe that whoever is doing this would target you, but I want you to be careful," he told her, his expression solemn. "Let me know if you see anything suspicious."

"I will."

His expression softened, and he reached out and touched her hand. "Everything's going to be all right, Ms. Black," he told her. Then, as if he'd felt the same jolt of awareness that coursed through her veins, he snatched back his hand, turned, and strode down the hill.

For a long time Kate stood there, warmth radiating from the fingers he'd touched and melting the chill his warning had caused.

She'd never felt so instantly attracted to a man before—any man, let alone a man who was miles out of her league.

She had the feeling Jake Green would eat her alive.

Kate laughed. She hadn't even been able to hold gentle, easygoing David, the only time she'd defied him and done what she had known was right.

She must be crazy, visualizing herself and this brooding scion of Texan oil royalty tangled up together in her sheets, skin to sweaty skin.

And fantasizing about the two of them in terms of romance, candlelight, and roses had to mean she was certifiable.

* * * * *

Soft music. Soft, naked skin pale under his hands. The smell of sex and some flowery perfume tickling his nose. The glow of flickering candlelight casting shadows on a face more intriguing than classically beautiful.

Kate Black's face.

The following morning Jake slammed his fist onto the desk, cursing at the stinging pain. He had better things to do than fantasize that the woman who owned this land was as hot for him as his cock was hard and aching for her.

Damn it, why was he thinking about her anyhow? And why in hell had the thought of her stuck him with a raging hard-on?

Adjusting his jeans, he tried to tell himself his condition was a natural reaction to too many months spent without a woman. Hell, Kate wasn't even his type.

He'd always gone for willowy blondes with long legs, big boobs, and slender hips. Not brunettes so tiny that he'd have to bend to rest his chin on top of their tousled curls. Or women so petite that the only way their bodies would fit together was fucking. With him standing up, holding her while she locked her arms around his neck and her slender legs around his waist.

They'd fit, too, if he took her from behind, lifting her cute little ass to keep her pussy lined up with his cock.

More blood rushed to Jake's groin when he imagined him and Kate on a bed, belly to belly, his cock buried balls-deep inside her while their tangled arms and legs held their bodies as close together as a man and woman could get.

What the hell was wrong with him? Here he was, up to his eyeballs in trying to stop this sabotage before it destroyed GreenTex, and drooling over a woman he didn't know and who by all that was holy shouldn't even appeal to him.

Pity Alice hadn't killed his libido along with his faith in women. If she had, he wouldn't be nursing this painful hard-on that wouldn't seem to go away.

Maybe after they caught the bastards bent on destroying the company his grandfather founded sixty-five years ago, Jake would stick around awhile and scratch the itch Kate Black had so inconveniently awakened. If he didn't come to his senses before then.

He picked up a core sample and tossed it between his hands.

Hell, maybe it was time he got married again, this time not for love but for the family his old man kept bugging him to start. The grandchild he never had the heart to tell his father Alice had killed before it had a chance to live.

Pounding boots on the wooden steps to the trailer distracted him.

"Jake?"

"Yeah, Skip?"

"Come on outside and take a look. If I'm not dead wrong, we're gonna have a gusher on our hands sooner than we thought."

* * * * *

"What's all that racket now, Katherine?"

Whatever it was, Kate was grateful for the respite it offered from the woman's diatribe about how the noise from the drill kept her neighbors from enjoying church services that were being held less than a mile down the road. "It sounds like men yelling, Ms. Gladys. And something rumbling up from deep down in the ground."

From head to toe, Gladys Cahill was at her Sunday best. Her blue-tinged hair was arranged in tight curls and waves, and the pale gray shirtwaist dress she had on fairly crackled with starch. Kate didn't know how she did it, but the woman's low-heeled walking shoes of white patent leather looked pristine — even though she'd trekked from her car across Kate's dusty gravel driveway.

Ms. Cahill had always known how to intimidate her. Kate shifted her weight from one foot to the other, painfully aware of the old shorts and T-shirt she'd put on to scrub her kitchen floor.

"A body'd think that oil company would give those boys a rest, let 'em praise the Lord one day a week anyway. What are they, a bunch o' heathens?"

Kate ignored the not so subtle barb. "I don't know. But I don't have any control over when they work."

"You don't? Well, you should make 'em stop. And you might even show enough respect toward your neighbors to put on some decent clothes on Sunday." Ms. Cahill eyed Kate as if she expected her to grow horns.

Damn it. Just once, Kate would like to tell the woman exactly what she thought of her meddling and harping, and her sugarcoated reminders that the Blacks had never really belonged in Groveland.

She swallowed the retort she itched to make. Ms. Cahill had been her fifth grade teacher. Being rude to the woman would go against all Pop had taught her. Deliberately, she pasted a smile on her face and spoke in a conciliatory tone.

"I told you, Ms. Gladys. When I leased the land, I gave the oil company the right to do their drilling whenever they feel like it. They've been here for nearly two months now, though, and this is the first time they've worked on a weekend. Maybe they're at a point where they have to keep going."

"Well, I'll never." Ms. Cahill's face turned an angry red, but her flat, slow drawl stayed the same. Kate had never heard the woman raise her voice, in all the years she'd known her.

"I'm sorry. They should finish the drilling soon."

"I hope so. We've got no use for heathens coming here, corrupting our children and our town." She paused, then continued her diatribe.

Kate stood silently, trying to ignore the woman's soft-spoken rant. Instead of focusing on Ms. Cahill's venomous expression, she stared over the short, squat lady's shoulder toward the noisy drilling site.

Suddenly the drone of the engines stopped, and a deep rumbling noise drowned out the men's raucous shouts. Jake Green was sprinting her way. As he got closer, she saw he was covered with black, slimy stuff from head to toe.

"Excuse me, ma'am," she told Ms. Cahill as politely as she could manage. "Somebody's coming up here from the well now."

"We've got us a gusher, honey, and it's a big one!" he yelled from halfway down the hill.

Before she could gather her wits, Jake leapt onto her porch. He lifted her high in the air, squeezing out her breath as he twirled her around in circles.

Her second to last conscious thought was that he was getting her positively filthy. Her last was that Gladys Cahill looked like a wide-mouth bass before she stormed away to her car, what with her vacant stare and her gaping jaw.

Then Jake kissed her, and Kate couldn't think at all.

Dazed, she watched Ms. Gladys's car wind down her driveway to the road.

She saw Jake kiss me. And what a kiss it was! She could still feel it, clear down to her toes.

Knowing Ms. Gladys would pass on what she had seen with malicious glee, Kate wondered how long it would be until everybody in Calder County would know she'd let a filthy roughneck maul her—and, incidentally, that her oil well had come in.

Still tingling from his kiss, she turned on Jake. "Why did you do that?"

"Hell, I don't know. To celebrate that gusher down the hill, maybe? Seemed like the thing to do."

His dark eyes glittered with apparent amusement, and when he shrugged she noticed the way the muscles in his shoulders and chest rippled beneath the oil-soaked T-shirt that was plastered to his big frame like a second skin.

"Oh." Emotions warred inside Kate. Embarrassment. Outrage. Desire for this enigma of a man to mold her to his hard, sinewy body and make her feel instead of think. "Pretty soon everybody in the county will say I'm having illicit relationships with all the men on the drilling crew."

"It was just a kiss, honey. And there's just one of me. Don't tell me no one's ever kissed you before." His whole face lit up when he grinned. "Besides, why should you care what a bunch of old busybodies think? Come on down the hill and get a good look at your new moneymaking machine."

"When?"

"Any time. Look, I've got to get back down there. See you," he told her, loping off as if that incredible kiss meant no more than a handshake.

It probably hadn't, to him.

As she tidied up her kitchen, killing time so she wouldn't appear too eager, Kate tried to banish the sweet sensation of strong arms surrounding her and amazingly soft lips caressing hers — but Jake stayed there, his mark indelible on her mind.

* * * * *

She'd felt almost as light as his seven-year-old niece when he'd lifted her in his arms, and she'd turned her face to his in apparent invitation before he gave in and tasted lips as soft as velvet. She smelled of spring flowers and tasted like sugared coffee. The feel of her hard little nipples boring into his chest had fueled yet another hard-on that wouldn't go away.

Why the hell hadn't he hauled her inside her antique southern farmhouse and fucked her 'til she screamed for mercy?

No. Why hadn't he taken that sweet morsel of a woman and loved her until they both got their fill?

Damn it, no way could her sweetness be real.

Jake stared out the trailer window, not ready to go outside and face the woman who was so inexplicably driving him mad.

She was working her wiles on Skip, her eyes sparkling with what he supposed was pure feminine greed. If his guess was right, she was already calculating what she'd do with the royalties that would soon be pouring into her bank account.

Assuming they caught the saboteurs before GreenTex went belly-up.

He took in her outfit of denim shorts and T-shirt — clothes Alice would have died before putting on her sleek, conniving body. Then he shrugged off a bit of sympathy that tried to rise in him for the hard times Kate must have endured. He'd learned the hard way that excusing women for their selfish ways got him torn apart inside.

Jake was up and through the door before his brain could persuade his cock that seeing Kate up close again was not a good idea. Making his way around a truck full of mud, he stopped just shy of the platform where Skip was standing with her and looked around.

Good, the armed security guards he'd hired surrounded the well site as they'd been instructed.

"I'd love to," he heard her say as he took the stairs two at a time.

"Jake. About time you got yourself out of that trailer. From the way you're acting, I gotta think you see a gusher like this one damn near every day. Sorry, Kate."

"I had to make some calls." The Old Man. Scott. Business calls, no matter that they were to his father and brother-in-law. Neither conversation had given him the rush he'd gotten earlier when he told Kate about the well. That had been business, too, but it had seemed damn personal.

"Is Skip showing you how they control the gusher?" he asked, blood speeding to his groin when he looked into her aqua eyes.

She nodded. "It's fascinating."

She turned him on.

If Alice hadn't taught him so well, Jake would believe this tiny sprite really gave a damn about how an oil well worked. "It is, isn't it? Skip, how's the pressure down there?"

"Just fine. I'm going to pump another couple truckloads or so of mud down the hole to make certain she doesn't blow again. Don't want to waste perfectly good crude. Kate here said she'd love to go with us later to celebrate. Says she knows a neat little bar in Hattiesburg. Why don't you clean up and take her in that fancy car of yours? Max and I will come along later in one of the trucks."

Jake could have throttled his friend—or hugged him, depending on whether he was listening to his brain or his cock. "Sure. Okay with you?" he asked Kate, telling himself that her answer didn't matter one way or the other.

She smiled again, that soft, sweet smile that could take a less wary man to his knees. "That's fine. I'd better get home and clean up," she said, brushing at a spot of mud that had somehow made its way to her satin-smooth thigh.

"I'll pick you up." Jake hoped she didn't notice the bulge in his jeans—or the tremor he detected in his voice that made him sound like a lovesick teenager.

"Want to bring me up to date on what's going on down there?" he asked Skip after Kate was gone, gesturing toward the well that would be Black-GreenTex Number One.

"Max and Harry just got back with two more truckloads of mud, and they'll go for more as soon as we pump out the trucks."

"How much pressure's she giving us?" As always when a new well came in, Jake worried about a blowout. "It's been a long time since I saw one blow as high as this one."

"Fifteen, sixteen thousand pounds. My guess is, we're gonna have to pump two, maybe three more truckloads of mud down the shaft to keep her stable. Did you arrange with the pipeline to hook us up?"

"They'll be here Wednesday. Will you be ready?"

The crew would be hard pressed to control the gusher, let alone worry about setting pipe and gas-lifting equipment. Jake hoped the around-the-clock presence of a couple of dozen roughnecks as well as armed security guards would discourage their saboteurs.

"Yeah, unless something goes haywire. Once we pump the rest of the mud on down, she should hold 'til we can tie her in to the pipeline and let her rip." Skip smiled broadly, his toothy grin reminding Jake of an old-time vaudevillian in black-face makeup. "You decide yet which well we're gonna drill next?"

Jake shook his head. "I want to take new soundings. Your hunch was right about this one, but you came too close for comfort. Five hundred feet more and we'd have had to stop drilling."

"Yeah. Don't think I didn't notice that permit was only good for ten thousand feet. I've been sweating it, too. We gonna go for another deep well, or is the next one gonna be shallow?"

"Shallow. Dad and Scott tell me GreenTex needs cash now more than it will, five years down the road. When you're ready, I'll show you the new spots I've picked. Right now, concentrate on getting this baby flowing into the pipeline."

"Okay by me. Want a beer?" Skip asked, his filthy hand already digging into the washtub full of ice that Jake had watched Max unload from his truck a few minutes ago.

"No thanks. Better not when I'm gonna be driving, especially since you volunteered me to take Groveland, Mississippi's newest future millionaire out to celebrate."

"Hey, I thought you could use a little contact with the gentler sex after spending all that time alone in the Saudi desert."

Jake grinned. "Who's to say I didn't find myself a sexy little houri over there? A whole goddamn harem full of them, for that matter?"

"Me."

Jake sobered when he took in Skip's serious expression. "You're right. There hasn't been anybody important since Alice and I split up." And there hadn't been any woman at all for a long time. His cock had been making that fact abundantly clear since he'd laid eyes on Kate Black.

Skip laughed. "Well, you look ready, my friend. Go on, lighten up a bit. I know what Alice did bummed you out, but not every woman's like her."

Not exactly, maybe. But after what he had been through, Jake wasn't anxious to take a chance that he'd be any better at choosing a mate the second time around.

"You may be right," he muttered before changing the subject. "The security guys look as though they can handle anybody that might have an idea of torching this baby. Want to let the whole crew come?"

"Nah. Just Max and me. We've been having a few drinks after bringing in a gusher ever since our first one ten years ago. And we can disappear fast if it looks as if you're gonna score with little Kate."

"Not likely. Hey, make sure your guys know to lay off that beer until they finish their shifts. We don't need anybody losing a hand or foot because they got boozed up and then tried to operate the machinery. And tell your foreman to make damn sure the security guys stay stone-cold sober."

"You got it. Watch out on the highway. Max said the state highway patrol's thicker than thieves out there. You better hurry. Ms. Black'll be wondering if you fell into the well." Skip downed the rest of his beer and turned to direct the men who were adding mud to the circulating pumps.

* * * * *

He'd said he'd come get her in two hours.

Still damp from her bath, Kate checked the time. Then she turned back to her closet and searched for something to wear. Why she should care what Jake Green thought of her attire, she didn't know. But it mattered. Sighing, she selected a dress she'd bought before her college graduation.

She hadn't worn it since she came back home. Longer than that. The last night she'd had it on was when David proposed.

Kate set the floral print sundress onto her bed. Funny. For the first time, thinking of her broken engagement hadn't made her want to cry.

Without trying, Jake had managed to shove David to the far corners of Kate's mind.

The idea of going out with Jake scared her stiff—but it excited her too. Despite her doubts, she wanted to experience the heady awareness he generated in her.

Awareness that was sexual. Carnal. Different from the quiet, comfortable kind of togetherness she'd enjoyed with David.

Once Kate had believed their kind of love would last a lifetime. David had been a steady anchor.

Jake was a tempest, a whirling dervish who would touch her briefly and leave destruction in his wake.

She shook off her misgivings. Today, she would celebrate life. While arrogant, earthy Jake Green wasn't the kind of man she'd dreamed of, he certainly was a man. All man. The most delectable specimen of manhood she'd ever seen.

Recalling how the skin-tight, filthy Levis and oil-soaked T-shirt emphasized every hard-honed muscle in his long, lean body, she touched her lips. Even now she felt the heated imprint of his hard, demanding mouth.

Damn. She'd never be ready on time.

Kate snatched up clean underwear and began to dress. Before she was done, she heard someone knock. She was gasping for breath by the time she snatched open the door and greeted Jake with a nervous smile.

"Come on in. I'll be just a minute."

He looked good enough to eat, freshly scrubbed and shaved. Designer jeans and a pale yellow polo shirt did little to mitigate the aura of danger she'd noticed about him from the first. "You look nice," she added as she led him inside.

"Yeah. Folks say I clean up pretty good." His hard but sensual lips curved in a devastating smile. "So do you, honey."

Her cheeks grew warm at his offhand compliment. "You can wait here," she told him, gesturing toward the old-fashioned parlor.

"No rush."

The echo of Jake's deep, smooth drawl stayed with her as she slipped her feet into high-heeled white sandals. In less than two minutes, she was back downstairs and ushering Jake out the door. She noted his casual good manners when he held the door of a dusty black Porsche open so she could slide onto its soft leather seat.

"Sorry about the car. There's no place around here to get it washed," he muttered. Then he closed her door and walked around to the driver's side.

A tingly sort of fear washed over Kate as she watched Jake fold his big body into the low-slung car. But the trepidation wasn't nearly as strong as her need to go for it. Enjoy every sensation she was confident he could hone to fever pitch. His hands were rough, a working man's hands, hands that moved steadily when he fit the key into the ignition and reached to grasp the gearshift knob beside her thigh.

Would he move his hand a fraction of an inch and touch her? She wished he would.

More than that, she wished she were the sort of woman who'd dare to edge her leg closer until it brushed against the callused pads of his long fingers. Or reach over boldly and stroke the soft denim that covered his rock-hard thigh.

Kate's nipples tingled. Dampness gathered between her thighs. She squirmed against the glove-soft leather seat.

Sexuality positively oozed from every pore of Jake's work-hardened body, each nuance of expression on his ruggedly handsome face. While he scared her silly, he made her ache in ways she'd never ached before.

"You're off in another world, honey," he said, startling her with his astute observation when he took a corner smoothly and guided the car out onto old Highway Forty-Nine. "Thinking about what you're going to do with those royalty checks we're gonna start sending you soon?"

"No. I was thinking about you." About his big callused hands and how they'd feel on her naked skin. About whether his muscular body would feel rough or smooth against her own softer curves. Of course she'd never confess her fantasies to him.

"Me? What about me?" Jake pulled out into the left lane and accelerated to pass a coughing old pickup truck. With a graceful move, he inserted a CD in the slot and adjusted the volume.

Soft instrumental music surrounded them, and surprised her since she'd braced herself to endure the loud lament of some country and western singer.

Kate wanted to peel away the layers, get beyond her fantasies to the real Jake Green. "I was thinking I don't know you. Where you're from. What it is you do." She paused, recalling something else he'd said. "For instance, I have no idea why you don't like women very well. Why you seem to think we're all heartless gold-diggers."

"I learned the hard way." Jake looked over at her and grinned. "Don't get me wrong, honey. I like women just fine. I'm just not about to let one of you get to me again."

A muscle twitched under the smooth-shaven, bronzed skin of his jaw, and Kate wondered what or who had hurt him and hardened his heart. "Okay. Tell me a little about yourself."

He glanced over and smiled, but the smile didn't quite reach his eyes. He had the longest lashes she'd ever seen on a man. Lashes she'd die for. For a minute Kate thought he was going to clam up.

Then he spoke. "I've lived in Houston all my life, but I spend most of my time on drilling sites. I've just come back from Saudi Arabia. Before that, I was in West Texas for a few months. I've spent time in oilfields in Kuwait, Venezuela, and offshore in the Gulf. I like being where the action is. If I didn't, I'd take my old man up on his standing offer of a vice presidency and a cushy office back home."

"What exactly is it that you do?"

"Me, personally?"

"Yes."

"I'm in charge of GreenTex's field operations. I decide where to drill, how deep to go, when we need to bail out of a dry hole. I analyze core samples as we bring them out of the ground. Then, there's the part I'm not too fond of—hassling with oil and gas regulatory agencies, and sometimes with landowners.

Whenever there's trouble, like this thing with someone sabotaging our wells, my job is to make it go away. We can't afford delays in exploration or loss of production." Jake smiled at Kate, then turned his attention back to the smooth blacktop road.

"Sounds as though you've got an interesting job. Lots of variety."

"Yeah. Over the years, I've done just about everything there is to do on oil rigs. When I was fifteen, my father made me spend the summer hauling and threading pipe, stuffing mud, all the dirty work. He thought he was punishing me for being a jock instead of a bookworm."

Kate smiled. She couldn't imagine Jake having spent a lot of time curled up with his textbooks. "Was it terrible for you?"

"It was the most fun I'd ever had. Dad's idea was that I'd come home and thank my lucky stars he was sending me to Houston Jesuit, and that he was willing to foot the bill for my MBA. But I loved the oil business—the puzzle of seismic readings, the excitement of bringing in a gusher like we did this morning.

"I didn't even mind breaking my back proving I could work as hard as the biggest, toughest roughneck on the crew."

Kate couldn't help noticing how Jake's expression softened when he talked about his work. "So did you quit school and stay out in your father's oil fields?"

"Not exactly. I went home and made a deal with the Old Man. I promised him that if he'd let me work the fields every summer and scrap the idea of sending me to the Wharton School of Business, I'd hit the books hard enough to get into petroleum engineering at Texas A&M. He was disappointed, but he agreed. Instead of a wizard financial analyst, he got a hell of a field engineer."

"So everybody got what they wanted in the end," Kate murmured.

"More or less. The Old Man still stews because his son won't be the one to take over the company. Deep down, though, he knows Scott, my oldest sister's husband, is far more qualified than I am to take over when he retires—at least, I hope he does."

"It sounds as though you have a wonderful family." Kate sighed, a little envious.

He shook his head. "You wouldn't think so if you heard my mother and sisters giving me hell."

"I'll bet you give them reason to."

"I guess so. Especially since my divorce. But it drives me nuts, the way they gang up on me. I've had every single female between eighteen and eighty paraded in front of me like a prize cow at auction. My old man's desperate for me to provide him with a grandson, and it seems like the rest of my family's obsessed with getting me settled down. You're an only child, aren't you?"

When he directed the question to her, Kate guessed he'd divulged as much of himself as he intended to. "Yes. I always wanted brothers and sisters, but it never happened."

As she watched the roadway sights pass by, Jake's easy silence and the soothing strains of a Gershwin medley lulled her out of her melancholy reverie.

* * * * *

When he pulled into the parking lot beside a club called the Sandcastle, Jake looked over at Kate. Suddenly he appreciated the quiet time they'd spent together for the last miles of the drive.

"Hey, we're here," he said quietly, sorry to have to break the silence.

"The place seems quiet tonight." She looked around, apparently checking out the few cars in the parking lot.

Jake smiled. "Yeah. Why don't we go inside and do something about filling our stomachs? I don't know about you, but I'm half starved. This place does serve food, doesn't it?"

"If you like barbecue or frozen pizza."

He saw her struggling to unfasten her seat belt and reached over to help. When their hands touched, heat sizzled through him like an electric current.

Jake told himself to cool it.

As he circled the car, he listened to his inner voice's warning. He'd enjoy a night or two of fucking around with Kate Black if she was willing, but he wasn't about to get involved.

Wrapping an arm around her slender waist, Jake led Kate into the club. Catching a whiff of the sweet flowery perfume that had kept him halfway hard all the way from her place, he had to fight the need to lean across the table where they'd just settled and bury his face in the tantalizing hollow between her breasts.

"What would you like to drink?" he asked instead.

"White wine will be fine."

A gusher and a possible seduction deserved something a bit more festive than that. "We'll have champagne."

"All right."

"I'll go see what they have." With that, he took off for the bar to place their order.

"Do they have any?" Kate asked when he came back to their table.

Jake liked the way she spoke, soft and gentle sounding. "Yeah. I can't vouch for the quality, but they've got a bottle of something the bartender swears is champagne. I ordered us some food, too."

Kate's smile brought his cock to instant attention.

It wasn't Kate. He'd been without a woman for too damn long. Any halfway attractive female would turn him on.

Testing that theory, Jake singled out a buxom blonde at the bar and imagined her writhing hot and willing beneath him. He pictured her glossy red lips locked onto his cock as she took him deep into her throat. His cock didn't rise to the occasion the way he'd told himself it would.

Hell, he didn't want just any woman. He wanted Kate. He looked back at her and frowned.

"Is something wrong?" she asked.

"I'm just hungry." And he didn't want to be that kind of hungry, not for this particular woman as opposed to any attractive female. "Where's our food?"

"It's coming now."

"Good," he growled at the moment his cell phone rang.

Welcoming the distraction, Jake snatched the phone off his belt and brought it to his ear.

He should have guessed. Skip and Max weren't coming to join them. Now there'd be just him and Kate. No buffer to take his mind off fucking her.

Was that good news—or bad?

Jake hated feeling ambivalent. "Okay," he said, ending the conversation and meeting Kate's questioning gaze. "It's just going to be us. Skip says they're having trouble controlling the gusher."

"Problems?"

"I doubt it. If I don't miss my guess, he decided I'd rather have you to myself."

"Oh."

Most women Jake knew would have laughed or made some coy little comment. But not Kate.

Jake's mood improved when the bartender showed up at their table with a bottle and two water-stained saucer champagne glasses. "This is fine," he said after tasting the no-name stuff and managing not to choke on it.

The effervescence of that first taste of dry, sparkling wine stayed on his tongue while a waitress set plates of barbecued chicken and beef on the table.

Kate took some meat and brought it carefully to her lips. "Watch out, honey, it's hot," he warned, imagining those soft, full lips closing around his cock the way she sucked the last of the sauce off her fork and into her mouth.

Hell, if he didn't put a lid on his imagination, he'd soon be fucking her right here on the tabletop.

Jake dipped a piece of chicken into fiery barbecue sauce and popped it into his mouth.

"Tastes so good," she murmured, flicking her tongue out to capture a spot of sauce that lingered at the corner of her mouth.

That tongue would taste delicious tangled up with his.

She didn't say much, but left him to enjoy his food in peace. He liked that.

Jake liked watching her, too. Would her dark brown, curly hair feel as silky as it looked? Would it crush beneath his touch like the rose petals in his mom's garden?

He imagined her legs wrapped around his waist and his cock buried to the balls in her tight wet pussy.

He wanted her tonight.

Chapter Three

But he wondered if one night would be enough.

He was pretty certain it wouldn't. A fast, easy fuck wouldn't satisfy his lust.

He wanted to learn the feel of her satiny skin against his own, to keep breathing in her clean, flowery fragrance until he had his fill.

He pictured how his dark, rough hands would contrast with the pale skin of her breasts—her slender hips and thighs. Tonight she'd taste like cheap champagne and spicy barbecue and hot, sexy woman. And her gentle touch would drive him crazy.

Damn it, he wanted to sample every inch of her sexy little body before digging in for the carnal feast he had in mind.

Even though he knew she was the last woman on earth that he should be lusting after.

The second-to-last, he amended, a bitter taste coming to his mouth at the thought of Alice.

Because he guessed he could easily care for Kate, Jake made a conscious effort to focus on the similarities between her and his treacherous ex-wife.

Country girls from the Bible belt, seemingly sweet and interested in simple pleasures. Both...he couldn't come up with any other parallels except the main one: they both had an uncanny ability to make him think with his cock, not his brain.

Willing his blood to stop flooding his already throbbing crotch, he looked away from her and scowled down at his plate.

"What's wrong?"

Goddamn it, even the apparent concern in her voice turned him on.

He grappled for a plausible excuse for his discomfort that didn't have to do with sex, love, or betrayal. "I was thinking about getting your well hooked onto the pipeline," he finally said, improvising.

"Oh." Leaving him to his own meal, Kate began to eat again.

He finished everything on his platter, but he hardly tasted a bite.

"Jake! That you?"

Glad for the distraction, he looked up and recognized Mel Harrison. Mel looked pretty much the same as he remembered, even though it had been years since their wild, summer roughnecking days.

"Mel. How are you?" he asked, pushing his chair back and coming to his feet.

"Great. Never better. You still hanging round oilfields?"

"Yeah. How about you?"

Mel's ambition twelve years ago had been to keep a band together and take it on the road. The big country boy had even tried to talk Jake into forgetting about college and joining up as his lead singer.

"Hanging in there. You've heard of 'Texas Fire,' haven't you?"

"Can't say that I have." Belatedly, Jake remembered his manners. "Kate, this is Mel Harrison. We used to work my old man's rigs together. Mel, Kate."

"Hello there, sugar. Old Jake's gone and got himself a pretty lady."

"I'm glad to meet you, Mr. Harrison."

Jake liked the way Kate's cat eyes sparkled when she greeted his old friend.

"Well, Ms. Kate, get your man to stick around. 'Texas Fire' is gonna be the entertainment tonight. If you sweet-talk ole Jake, I bet you could get him to sing for you. He never could play guitar worth a hoot, but his voice used to make the ladies shiver clean down to their toes."

"You sing?" Kate asked. "I'd never have guessed."

"I don't. Not for years. This worn out old roughneck conned me into trying it, back when I was wet behind the ears. The summer between high school and college, we worked on the rigs all day and played sleazy honky-tonks half the nights."

Jake sat back down and gestured toward an empty chair. "Join us."

"Just for a minute. Gotta join the boys and get warmed up. Stay, you can listen and dance. That is, if you're too much the big bad oil man to come up and do a number with us for old times' sake." Mel sank onto the straight-back chair.

"Jake, go on. I'd like to hear you sing," Kate said, her quiet words as soft and melodic as any Jake had ever heard.

"You heard your lady. Hey, it'll help us out, too. Libby, our singer, is down with a bad cold. She's gonna try to make the second set, but I'll just have to fill in until she comes."

"You? You can't carry a tune in a bucket."

"Damn. 'Scuse me, sugar. I sing better than you ever thought of playing guitar, you conceited polecat."

"Compliments like that won't get you jack shit—sorry, honey. You wouldn't mind?" Jake asked, knowing he'd be better off singing with the band than holding Kate in his arms on a public dance floor.

"I'd love to hear you."

"Then it's settled," Mel said. "You remember the old songs, Jake?"

"I remember how to read a fake book. I think. You sure you want to chance it?"

"Yeah. We'll do the lead-in, then call you up."

After Mel had left, Jake told himself it was okay to want to fuck Kate. Not to start caring about her.

The hell of it was, he liked Kate. Couldn't help himself. Her excitement at the prospect of hearing him sing had thawed some of the ice his ex-wife had left around his soul. Alice would have gone berserk if he'd ever suggested leaving her alone at a table while he took a trip down memory lane. The contrast made him smile.

That summer he'd filled in with Mel's band had produced some happy memories. He wished when he looked at Kate that he could roll back the years.

"You really want to see me make a fool of myself?" he asked instead.

"I'm sure you won't do that. What kind of music do they play?"

"We used to play light rock, a little country and western, easy stuff. I doubt if Mel's changed his style much." Jake relaxed while they finished off the bottle of cheap champagne, and after laughing at some jokes the lead-in comic had told, he was downright mellow.

Kate couldn't help smiling. Jake was showing her a side of him she hadn't imagined he possessed. Yes, he was arrogant and cynical. The more she saw of him, though, the more she believed she hadn't scratched the surface of who he was.

One minute he'd come across as selfish and unfeeling. Then, before she could bring herself to dislike him, he'd say or do something that revealed a deep-down basic goodness.

Every once in a while, a look of pain would cloud his expression, giving her a fleeting sense of his vulnerability. She recalled him mentioning a divorce, and she wondered what kind of woman had let Jake Green slip through her fingers.

When she glanced up at the band platform a few minutes later and saw him looking straight at her, she sensed this song would be for her. He'd just done an upbeat version of "Take It Easy," and his deep, mellow voice had teased her senses, made her feel every nuance of longing for home that the long distance trucker in the song must have experienced.

Jake turned to Mel and said something before picking up the microphone. Caught in a magic spell, Kate barely heard the slow cadence of the melody.

In the shadowed lounge, muted spotlights lit his face. The passion in his gaze made her blush. And the lyrics—Kate pretended Jake had written them just for her.

While he sang of making love, sharing more than an affair, she imagined them alone together, him touching her with his callused hands—his expressive mouth—his big, hard body. Caught up in her fantasy, she was sorry when the song was done and he stepped down from the stage.

"Well?" he asked, bending down and brushing a lock of hair back from her cheek.

"You're good. Really good."

His touch warmed her, and she had to restrain herself from covering his hand with hers to prolong the tingly sensation that radiated through her body. It was as if he transformed her with his presence, changed her from the shy, gentle woman she'd always been into a sensual being who could meet all his unspoken demands.

"Thanks. Let's dance." Smiling, he held his other hand out to her to help her from the chair.

And the fantasy went on.

Kate knew she should stop dreaming. Hold onto her sanity. Jake Green was way, way out of her league.

Big city, big money, big chip on his shoulder.

But there was no way Kate could stop herself from drifting into his arms.

She rested her head on his broad shoulder, molding her body tightly to his tough, powerful frame. The feel of his hard, work-toughened body stoked the fire in her soul.

While the music played, she savored her sensual awakening.

"Honey." His voice was as sweet and languid as the casual endearment he used so often.

She tilted her head back. The blatantly carnal look on his face almost took away her power of speech.

"What?" Her voice was little more than a croak.

"I want you. Let's get out of here before I do something that will get us both arrested."

He nuzzled her cheek, bathed her skin with the moist warmth of his breath. Unresisting, she followed him to their table and picked up her purse while he tossed down some bills.

She loved the feel of his hard-muscled arm around her waist. And when he took her in his arms and pressed her against the car door, she forgot to breathe. The searing hardness of him ground into her belly, setting her afire.

God, she wanted him.

But she was afraid of him and of herself, of the fiery passion within her that he so easily awakened.

* * * * *

She's scared.

The realization hit Jake as he was closing the car door. Kate had trembled when he'd ground his erection into the inviting softness of her belly. And the timid way she'd met his marauding tongue spoke of more than shyness.

It damned well shouted innocence.

He groaned, shifting in his seat to accommodate his swollen cock. He might be a cold bastard, but he couldn't slake his lust on someone so blatantly unsophisticated. Not when Kate could have no place in his life beyond a few nights of mutual pleasure.

The Porsche's powerful engine roared to life when he turned the key in the ignition. Within minutes they were speeding down the highway.

"Where are we going?" Kate's voice sounded different, huskier and more inviting even than her gentle touch on his arm.

"I'm taking you home," he said through clenched teeth.

"B-but I thought…"

"I know, honey. I thought so too. But you're obviously not a woman who's into one-night stands. And I've got nothing more to offer. I don't want to use you and leave you. So I'm backing off."

"Oh." Kate sounded disappointed.

His cock was disappointed, too.

Too bad. No matter how much Jake wanted her, there was no way he'd risk coming to care deeply for Kate or any other woman. Not after the painful lessons Alice had inflicted on him about women and their treachery.

But Jake wouldn't knowingly do anything that would cause Kate pain. His conscience wouldn't let him.

As he drove along the darkened highway lined with tall, spindly pine trees, he tried to curb the desire she'd roused in him so easily with just a word, a simple touch. It had to be horniness born of long deprivation.

The comfortable feeling of rightness he had when he was with her could be nothing but a painful illusion.

* * * * *

For a few hours the other night, while they'd talked and danced and got as close as she figured a man and a woman could while they still had on their clothes, Kate had let her feelings lead her.

But Jake had shattered those fledgling dreams before they had a chance to grow.

The fire he'd set inside her still burned so hot that she could barely function. Her trip to the grocery store this morning, necessary as it was to replenish her empty larder, had intruded on the persistent tingling longings that were half pleasure, half torture.

Mechanically, she emptied the bags of groceries onto the kitchen table. Pouring herself a glass of cola, she took it with her and went upstairs to brood.

What was wrong with her?

She'd practically thrown herself at Jake—no, she'd definitely done her damnedest to seduce him.

Too bad it hadn't worked.

When he'd backed off and headed for home, Kate had nearly bitten her tongue off to keep from begging him to stop at one of the motels they passed along the highway.

She still wanted to go to him now, beg him to fulfill the promise in his kisses. Her nipples still tingled when she remembered how they'd felt, pressed into the hard muscles of his chest.

When every cell in her body was calling out for Jake like this, innocence seemed highly overrated. She couldn't help imagining how it would feel to experience all the mind-boggling sensations she'd read about. The glow romance heroines always seemed to have after their heroes claimed their bodies the way Jake had already laid claim to her senses.

Sitting beside the window, Kate tried not to look toward the drilling site. Instead, she picked up a small framed picture and tried to summon up the pangs of regret that looking at David's solemn image always evoked.

But her mind was so full of Jake, she could hardly recall why she had ever fallen in love with David. His quiet, self-assured manner had soothed her, but he never had coaxed tingly, frantic sexual arousal from her the way Jake did without even trying. He'd never had her hot and wet between her legs from wanting him.

She hadn't been panting to share David's bed even after dating him for six months and accepting his engagement ring. Kate imagined their lovemaking would have been peaceful and restrained. Boring.

Nothing remotely resembling what she imagined sex would be like with a man like Jake.

David would have made a good father for their children, though. Tears welled up in Kate's eyes, for all she'd ever wanted had been a home and family of her own. David had fit her picture of the perfect dad, but his love for her hadn't been strong enough to encompass her ailing father.

She wiped away her tears. It hadn't taken her much soul-searching before she'd said goodbye to David and come home to care for Pop. Her decision wouldn't have been nearly as easy if David had ever aroused her senses the way Jake Green did.

"Why didn't you make me want you?" she asked his silent image. "I loved you for your intelligence, for your kindness. You'd have been a good husband, a good father, and a wonderful companion. I'm sure you'd have been a gentle lover, too. But your kisses never made me want more. You never showed me there could be fire."

Kate set the picture down and turned, drawn irrevocably toward the towering derrick, toward the tall, dark stranger whose image seared her soul.

Jake wasn't the kind of man to settle down. She should be grateful he had the decency to bring her home and turn down what she'd so freely offered.

Never before in her twenty-eight years had Kate ached for a man. Not even the man she'd once planned to marry.

But she ached for Jake.

She straightened her shoulders. She had to get over this obsession and stop wanting a man who'd told her straight out they had no future together. Forcing herself not to stare out the window, she focused instead on the patterned quilt on her bed.

When the phone rang, she answered it eagerly, anxious for the momentary distraction from fantasizing about Jake.

"Hello…oh, hi, Becky. How's Stan? And the kids?" Kate listened while her friend gave a nonstop report on her family's activities.

"Where were you Sunday? We'd all gone out for a ride and we stopped by your house. The fellow in charge down at your oil well said you and some boss from GreenTex had gone to celebrate the well's coming in."

Kate held the phone away from her ear. When Becky was excited, her tone of voice got shrill. Someday Becky was going to rupture somebody's eardrum.

"Calm down," she said as soon as she dared bring the receiver back to her ear. "I didn't know you were coming or I'd have stayed home. I just got caught up in the excitement when the well came in. Jake Green and I drove over to Hattiesburg to a bar and grill close to the university. He's one of the owners of the oil company that bought the leases."

"Ooh. I like his name. Do you like him? Is he nice?" Becky's tone had lightened, but Kate was fairly certain her curiosity hadn't abated.

"'Nice' is not a word I'd apply to Jake. He's obviously well-educated and well-heeled, but he's as tough as you'd expect any roughneck to be." Heat came to Kate's cheeks when she recalled just how willing she had been for that particular roughneck to haul her off to the nearest motel. "He's fun to be with. Jake is—well, I guess cynical's the right word. Of course, he's worried about that explosion I told you about—he thinks it's sabotage. And I get the feeling he isn't comfortable, having to be here. But he's not *all* tough."

"Hey, I'm happy for you. You should get out more, meet more people. It's dumb for you to stay out there in the middle of nowhere. I know you had to take care of your pop, but he's gone now. It's time for you to start living."

"I know. But Jake already said he wasn't interested in any more than a one-night stand."

"He's not married, is he?" Becky sounded concerned.

"Divorced." Kate shut up abruptly. She'd already told her friend enough to keep her speculating for weeks.

"So? Look at Frank and Gilda. He was married before, and they're as happy as any couple I know. I hope you told him where to go, though, when he mentioned a one-night stand."

"No. I didn't." Kate wasn't about to admit to Becky that it was Jake who'd backed off, not she. "He was being honest. Anyhow, I doubt I'll see him again except about the well."

It hurt to realize Jake was only a stranger who had briefly touched her life. In spite of the fact that he had made his feelings crystal clear, Kate craved him the way she imagined an alcoholic pined for his liquor.

"I'm sorry I missed you Sunday. Give the kids a hug for me. I've got to go." Kate needed to end the conversation before she broke down and cried.

When she hung up, she stared out the window at the place five generations of her family had called home. The place Pop had begged her never to let go.

He'd die again if he knew she was on fire for a stranger whose traditions were rooted far away from Groveland, Mississippi.

Kate tried to picture her father, but the image that came to mind was a hard-hewn body with the face of a dark angel, eyes that twinkled with amusement one moment before becoming shadowed with emotions from someplace deep inside him where she couldn't reach.

Going back to the window to stare at the drilling site, she let herself hope for a glimpse of Jake.

This yearning was insane. Kate could tell herself that, but knowing didn't erase the feelings that had begun the moment she'd seen him from a distance.

She craved the solid thump of his heartbeat beneath her hands, the spicy smell of his aftershave. The sight of hard muscles rippling in his arms and shoulders and the velvety feel of his tongue stroking hers. Even if it was only for one day or one hour, she wanted to enjoy the sensual feast she sensed this man could bring her. What was that man doing?

Seeing a stranger sprinting out of the barn and down her driveway shocked Kate back into reality. Before she could get a good look at him, though, she noticed flames licking hungrily around the empty stable.

For a moment, she was too stunned to move. Then she bounded outside toward the burning building where some men from the oil well crew were working frantically to put out the burgeoning fire.

Standing back so she wouldn't hamper the men's efforts, she searched each sooty face. Finally she glanced down the hill. She needed Jake to help her cope. Heeding that desperate need, she took off running toward the well. But he wasn't there.

* * * * *

Not caring at the moment whether Blake thought he was enjoying a tantrum much like one of his nieces might throw, Jake slammed his briefcase onto the small back seat of the Porsche.

It was going to take some time for him to put a lid on the fury he'd worked up for the stalling bureaucrats on the state's Oil and Gas Board. If the cocksucking politicians had their way, it would be months before GreenTex could start drilling on more of the properties they had leased.

All he could do now was sink more wells on Kate Black's land. At least his lawyer, Blake Tanner, had managed to talk the Board out of rescinding drilling permits they'd already issued for seven additional wells there.

"We didn't have much luck today," he commented to Blake as he revved the car engine.

"Sorry. That explosion has them spooked. Just be glad they didn't rescind the permits we already have. In spite of all the points I argued, the'd have been within their rights to do that."

"Yeah, sure. I appreciate your flying over here this morning. Not to mention keeping me from cutting loose with a major temper tantrum in that meeting," he said after starting the car and pulling out into the downtown traffic.

"I need to pick up a drill bit, if you can spare the time," he added when he noticed Blake's apparent confusion at the direction he was going.

"I'm in no big hurry. Erin isn't expecting me home until this evening." The lawyer's expression softened when he mentioned his pretty second wife.

Jake focused on the scenery. He shouldn't envy his good friend Blake, who'd gone through hell before finding love again after his wife's death, with the surrogate mother of his child.

Downtown Jackson, except for the Capitol and State office buildings where they'd spent the morning, reminded him of an oversized ghost town. As in many fast-growing southern cities, the better stores had moved to sprawling malls. Jackson was worse than most, with its abandoned King Edward Hotel across the street from an ancient, dilapidated Amtrak station.

The ever-present scene of decaying buildings depressed Jake almost as much as wondering how he had managed to be as unlucky in love as he was lucky at finding oil underneath the ground.

Silently he searched for the machine shop where he was supposed to pick up a custom drill bit Skip had ordered. By the time he found the dingy building west of the railroad tracks, he didn't much care if the damn bit was ready or not. It was, though, and he stashed it in the trunk before heading southeast toward Groveland, via the Jackson airport.

"How's the family?" he asked Blake. He guessed that since his cousin Greg had married Blake's sister-in-law, he and the lawyer were shirttail relatives of some sort.

"Growing. Erin's due again in September, a month after Sandy. But I suppose Greg's told you all about the boy they're expecting." Hank grinned as Jake pulled up to the small metal hangar that served as a terminal for noncommercial flights.

"Yeah. Guess I'll be coming out to Dallas next month to meet the remarkable little guy." Jake wondered if the baby Alice had destroyed would have been a boy or girl.

"See you then." Blake slid out of the car, reaching back inside to get his briefcase. "Hey, Jake, it's good to have you home again," he said before he strode away toward his twin-engine Cessna.

Alone now with the sound of old show tunes surrounding him in the car, Jake let his thoughts wander. Hell, he'd barely been able to function the last three days, between trying to figure who was out to destroy his business and having a constant hard-on for Kate Black.

For the moment it wasn't the saboteurs as much as it was Kate boggling his mind. And that made Jake furious. He should be putting all his energy to stopping the attacks on GreenTex before there wasn't any company left to save.

If he'd had a lick of sense he'd have taken her to a motel the other night and fucked her brains out. Maybe then he'd have gotten her out of his system.

But he hadn't.

And the itch was still there. Just thinking about her had his cock hard and throbbing against his zipper. He groaned, shifting against the leather bucket seat to find a more comfortable position.

He wanted Kate. Not just her pussy, either. That's what scared him. He wanted to talk with her, look at her, share her thoughts and dreams as well as her sexy little body. He'd felt that way about Alice, too, and look where that got him. No way would he set himself up for more broken dreams.

They'd had eight years together. Jake had thought they were good ones. Until Alice had torn his heart out eighteen months ago.

Ironically, she'd done it while they played the happy couple at Greg's wedding celebration. After the rehearsal dinner, when he'd tried to take her in his arms, Alice had shattered the last of his youthful illusions.

Her words were stamped indelibly in his memory. "I'm done with this farce of a marriage. I'm leaving in the morning. I filed for divorce last week. If you hadn't come back early for Greg's wedding, I'd have been gone when you got back to Houston."

Jake slammed his fist into the padded dash.

He'd made a fool of himself that night, begging her to stay for the sake of the unborn baby she'd told him about just three weeks earlier before he took off to solve some problem in a Venezuelan oil field.

His child. The baby who would never have known anything but love from him, never have felt pressure to become something he wasn't. The baby Jake had wanted since early in their marriage.

The baby Alice had tossed away like an unwanted toy when she decided he was no longer the hero she'd fallen in love with eight years earlier when he'd been tossing touchdown passes for the Aggies.

Part of Jake had died when she told him about the abortion, and not just the son or daughter Alice had tossed out like garbage. She'd destroyed the part of him that believed, that loved, that trusted in the goodness of his fellow man.

He gripped the steering wheel so hard that his knuckles turned white. "Goddamn it, I loved her."

Now he didn't even hate her anymore. But it would be a cold day in hell before he'd give another woman his trust.

He certainly couldn't trust Kate, whose soft drawl and rural lifestyle reminded him of Alice when they'd first met.

Jake expected to marry again one day. Hell, he was an only son, and his old man was desperate for a grandson to carry on the family name.

But his next marriage wouldn't be for love. The wall he'd built around his wounded heart would keep him safe. He'd find a woman and give her his name and his children, but never his heart.

She'd have to accept his work, share his interest in sports and rugged outdoor pursuits. Most of all she couldn't demand more of him than he had to give.

"Damn it to hell." Jake glanced at the rolling meadows on either side of the two-lane blacktop road. "Why do I keep thinking Kate's different from Alice?"

When his only answer was the powerful roar of the Porsche's engine, he let out a stream of vicious curses. Then, powerless to prevent his mind from wandering, he mulled over what he knew of Kate Black.

He couldn't figure exactly what made him want her. Unlike his bitch of a former wife, she wasn't knockout gorgeous. While he had no trouble imagining how her petite body would mate up with his when they got horizontal, and while just thinking about her kept him hard as a horny teenager, Kate's wasn't the sexiest body he'd ever seen. Or had, for that matter.

Maybe it was her eyes, soft blue-green, slightly tilted cat eyes on a delicate, fine-featured face. Or that curly mop of dark brown hair that tempted him to reach out and fondle it, to bury his face in its softness?

Might Kate make him a decent wife?

She'd sure as hell please him in bed. Just rubbing himself against the convex plane of her slender belly the other night had gotten him hard enough to burst.

Damn it, Jake. You've got more sense than to let your cock do your thinking. You can find hundreds of women who look pretty and will give you a good ride. Those are the least important qualities you're looking for in a woman.

His cock obviously disagreed. It ached and throbbed so painfully that he unzipped his jeans to ease the pressure.

Kate would be a good mother, he imagined. She'd told him enthusiastically about the children she'd taught before coming home to care for her dying father. That was important. He didn't want his kids having a mom who would leave their upbringing to maids and nannies. And he damn sure didn't want another woman who would callously destroy his baby.

Unlike Alice, who hated that she'd grown up poor and had never let him forget it, Kate didn't seem particularly greedy. In any case, Jake had enough wealth to gratify any but the most avaricious of women.

He sensed she'd be satisfied with home and hearth—and bringing up a family. Unfortunately homebodies had a nasty habit of wanting their men home every night. Jake didn't imagine Kate would like him running off, drilling wells all over the world, any more than Alice had.

When his car phone beeped, Jake pushed a button to activate it, still caught up with thoughts of Kate.

Chapter Four

"Jake here."

"This is Skip. Where are you?"

Jake looked out the window at scenery he couldn't place, then at the trip odometer. "About five miles out of Groveland."

"Step on it, then. We've got a helluva fire on our hands."

Shit! "The well?"

"The woods. Sparks must've got away from us when we were putting out a fire in that old barn behind Ms. Black's house." Skip sounded frantic.

Jake pressed the accelerator to the floor, then leveled the speed off at ninety miles an hour. "You got help?"

"County volunteer fire department's here with a fifty-year-old pumper truck. Forest service has helicopters on the way to spray the trees."

"Good. Get one of the wild well control outfits to stand by in case we need them. And put your people to work keeping that fire away from the well."

"Already done. The PIs are out, trying to catch the son-of-a-bitch Kate saw running away from her barn early this morning. Anything else?"

"No. Damn it, yes. Did you get Kate out of there?"

"We tried. Haven't been able to find her," Skip said, his voice almost drowned out by the sound of a helicopter that was flying low over Jake's car.

"Go look for her."

Jake shut off the phone and floored the accelerator again. He clutched the wheel and fought the bumpy road in spite of the tight, constricting fear that clutched at his chest.

His fury rose, along with terror. Six fucking expensive armed security guards on site, and they hadn't managed to nab the saboteur.

Somebody had to have seen their arsonist. Why in hell couldn't one of the lazy private cops have managed to snare this bastard pyromaniac the minute he'd set foot on Kate's property?

He watched the speedometer edge up over a hundred-twenty.

The two minutes it took to reach the well site seemed like two days in hell. Ominous black smoke thickened, scorching his eyes. Burning tree limbs crackled all around him as he approached the turnoff.

Jake applied the brakes and downshifted as he executed the sharp curve into Kate's driveway. Dust swirled from where the tires grappled with the packed clay road.

Screeching to a halt, he saw the ruin of the barn that stood halfway between Kate's house and Black-GreenTex Number One. Old and rickety to begin with, the structure was now nothing but a mass of smoldering embers being tended by two of Skip's drillers.

A forest service chopper circled overhead, spraying water over the burning woods that ringed the well.

When Jake saw movement from the corner of one eye, he looked closer. A brute of a man charged up a narrow path toward the driveway. Smoke billowed, and fresh flames crackled in his wake.

The red gas can the bastard clutched in one meaty fist gave him away. Bracing himself, Jake waited for his chance.

When the man was barely six feet away, Jake lunged. He caught the guy in the belly with his left shoulder, knocking him to the ground. Jake came down on top of him, slammed a fist into his beefy face and a knee into his groin.

But that didn't take him out.

The arsonist connected with several bruising blows to Jake's ribs and jaw before Jake laid him out cold with a vicious chop to the neck.

His energy depleted, Jake sank back onto the rain-starved grass along the pathway and yelled for help.

Then he heard a faint moaning sound.

He forced himself to sit up.

There it was again, an almost human plea coming from the burning woods.

Leaving his unconscious prisoner for the security men who were headed his way, Jake staggered to his feet and limped toward that pathetic sound.

Kate.

The bastard had hit her and left her to burn.

He uttered a vile oath at the pain that radiated from his gimpy knee when he tried to run. Gritting his teeth, he forced himself to keep going, then sank down beside her and began to check for obvious injuries.

She couldn't die. Didn't deserve to die.

Fuck! He couldn't lose her.

The flames licked at the dry underbrush. Close. Too close.

Crackling.

Coming closer now.

He beat at the tiny flames with his hands, tried to ignore the searing pain.

The wind fanned the fire and spread it, in spite of the steady stream of flame retardant that dripped on them through limbs of the trees.

They had to get out of here.

Now.

Snatching Kate up in his arms, Jake stood and staggered out of the woods.

"You!" he yelled through parched lips at the guards who had left their unconscious prisoner and come to lend a hand. "I'll take care of her. Get that bastard to the trailer. Call the sheriff. For God's sake, don't let him get away!"

Inside Kate's house, he collapsed on a worn couch, cradling Kate in his arms.

Damn it, he should have protected her.

He should have killed the bastard who hurt her.

But now, with any kind of luck, GreenTex's sabotage problems would be over.

Kate stirred in his arms, opened her eyes.

"Are you all right?" he asked, surprised at the hoarse sound of his own voice.

"I—I think so." Kate coughed, then shot a horrified look toward the woods. "Jake, the fire!"

"It's under control." He hoped to hell that was true.

Suddenly he was furious. She could have been burned alive. "What were you doing out there?"

She shook her head. "That man. I saw him heading back into the woods. He didn't look like one of your workers, so I followed him. Jake, I was scared."

"He knocked you out. You could have been killed."

She gave him a watery smile. "But you saved me."

"Damn it, lady, that was blind luck. Don't you have more sense than to go chasing off into burning woods after some stranger three times your size?" That SOB must have been six-six or more, and from the way he'd thrown punches Jake figured he had to have weighed three hundred pounds. If not for that knockout punch Jack had landed, he and Kate both could have died on a smoldering bed of pine needles in the burning woods.

"He hit me from behind," she said, her voice conveying disbelief. "Did you catch him?"

"Yeah." His knee throbbed as though somebody had stabbed it.

"Jake. The fire…" she said again.

"Will be out soon if it isn't already. Honey, I'm sorry." He shifted a little, trying to ease the pain in his bad knee.

"Why are they doing this?"

"I don't know. But I intend to find out. I'm certain it has nothing to do with you, or with this particular drilling operation, if that makes you feel any better. GreenTex has been hit with too many disasters the past year or so for me not to believe somebody's trying their damnedest to put us out of business."

"Oh."

"Do you feel up to taking a look at the guy who set your woods on fire and seeing if he's the same one who torched your barn this morning?" Though he needed her input, he hated to put her through more grief.

"I guess so."

Jake hated it when she pulled away and stood on shaky feet. But his own bumps and bruises distracted him as they made their way down to the drilling site.

* * * * *

When Kate sadly shook her head and told them their prisoner was not the man who had set her barn on fire, Jake felt as though he'd just taken another blow from the brute's meaty fist. The fire was under control now, but the trouble wasn't over, after all.

"Talk," he snarled as he grabbed the man's grimy shirt and jerked him onto his feet. "Who hired you?"

"I ain't saying nothing without a lawyer."

Jake drew back his right fist. He would have nailed the guy in the mouth if Skip hadn't grabbed his arm.

"Jake. His hands and feet are tied. Let the sheriff handle him."

"Damn." Jake should have killed the son-of-a-bitch when he had the chance, out there on the path to the woods.

He didn't need any help figuring out that the sheriff wouldn't appreciate him beating a helpless prisoner half to death. But he didn't much care.

The bastard had set a fire that could have blown the oil well over half of Mississippi. He might have set off the explosion that killed Dale Martin last month. And he'd come too damn close to killing Kate.

Jake strained against the hands that held him back. "Let go," he rasped, his breath coming fast and hard.

"What's going on?"

Jake gave Sheriff Jones a quelling look when the lawman ambled in as if he hadn't a care in the world. "We caught you an arsonist, Sheriff. You might want to see if you can get him to tell you who put him up to it."

"Looks like he might've given y'all a bit of a tussle." Jones looked pointedly at the cuts and bruises on the prisoner's face, then glanced at Jake's bruised jaw before turning back to the arsonist.

"What you got to say for yourself?" he asked the man gruffly.

"I want a lawyer."

The sheriff laughed. "Well, folks in hell, they want ice water, son. The public defender's out fishing for catfish this week on the Alabama River, so unless you get yourself a high-price, hotshot mouthpiece, you're gonna be waiting awhile. Why don't you just do yourself a favor and 'fess up? Don't want to miss my supper because of some no-account jailbird like you."

"Fuck you, too, cocksucker." The prisoner strained at his bonds, spat at the lawman.

When Kate gasped, Jake turned and saw the look of horror on her pale face.

Damn! He should have taken her home as soon as she got a look at the man they'd captured. He certainly shouldn't have let her watch him practically assault their prisoner or made her stay and listen to the bastard's filthy mouth.

"Come on. I'll take you home," he said, crossing the room to meet her halfway. "There's at least one other one like him, running around causing mayhem," he told Jones as he ushered Kate out.

"Until this is over, I don't want you in that house by yourself," he said to her.

"Does that mean you're going to stay?"

"For now, at least."

"Thank you." She managed a shaky smile.

Jake wrapped an arm protectively around her shoulders.

* * * * *

"You're hurt."

Kate stared at his legs when he limped across her living room toward the sofa. "It's nothing," he said, cursing the weakness he didn't like her noticing. "How's your headache?"

"Better." She looked at him, worried her lower lip between her teeth. In her eyes he saw trust—and the beginnings of something more.

Suddenly the pain in his knee seemed unimportant, the urgency to end this trouble less intense.

"Hey, I'm sorry you had to witness that scene," he told her.

Jake had flat out lost it, said and done a bunch of things he knew damn well he never should have. Not in front of a decent woman like Kate. "I've been brought up better than it must have seemed when I tried to beat up that guy."

Kate gave him a tentative smile. "It's all right. If I could have, I'd have liked to give him a bump on his head, the way he did to me. Somebody could have died. And he hurt you."

She reached over and touched his face, and he couldn't stop himself from pulling her close.

"Calm down, honey," he murmured, trying not to dwell on the fact that at least one person had already lost his life because he'd gotten in the way of whoever was out to destroy GreenTex, and he and Kate had just had a close call. "Why don't you pack a bag? Go to a friend's house. I'll take you."

She shook her head against his shoulder. "No. Just stay with me for a little while."

"All right."

The thought of her getting hurt ate at Jake. No way was he going to let her far out of his sight as long as another madman was on the loose. He stroked her back, trying not to think about the way his body was responding, just to being close to her.

Damn! She made him ache in all the places that had escaped the arsonist's flailing fists and legs. Her nipples hardened and burrowed into his chest like tiny needles of fire. Flames that spread straight to his cock.

Now was not the time for this, he told himself, but his hands didn't work when he tried to push her gently away.

"Please hold me."

Her warm, damp breath tickled his neck and made him forget time and place—and the madmen bent on destruction. Her soft voice soothed his mind and torched his senses. And the feel of her, pliant and giving in his arms, was driving him insane.

"Sure." *I'll hold you, honey. For starters.* He tightened his arms around her.

Cradling her in his arms this way, while she snuggled up so close that he could practically feel her heart beating against his chest, had the blood coursing straight to his cock. He had to have more. And he didn't give much of a damn about the consequences—or anything but hauling Kate to the nearest bed and putting out the blaze.

"Take me to your room."

"The other night you said you wouldn't pay the price," she reminded him, but her soft voice sounded like a caress.

He had to have her. He craved her touch. He wanted her pussy wet and throbbing around his cock. "You're right. I did. But damn it, honey, I was a fool."

As he stood and set her down beside him, he caught a whiff of her flowery perfume mingled with the smell of burning pine branches.

Hell, she could have died out there!

He had to touch her, reassure himself they had both survived this time.

Dragging her back in his arms, he held her close and fed his own hard need. "Do you want this?" he asked, cupping her bottom in his hands and nudging her soft, inviting curves with his erection.

She just trembled in his arms, but when her hips shyly moved, brushing his cock with a tantalizing kind of fire, he sensed that she wanted him, too.

And he couldn't fight her and the potent attraction any longer.

"Make love with me, honey," he whispered in her ear, savoring the way her nipples responded to his searching fingertips when he cupped her breasts in his hands.

"Yes."

It was just one word, spoken so softly he could barely hear it. But it was all he needed.

Ignoring the ache in his knee, he scooped her up in his arms and carried her upstairs.

* * * * *

"I'll close the curtains." Kate averted her gaze from the man whose presence made her roomy bedroom feel as if its walls were closing in on her.

As long as he was holding her, she had no doubts about what they were going to do. But now that he'd set her down in this familiar room, it struck her that he'd never said a word about his feelings for her.

"You got second thoughts, honey?"

He came up behind her and nuzzled at her neck, his warm breath sweet-smelling despite the lateness of the day. His five o'clock shadow tickled her jaw.

He was giving her a chance to change her mind.

She should. But she couldn't. Today she had seen how fleeting life could be. She wanted to live, to feel the joy of Jake's hot passion before her chance was forever lost.

If she could only have him now, like this, it would have to be enough. He made her want his fire to consume her like the actual flames that had threatened them hours earlier. She took his big, callused hand and brought it to her lips.

"No. But Jake, I don't know much about this." She hoped her inexperience wouldn't turn him off.

"I know."

She shuddered when he turned her around and wrapped her in his arms, crushing her against his big, hard-muscled frame. They were so close, she felt each strong beat of his heart through his soft cotton-knit shirt.

His steely arousal nudged her belly, graphically demonstrating that, at least for the moment, he wanted her as much as she wanted him. Her blouse fell away with a brush of his big hands. Then she felt her bra straps sliding down her arms. Kate gasped for breath.

His mouth descended on her bare breasts nipping and suckling at one tingling nipple and then the other while he tugged at the waistband of her shorts with both hands. His velvety lips soothed the places where he'd nipped her with his teeth, and when he closed them over one nipple and sucked it into his mouth she gasped at the new, sizzling sensation that slammed into her belly and made her want more.

Mindlessly, she began unbuttoning his shirt. She wanted, needed, to touch him the way he was touching her.

"My God, honey."

"I-I'm sorry," she stammered, snatching her hand away from his chest as he shrugged out of the shirt and tossed it to the floor.

"Don't stop. For God's sake, don't stop." Sounding as though she were torturing him, he groped for her hands and pulled them back to skin as soft as textured silk stretched taut over rock-hard muscle.

Then another sudden jolt of sensation coursed through her body. He'd moved his hand between her legs, and his long, callused fingers were doing something wonderful, something that made sizzling, sparkling feelings grip her in their hold.

"Jake."

She hardly recognized the husky sound of her own voice. Soon, though, the emotions he was arousing in her swept away her ability to think at all. All she could do was hold onto him and drown in the heady vortex of newly discovered passion.

"You like that."

He sounded hoarse, almost as if he was choking. She let her hand drift down, away from his flat, masculine nipples, and her fingers combed through soft, dark hair that thinned into a fine line before it disappeared into his low-riding jeans.

"I like touching you. A lot," she murmured. He felt good. Warm and alive. His power was barely leashed under her seeking hands. She delved shyly with her fingers beneath the waistband of his jeans, and he sucked in his taut stomach muscles to give her room.

"I want you naked," he said gruffly, and she stood still while he drew her shorts and plain cotton panties down her legs.

Without any of the shyness she had thought she'd feel, she stepped away from the puddle of clothing at her feet and stood bare and trembling before his hot gaze.

"Beautiful. You're beautiful. So sexy."

She watched his handsome face, saw his dark eyes grow almost black with passion. Would he stand there, as if transfixed, forever? She wanted him to undress.

"I want to see you, too," she said, deliberately feasting her eyes on his big, muscular body.

When he moved, it startled her. His usually fluid motions were abrupt. She watched him bend over and tug off first one boot and then the other. Next came his socks.

She drew in a deep breath when she realized the significance of the huge, hard bulge that strained against the zipper of his jeans. Would he finish undressing now?

He didn't. She saw him reach into his pocket and withdraw several small packages. Only after he'd tossed them onto the night stand beside her bed did she realize that not once had he stopped looking at her.

"You can put one on me, honey."

"What?"

"A condom. I don't have sex without one. Ever. Not even if you're on the Pill."

Kate's cheeks grew hot with embarrassment. "I'm not."

"I didn't think so." He moved back within her reach and took her hands. Bending to brush his lips across hers, he dragged her hands to his waistband.

"Feel what you do to me," he rasped, moving one of her hands down until it rested on his distended fly. "Have you done this before?"

"No." She'd never considered herself a sexual being before she met Jake. But when he strained against her hand like this, all she wanted was to take his hot, heavy sex inside her.

"I'll go easy." His uncharacteristically gentle words poured over her like warm, sweet honey. "I'll make it good for you."

"I know."

"Undress me. Touch me," he whispered.

She rubbed her palm against the heated ridge of his sex, felt him grow even harder at her touch.

"That feels like heaven, honey. Take off my pants. Please."

Kate hesitated. Then, with shaking fingers, she managed to work the metal button loose. The zipper wasn't as easy. She wondered why its straining teeth hadn't already split apart.

Finally the zipper gave way. With shaking hands, she drew his snug jeans down thighs bulging with muscle and cushioned with soft, dark hair.

He shuddered when her knuckles brushed intimately against his taut male flesh without the impediment of heavy denim.

Knowing her touch affected him so strongly encouraged her to peel off his jeans quickly. When she stood again, she couldn't help gasping at the way he looked, magnificently sculpted and naked except for the tight, navy briefs that emphasized his masculinity.

"Don't stop. The rest comes off easy."

"I-I can't." She couldn't bring herself to strip away his underwear as brazenly as he seemed to expect her to.

"Okay. We'll wait."

"I'm sorry. Do you want me to lie down?"

"Not yet, honey. Come here."

Instead of taking her in his arms, he knelt at her feet and began stroking his way up her legs. The touch of his rough, warm fingers on her own much softer flesh was incredibly arousing while at the same time it served to soothe her fears.

"What are you doing?" she asked when he moved in closer and blew gently on her pubic curls.

"Making you feel good. Come here."

Puzzlement turned to embarrassment when he cupped her buttocks in both hands and started nibbling at her inner thighs. But it felt delicious. Tingly and hot and…

Still she almost stopped him when he nudged her legs apart and started caressing her between them with those gentle, work-roughened fingers. She burrowed her fingers into his thick, dark hair and reveled in its silky texture.

The sensations bubbling inside her felt…unbelievable. Like fire and ice, burning and chilling and making her seek something—something more she sensed lay just beyond her reach. "Don't—don't stop."

"I've just started, honey."

By the time his mouth took over for his nimble fingers, she was burning as much with embarrassment at the unexpected intimacy as with the pleasure-pain from thousands of sparks converging inside her.

This couldn't be right. She should stop him.

"Jake…" Oh, God, his tongue felt like hot wet velvet licking her clitoris and making it swell and harden. "Don't…don't stop," she croaked as this incredible sensation of pleasure began there and cascaded through her body in undulating waves of white-hot, pulsing pleasure.

She'd waited all her life to feel this way. And they hadn't even made love yet.

So hot he was damn near ready to explode, Jake raised his head.

Seeing Kate trembling, flushed and oblivious to everything except the release he had just given her, almost sent him over the edge. The flowery scent of her perfume mingled with smoke, with her sweat and his. He ought to bottle up the smell and sell it as an aphrodisiac.

Barely in control now, he scooped her up and set her on the edge of the bed.

He was beyond ready, so hard he hurt when he shucked his underwear and grabbed one of the tiny packets. Standing nude before her, he dropped the wrapped condom between her legs.

"Look at me, honey."

When her eyes widened as she stared at his throbbing cock, he vaguely recalled through a haze of need that this sexy, sensual creature who had just climaxed at the touch of his hands and mouth was still a virgin.

He should run, get away. Escape from this woman who apparently was determined to give him much more than he was willing to return.

But he couldn't.

He had to have her. Bury his cock inside that soft, welcoming warmth and ease the agony in his groin. Agony that spread like wildfire to every cell in his body.

"Touch me. You think I gave you pleasure, touching and kissing your clit? It's nothing compared to how you'll feel with me inside your tight little pussy." God, but her hesitant stroking was going to make him come if she kept it up for long.

Her touch was warm, gentle, almost soothing. But when she touched him with her tongue and sucked the tip of his cock between her lips, he jerked away. He couldn't take any more.

"Enough. Lady, you drive me wild. Put that condom on me now, or it'll be too late." He watched her fingers flutter when she ripped away the wrapper.

"Like this?" She positioned the rolled prophylactic gingerly at the tip of his erection.

"Yeah, honey. Roll it on down." Deliberately, stroking the thin latex over his cock, she sheathed him with a tenderness he could feel.

"Hurry!" She was driving him crazy with that condom.

Before she finished getting it just right, he had two fingers inside her, and the dewy wetness he found there told him she was ready. He shuddered when she traced his length and thickness again with trembling hands.

"You're so big." Her voice was tiny, quivering, as if she was afraid.

His cock was getting harder and hotter by the second, and the way she was stroking it was about to send him over the edge. "Just the right size to give you pleasure," he muttered, hoping he could last long enough for that to happen.

He couldn't if he waited any longer. As gently as he could, he pushed her down across the bed. Then he spread her legs and knelt between them. Slowly, carefully, he pressed into her hot, tight pussy.

As she let him in, he cursed the latex barrier that dulled sensations. Then, he blessed it, for she felt so unbelievably good. If he'd sunk his cock inside her pussy skin to skin, he'd have been lucky to last two minutes.

She thrust upward with her hips and wrapped her slender thighs around his waist. He was in heaven, buried to the hilt within her satin embrace.

God, she was tight. She fit him like a glove. Groaning, he wished again that he could feel her hot, wet dew easing his way.

He wanted to savor her slick, hot moisture on the bare flesh of his cock.

He craved more contact. Supporting most of his weight on his elbows, he lowered his body to rest on hers. While he rotated his torso enough to tickle her taut nipples with the hair on his chest, he clamped his mouth over hers and plunged his tongue inside.

He needed to explode in her. But he wanted to stay buried inside her forever.

"Honey, you feel so damn good." The effort of holding back his climax made him tremble all over.

Hips moving in tandem with the deep thrusts of his tongue in her mouth, he coaxed her to respond. And when she rose to meet him, he drove harder, faster. He gave her all she demanded.

Her fingernails raked his back. Her body quaked. The muscles inside her contracted violently around his cock.

Shuddering at the power of her orgasm, he thrust once more and came. Then he collapsed, pinning her under his nearly dead weight.

When he could breathe again, he looked into her passion-glazed eyes. "You're something, honey." Taking her with him, he rolled to his side.

Their bodies were still joined, her legs still wrapped tightly around his hips. Her softness still surrounded his wrung-out cock. For a long time, Jake stayed in Kate's embrace, reluctant to lose the closeness.

Damn it to hell! He didn't want to feel closeness. Just the release he'd sought and found. The feelings he couldn't suppress reminded him too much of how he had cared for Alice. How much her betrayal had hurt.

He pulled away. When he did, her dreamy expression turned sad.

He felt guilty. But not guilty enough to throw good sense out her bedroom window.

Naked, he stood and touched her shoulder. When those aqua cat eyes opened and focused on his wrung-out cock, he grinned. "I'll be back, honey. I need to check out our protection. Where's the bathroom?"

Her face suddenly reddened, and she seemed unable to find her voice. As he limped off in the direction she had pointed, he thought idly that it had been a long time since he'd seen a lover blush.

* * * * *

Kate lay back, still caught up in the magic. Finally she knew what it meant to be a woman. To love a man.

And what a man Jake Green was!

He was big and tough and earthy. With a body like a statue of some ancient god. Perfectly honed, beautiful in spite of the bruises that awful man had put on him from head to toe. The crisscrossed mesh of scars on one of his knees reminded her he was human, not the invincible hero he had first appeared to be.

And she had trouble believing how fantastic he'd made her feel.

Nothing in her previous experience compared with the sensation of having him inside her. Even if she could never experience his touch, the physical power of his work-hardened body again, she would be glad for having shared his passion.

But she couldn't help dreaming that Jake would come to love her. Her eyelids fluttered and closed, and she tried to hold on to impossible illusions.

The cotton sheet slid away, followed by the rough-soft warmth of a damp cloth that moved gently from her belly to the tender, sensitive spots between her legs. Kate opened her eyes to feast on the naked beauty of the man who filled her heart as he had fulfilled her body.

"Sore?" he asked, his tone as intimate as the word was casual.

"N-no. Well, maybe a little." She flinched slightly. The moist heat soothed her, but she wished it were his bare, callused hand — or his hard, throbbing penis with its satiny smooth heat.

"Keep looking at me like that, honey, and I'll forget I need some time before we can do it again." Jake finished bathing her and set the cloth on the nightstand. "Once wasn't enough, was it?" he asked softly, and from his expression Kate guessed that his question disturbed him.

"Was it for you?"

"Damn it, no."

He stood and stared at the clothes they had so carelessly strewn across the floor.

Then he came and sat beside her on the bed. "Look. I don't want to leave you here alone. Isn't there a friend or neighbor you could stay with for a few hours?"

"You can't stay?"

He shook his head. "I've got to go see what's going on down at the well. Come on, get dressed. I'll run you over to a neighbor's."

"I'll be all right here. You don't need to worry about me." Kate forced a cheerful smile that didn't reach her heart.

"Yes, I do, for more reasons than the fact that at least one of our arsonists is still on the loose."

Kate watched him pull up his briefs and jerk his jeans up. She couldn't help reaching out and stroking the silky skin of his bare back when he sat beside her to put on his socks and boots.

"You're so big, so beautiful," she said, tracing well-defined cords of Jake's shoulder muscles down to where they converged at his spine. She felt each nervous twitch, each subtle movement beneath her fingers. Maybe her touch affected him more than he wanted it to.

"I'd stay if I could. Believe me, honey, there's nothing I'd like better than to crawl back into that bed and mess around with you all night long." He reached out and tugged at her hand, pulling her up with him. "Come on, now, get dressed and I'll drop you off with one of your friends."

Kate dragged the sheet around her when she realized she was still naked. To her surprise, she found that her still-tingling legs could support her weight. "I'd really rather stay here."

"Not as long as we've got a firebug running loose." Jake bent and picked up the clothes he'd stripped off her not long before. "Here. You want to call first?" he asked, glancing toward the small table that held David's picture—and a phone.

She couldn't think of anyone closer than Becky who would welcome her gladly into their home. "I have a friend in Laurel," she murmured. "But I can drive myself there."

"No."

* * * * *

Within minutes Jake had settled Kate into his car and was headed toward Laurel. They'd stopped at the well to drop off the new drill bit he'd brought from Jackson and find out what progress the security men had made toward catching their other arsonist. With determination, he pushed aside the memory of what he and Kate had just shared—and the nagging urge to fuck her again and again—while he tried to concentrate on stopping the sabotage once and for all.

"Why did you need another bit?" Kate asked, her soft drawl shattering his shaky willpower as it sent a jolt of need straight to his groin.

"For the new well we're going to start drilling next week."

"You're going to put in more wells?"

He glanced her way. "Yeah. We'll be drilling wells in this oil field for several years, at least."

"You mean, you'll be around here that long?"

"Would it bother you if I were?"

"No. I just didn't know you'd leased any other property around here."

"We have leases on around five thousand acres, more if the land man's been doing his job for the past two or three weeks. If the price of crude goes up, we could be putting as many as a hundred wells in this part of Mississippi. Even with prices depressed the way they are now, we can make money on fifteen or twenty if we put them in the right places. Assuming we can stop whoever is trying to put the company six feet under."

Kate smiled, that gentle smile that lit her whole face up. "You'll catch them. I'm sure of that."

"Yeah. We will. Whatever it takes. The Oil and Gas Board's refusing to grant us any more drilling permits until we do."

Kate frowned. "I'm surprised that you've been able to lease so much of the land around here. Some of my neighbors have been up in arms since I opened my place up for oil drilling."

"There are some who are holding out. Mostly bigger landowners like you. But in the end, they'll prove they're as susceptible to the lure of money as anyone else is. Their crops have failed too many times in recent years. Their land is farmed out, and they can't eat their principles or their long-dead ancestors forever. Everybody needs money, and leases provide it. Oil wells on their land will make them rich. You certainly weren't the only one to lease us a good-size section, honey, just the first."

"Then why are my neighbors being so mean to me? It's as though I'm the only person within a hundred miles who's put oil leases out on their property."

"I don't know," he said, thinking idly that it was weird that Kate apparently had to go twenty miles from home to find a friend to put her up for the night. "Did some long-dead ancestor of yours make the mistake of fighting on the wrong side of the Civil War?" he asked, hoping his question would make her smile.

"Not exactly. My great-great grandfather bought this place for taxes after the Civil War. And he made a success of himself with his store in Laurel when I guess lot of folks were suffering."

"A carpetbagger, huh?"

"No. He didn't fight in the war at all. He was a Jewish peddler who came here when he emigrated from Germany."

"I didn't realize you were Jewish," he said matter-of-factly. "I don't imagine many Jews live around here."

"No. Oh, Jake, I should have told you before we…"

Jake watched Kate's cheeks turn a becoming pink. It amused him that she apparently couldn't come right out and say they'd just had mind-blowing sex.

"Why?" He'd never felt the need to discuss religion with the women he took to bed. Except Alice, and not even her until they'd decided to get married.

"Would you have wanted me if you'd known?"

Jake devoured her body with his eyes and grinned. "Honey, I'd have wanted you. You can take that to the bank. I'm Jewish, too, but religion has nothing to do with what you do to my libido."

* * * * *

After leaving her at the door of her friend's modest white brick house, he tried hard to put Kate out of his mind.

He didn't want to care that she lived alone, not close enough with her neighbors nearby that she could go to them when trouble loomed. And he certainly didn't welcome the anger that bubbled up in him when he pictured some narrow-minded rednecks hurting Kate's feelings with their sharp tongues.

But he knew all about the subtle forms of disapproval that fundamentalist rural Southerners could express toward someone who, to them, was different.

Heathen.

That was the word they'd used then, and the one he had heard that disapproving old woman mouth at Kate the other day when she'd described the roughnecks who were here to drill the wells.

A word that Jake had more than passing familiarity with.

He'd liked the close-knit, down-home friendliness of Alice's friends and relatives when she took him home to meet her folks long years ago in tiny Thayer, Georgia. At first they had seen him only as the Aggies' star quarterback—a fitting match for their hometown beauty queen. And he'd pictured himself with Alice, living a simple rural life away from the pressures of Houston society and his overachieving, ambitious family.

It hadn't worked out that way, though. The good folks of Thayer, Georgia had cooled to him damn quickly when they found out he wasn't a card-carrying member of the Baptist church. Not even marrying Alice in that church had persuaded some of her parents' friends he wasn't a "heathen" out to corrupt their pampered darling and destroy their simple way of life.

Fortunately he'd only had to put up with that subtle prejudice a dozen or so times, when he and Alice had gone to visit her folks. Kate must have lived with it all her life.

Jake shouldn't give a damn.

After all, Kate had left Groveland but returned by her own volition. She had apparently decided to stay after her father died, even though her family was gone and her only ties here were to her land. It had been her choice to sign oil leases, her decision that made her set herself up as her neighbors' pariah. He shouldn't give a damn if people treated her badly.

But he did.

He could take her away from here.

What the hell was he thinking? Just because she made him feel like they were making love instead of fucking was no reason to start thinking dumb things like that.

* * * * *

Determined not to let his thoughts continue on their dangerous path, Jake tried to think of incidents with former employees, problems with landowners and their neighbors at any of GreenTex's domestic fields—anything that might have triggered this sudden outbreak of sabotage. Anything that might keep him from reliving his time this afternoon in Kate Black's bed, and the most satisfying fucking he'd had in years. Maybe ever.

Pulling in and stopping beside the derrick, he greeted Skip once he'd gotten out of the car.

"Did Sheriff Jones finally haul our firebug off to jail?" he asked.

Skip grinned. "Yeah."

"Is the fire completely out?"

"Uh-huh. But Ms. Kate's pond's damn near dry. We had to pump water out of it, onto the brush fire our friend set in the woods."

Jake nodded. "We're lucky she has that pond. Otherwise we'd be calling out the wild well control folks."

"They give you a hard time up in Jackson?" Skip headed for the trailer, Jake at his heels.

Suddenly exhaustion overtook him. Jake sank onto the lumpy sofa bed and opened the beer Skip handed him. "They didn't jerk the permits we already have, if that's what you mean. But the Board refused to grant any of the new ones Blake and I applied for. They made it damn clear there won't be any more permits to drill on GreenTex leases in Mississippi until the sabotage stops."

"Damn. I was planning to bring a second drilling crew over here pretty soon."

Propping his bum leg up on an overturned trash can, Jake shrugged. "We've got to stop the bastards soon, or GreenTex won't have enough assets left to fund the drilling. Did that guy we caught finally start talking?"

"No. Not even when the sheriff told him he'd be doing ten to twenty years of hard labor on an old-fashioned Mississippi chain gang."

"Will he?" The idea sounded good to Jake.

"Hell, I don't know. I hope so. It's no more than the son-of-a-bitch deserves. Bob Wallace needs to talk to you before you leave," Skip said when the middle-aged investigator joined them in the trailer.

Jake sat back and listened while Bob brought him up to date on the nationwide search for information about the guy they caught this afternoon. While the dry-voiced security chief droned on about fingerprint searches and background checks, Jake found his thoughts drifting back to Kate.

"Ms. Kate's gotten to you, hasn't she?" Skip asked after Wallace left. "You going back up there tonight?"

"Why?"

"Because if you are, you might tell her we'll be sinking seismic holes starting bright and early tomorrow morning."

"Already? I thought, since you had to get that barn fire put out this morning, you'd still be struggling to get this well hooked up to the pipeline."

"Nah. We finished up about an hour ago. Thought you might be interested. Black-GreenTex Number One is flowing into the pipeline." Jake saw the look of pride on Skip's face.

"How much?"

"A little over thirty barrels an hour and going up. We're getting a good flow of liquid gas, too."

Jake let out a whistle. "Close to seven-fifty a day. Not bad. Pretty damn good, in fact. Go call and tell Susie you've got a bonus coming, so she can spend it," he told his friend.

"I already did. Hey, I almost forgot to tell you. Susie told me I'm gonna be a daddy again."

Jake couldn't help it. He was jealous. Jealous of Skip for his pretty, loving wife and his two sturdy sons. Jealous of his friend's joy at the prospect of having another child to add to his happiness. He forced himself to smile and extend his hand.

"Congratulations."

"Thanks. We're hoping for a little girl this time."

Jake hoped Skip hadn't sensed his envy.

"Hey, you didn't answer me. Are you gonna see Ms. Black tonight? If you aren't, I'd better high-tail it up there and warn her we'll be traipsing around on her property with the portable rig."

"You don't have to. She's not there. But I'll tell her when I bring her home."

"So you took her somewhere for the night?" Skip asked, a big grin spreading across his face.

"Not exactly. I didn't want her up at her house alone, so I took her to Laurel to see one of her friends. I told her I'd pick her up about nine tomorrow." Jake didn't know why, but he was reluctant for Skip to know he and Kate had become lovers.

"What's the problem, Jake? Afraid to admit you might be feeling more than an itch in your jockstrap for Ms. Kate? Are you scared you might just have to toss that chip off your shoulder and let yourself care for somebody again?"

"What the hell do you mean?" Jake's fists clenched, and he stepped within striking distance.

Skip held his ground, and Jake knew from experience that he wouldn't back down. He watched Skip sift a hand through his hair before looking him in the eye.

"You know, Jake, you may be the best damn petrochemical engineer in the world, but you don't have a lick of sense if you don't know what I meant."

"Spell it out, pal."

"If that's what it takes."

Skip ambled casually over to the refrigerator and grabbed another beer. "This is gonna take some time. Might as well sit back down and relax."

Jake shrugged. He and Skip went back a long way, back to when they had shared an apartment at college. Jake had learned the hard way that when Skip had something on his mind, he might as well listen from the outset. His friend wouldn't let go until he'd said his piece.

Chapter Five

"So what's on your mind?"

Jake had an overwhelming urge to get back to Kate, and he didn't much like the feeling. It was too much as if he needed the woman.

He watched Skip down half a beer before he set the bottle down and turned to him. Finally he spoke up.

"You know, we've been friends a helluva long time. I think I know you better than your own kin."

"Get to it, my friend. I haven't had free psychoanalysis from an overeducated roughneck for a good long while. But I don't have all night."

"Okay. Ever since you dumped Alice, or she dumped you, whichever, you've been a damn hypocrite. You come home with me and envy me for Susie and the kids. You say you want a wife, a few children of your own. But you don't. Not really. Since your divorce, you've been using and discarding women right and left. You've set standards so high not even your matchmaking mama and sisters can find you what you want..."

"Hold it. You don't think I've asked my mother to go scouting out women for me, do you? Let alone Shana, Leah or Deb?"

"You haven't stopped them."

"I'd like for you to try stopping them. At least I escaped the minute I could, when our Saudi field manager decided to take early retirement."

"You haven't stopped them the only way you could — by finding your own woman or shutting up and admitting you don't want to take a chance on marrying again. You've deliberately hit on sluts and ice princesses so you wouldn't be tempted to waste any tenderness on them."

"So? Maybe I like those kinds of women." The accusation stung, though, because Skip's description pretty well fit the women Jake had slept with after his divorce — until he'd skulked off to the Saudi Arabian oil fields to lick his wounds.

"If you do, why are you sniffing around Kate Black? From what I can see, she just might be that one in a million woman. If it weren't for Susie, I could get real worked up over her, myself. She's no porcelain doll like the ones your mama sets you up with, but she doesn't strike me as being an oil rig groupie either."

"Shut up, Skip."

But Skip was right. Kate was different from the women he'd dated since his divorce. What he wasn't so sure of was that she was different enough from Alice. "I like her," he admitted to himself as much as to his friend.

He watched Skip's eyebrows lift. "Don't go reading more to that than is there."

"Well, at least you aren't looking at her like she's a quick, convenient fuck — or a broodmare for the next generation of Green oil millionaires."

"No, she isn't." Suddenly Jake pictured Kate as she had been this afternoon, wild and innocent at the same time when she'd made love with him in her narrow bed.

"Well, do you love her?"

Jake snorted. "You know me better than that."

"You loved—"

"Alice," Jake spat out. "Yeah, I know. And what, I ask you, did that get me? Besides royally fucked over?"

"Bitter, pal. It got you cold and bitter. You're not yourself anymore. What the hell do you expect in a woman?"

"One who wants me for who I am, not what I am or how much money I've got. One who judges people the same way I do, who doesn't let prejudice get in the way of how she feels. One who won't be on my back about the work I do, and who'll love living at the ranch instead of in some Houston palace." *One who won't kill my kid and leave me for another man.* "You're being obtuse. You know exactly what I want," Jake concluded, scowling at his friend.

"You want a woman like Susie." Skip's eyes were unnaturally bright. "She's no big city girl."

"Neither was Alice. At first, I guess I was a novelty to her. And then we fell in love. Getting married when we finished college seemed like the right thing to do."

"Before long, she got to whining that I spent so much time out in the field. She got uptight about my being in the oil business when she thought I should have been playing pro football, and even more upset that I wouldn't give up working in the oil fields and take a job of some kind in the Houston office."

Skip shook his head. "Why didn't you have kids? They would have kept her busy at home when you were gone."

Jake flinched. He'd never told Skip exactly how his marriage ended. Maybe it was time. But the words damn near stuck in his throat. "She didn't want kids right away, and that was okay with me. But when I started pushing for us to start a family, she balked. By that time, I guess, we really didn't have much of a marriage left."

"That was when you started spending months at a time over in the Middle East, wasn't it?"

"Yeah. Alice must have gotten careless with her pills while I was gone, because the second to last time I came home from Riyadh before the divorce, I got her pregnant. She wasn't happy about it, but I was thrilled. Afterward I flew out to Venezuela to take care of some problem. Hell, Skip! I was only gone two weeks, because I had to be back in time to stand up at my cousin Greg's wedding. When I got back, she told me she'd gotten an abortion and filed for divorce."

Jake's hands shook, and his words caught in his chest. "She married Durwood Yates the day the divorce was final." He looked up and saw his friend's shocked expression.

"That cocksucker." Skip's fist slammed down onto the table. "I'd have killed him. Her, too."

"Sometimes I wanted to. At the time, though, I loved her."

"Do you still?"

"Hell, no," Jake growled. "I don't even hate her much anymore, except when I think about her killing my flesh and blood."

"I didn't know you felt so strongly about abortion," Skip said, rubbing a hand across his brow. "But I'd have thought Alice would have, her being raised the way she and Susie were."

"I didn't—at least, I'd never thought much about abortion one way or another." Jake couldn't say the word without hurting. "I never thought Alice would consider it, either. If I'd had any idea she was going to kill my baby the minute I left town, I never would have gone."

"So you've let that bitch turn you cold and bitter and afraid to take a chance on being happy with someone else? Are you scared, Jake? Is that why you've gone out of your way to fuck around with sluts and date society girls who would die if you took them away from the stores and parties and all the other glitter of the city? Is that the reason you've hauled the ones you've slept with out to your ranch afterward and told them that's where you're gonna stash them while you go all over the world drilling for oil? So you won't be tempted to take another chance on love?"

"No, goddamn it. Alice did a good job, taught me love is for kids and fools."

Jake drained his beer and got up to replace the bottle in the empty case. Without having to turn in the tiny kitchen, he opened the refrigerator and retrieved two cold sodas. He sat back down and handed one to Skip, who seemed for once to be searching for words to say.

"If Susie and I don't have love between us, just what do you think we have?" Skip finally asked when Jake looked him in the eye.

"Compatibility. Good sex. Your two little boys and the new kid that's on the way. Respect for each other and tolerance for the differences between you. If there are any differences, that is."

"Well, you just defined what Susie and me call love, old buddy. And all I've been saying is that I think you've been looking in the wrong places for the lady you want. If you really want one."

Skip headed for the door while Jake tried to tell himself Kate Black wouldn't, couldn't heal the kind of emotional wounds Skip couldn't possibly understand. Wounds Jake would never risk opening up again.

* * * * *

Jake had been quiet when he picked her up at Becky's house the next afternoon, and when they got back here he'd holed himself up in her bedroom to make some calls he'd told her couldn't wait. Still, Kate liked having him with her, even if he had obviously chosen to put some emotional distance between them since they'd made love.

She hurried around the kitchen, checking the potatoes for doneness with a two-pronged fork and stirring the beans one more time, before lifting chicken-fried steak pieces onto a platter. The gravy was too thick, so she added a little more milk from the carton on the counter.

Good, it didn't turn lumpy this time, she noted with relief. She hoped Jake would come downstairs soon, before everything got cold and unappetizing. For the first time since Pop had died, she enjoyed fixing a meal. She hated cooking just for herself.

Shyly, she touched her breasts through the barriers of her clothing. They were sensitive, a little sore from Jake's rough hands and the abrasion of his shadowed chin. Still, she had no remorse. She'd loved every minute of making love with him and could hardly wait for more, even though she knew that playing with Jake was like playing with fire—in more ways than the obvious one.

What was Jake's magic? There was something about him, so much more than his dark, handsome face and a body that reminded her of a classical statue. His physical attributes alone hadn't lured her into his arms.

If anything, Jake's towering height and rippling, work-toughened muscles intimidated her. She decided it must have been those fleeting glimpses of his sensitivity and tenderness that had eased her qualms and released her inhibitions.

As she stirred the gravy, Kate sighed. Unlike most of her friends at college, all she'd ever dreamed of was nurturing a husband, making him a happy home and being a loving mother to his children.

Pity, Jake Green didn't seem to be a man who'd take to nurturing, though he certainly made her want to sweep away that cynical attitude and earn his love and trust.

Kate shook off her futile hopes. To wish for what would never be was hardly productive. For now, she'd accept what Jake offered and give him as much as he'd take from her. She'd store up memories to hold her when he'd gone to drill more wells and enchant more faceless women. Turning back to the stove, she ladled beans into a bowl.

When she looked up, her heart beat faster. She smiled. Jake's jeans-clad body was framed in her kitchen doorway. He answered her welcoming smile with one of his own, but the brooding expression that darkened his deep brown eyes made her wonder if seeing the domestic scene she'd set had raised his defenses.

"Something smells good," he said as though he'd suddenly developed a keen interest in what was in those platters on the counter.

"I hope you like it."

"I will. Can I help?"

"No. Everything's ready. Just sit down and I'll put it on the table." Kate hesitated. "Would you rather eat in the dining room? I could set the table there."

"Honey, don't do anything special. Here's fine." His voice was mellow, soothing, but she sensed his wariness. After watching him settle his long, lean body at one of the places at the table, she started setting out the food.

"Would you like a drink? I think there's a bottle of wine here somewhere," Kate said as she rummaged hurriedly through the old-fashioned cabinets. "Or I've got tea. And cola. I could make some coffee if you'd rather have that."

"Tea's fine. You don't have to go to any trouble, honey."

"It's no trouble…"

He's never called me by my name. Not even when we were making love.

At that disturbing realization, Kate set the pitcher on the table.

She tried hard to think of something else. Dinner, for instance. Had she forgotten anything?

The biscuits. Grabbing a hot mitt, she hurried to the stove and snatched the pan from the oven. After dumping the biscuits onto a plate and setting it down in front of Jake, she sat and served herself from the steaming platters.

The hearty appetite he exhibited in bed carried over to eating, apparently, because he was making quick work of the hefty portions he'd put onto his plate.

"Do all country girls cook like this?" he asked as he split a biscuit and poured creamy milk gravy over it. "I haven't had chicken-fried steak and gravy this good since the last time I was at Skip's ranch."

"I'm glad you like it." But she still wished he'd call her by name.

"What's wrong, honey?" he asked, as if he'd noticed Kate's uneasiness.

"Nothing. Can I pass you more beans and potatoes?"

"Sure."

Kate handed him the bowl. Her conscience was getting the best of her. She had tossed good sense out the window and crawled into bed with this handsome stranger who had taken her heart while giving only his body.

Her cheeks growing warm, she recalled the half-a-dozen foil wrapped packages he'd tossed onto her bedside table. How she'd melted when he touched her with his hands and mouth. And the delicious feelings that had burst inside her when he'd filled her with his hot, heavy sex.

Maybe there was something to be said for pure, uncomplicated sex.

But he has never called you by name, just "honey" or "lady" or some other offhand endearment. Not even the memory of all those sensual delights could make that stinging thought go away.

Jake looked up, apparently amused, and Kate met his gaze. "You know, honey, you'd think after what we shared upstairs yesterday afternoon, we wouldn't be stammering around like strangers," he said, and his voice was like a caress.

There he goes again. Kate felt the heat on her cheeks.

"But we are strangers, aren't we?" She set her fork down on her nearly untouched plate of food. "You don't even use my name," she blurted out before she could stop herself.

He looked surprised. "Why, sure I do. You think I don't know it's you making my cock hot and hard? That I'd have been just as horny for any woman I might have run across?"

"Yes. No. I don't know. Jake, I've never..." His explicit comments confused and embarrassed her.

"I know. It meant a lot to me—you know, that you wanted me the way you did. Come on now. Don't get all uptight on me. Dinner is delicious." His lips curved in a cajoling grin, and she thought when she looked at him that some of the moody darkness had left his eyes.

"All right." She picked up her fork to muss her food around her plate, watching Jake eat with apparent gusto. As far as she could tell, he was oblivious to her discontent.

But she'd gone and fallen in love with him. No matter what he said, it hurt to think he might have made love as easily and pleasurably to any woman—that she'd just been handy at the time.

* * * * *

"Let's take a walk. I need to work off some of your good food." He also wanted to be damn sure the fire hadn't started up again in the woods behind the house. And he wanted to ease this sweet woman's conscience, too. That surprised the hell out of him.

Ordinarily, Jake walked out when a woman pulled a sulky act on him. With Kate, though, he figured her silence stemmed from embarrassment at the way she'd come apart in his arms.

He was certain he hadn't hurt her physically. She'd taken as much as she gave him yesterday afternoon. He was pretty certain that the climax she'd enjoyed with him had been her first—and he granted that her inexperience gave her license to have a few recriminations.

"Ready for a little exercise?" he asked when she didn't respond.

Her reply was a silent nod and a subtle movement toward the kitchen door.

"Is it easier for you to call all your women 'honey' than to try and remember their names?" she asked tightly when they paused in front of her house.

"Hey! What kind of rotten bastard do you think I am?"

He grasped her shoulders and turned her to face him. Suddenly feeling cold inside because their bodies weren't touching, he reached out and pulled her into a loose embrace.

"I'm sorry. I have no right to complain."

She trembled in his arms. Knowing she was hurting did strange, unwelcome things to him.

"I told you, I wanted you. That once was not enough. Don't you know, Kate Black, that you've got me damn near obsessed? Don't you realize I don't want to feel the way I do when you're in my arms?"

Jake knew his words had come out sounding harsh, and he imagined Kate thought his anger was directed at her. Deliberately, he soothed her with slow strokes of one hand and along her spine.

When he spoke again, he gentled his tone. "Lady, it's been a helluva long time since a woman has made me want her the way I want you."

"It has?" She sounded hopeful but skeptical.

"Yeah. I don't like the feeling, but I can't walk away. Not yet."

Jake wouldn't lie. He wouldn't spout the pretty words he imagined would have Kate crawling all over him the way he wanted her to. But damn it, he wanted her again. She kept him horny like no one had for a long time. Since those few good years with Alice, he reminded himself, but his half-hard cock was in no mood to listen.

"When will you walk away, then?" When Kate tilted her head back, he looked into her solemn aqua eyes.

"When the drilling is done. Or when I quit burning when I look at you. Or when you take yourself off to the city and start enjoying the life your oil money's gonna bring you. What are you going to do, Kate?"

"Nothing different. This is my home. I've put in an application with the Calder County Schools for next year. Not that I think they'll have any openings for primary teachers any time soon. Since the well came in, I can afford to wait until they do. I'd like to teach again."

She sounded wistful. "I love kids. At one time, I thought by now I'd be married and have a house full of my own."

Jake swore under his breath, mentally replaying their conversation yesterday about her neighbors leasing their land. As far as he could recall, he hadn't said anything specific about the new wells he was planning to drill on her land. Had someone given her the impression that Black-GreenTex Number One was going to be it on Kate's entire three hundred sixty acres?

No. He was being paranoid. The land man would have been certain to spell out exactly what rights he was asking a landowner to give over to the company. He shoved his suspicion to the back of his mind.

"Could we go back to the house and sit on the porch awhile?" Kate asked. Jake detected sadness in her expression as he watched her stare out at the charred underbrush and mud that marked where fire had licked out at the edges of the clearing around the house.

"Sure."

He let his arms fall away, but when she turned, he took her hand. He had to touch her, to maintain contact with her soft, giving body.

* * * * *

"You know, you really should think about leaving here, going to New Orleans or Houston or Atlanta and enjoying the fruits of my labor. For the next few years, until we finish drilling wells, this isn't going to be the most pleasant place in the world to live."

Kate turned and looked at Jake, shifting her body but keeping it cradled snugly against his muscular frame as they sat on the creaky front-porch swing.

"I don't mind your well," she replied lazily. His nearness and the hot, humid summer air had lulled her into a sense of easy peace.

"I'll grant you, it's not too annoying to have a free-flowing well like Number One. All it does is gush oil and wet gas out into a pipeline, nice and quietly. Until something goes wrong. Then, we'll have to bring the heavy equipment back in so we can rework it. Number One came in fast, too, and we didn't have to bulldoze access roads all over the place to get equipment to the site. You may not be so lucky with the next wells."

"The next wells?"

Surprised, Kate pulled away to look more closely at Jake.

He seemed puzzled. And a little angry, though apparently not with her. "Yeah. The next wells. You've got three hundred sixty acres here, honey, and all of it is under lease to us."

"What does that mean?"

"It means there are between five and nine drilling units on this place, depending on how we set them up. Number One is on an eighty-acre unit, so there are two hundred eighty acres left. We already have seven permits to drill wells on your land, and I wouldn't have a lot of trouble getting a couple more if I applied for them.

"We're going to sink more seismic holes so I can decide where we'll be drilling next. From what I've seen so far, my plan will be to put in two or three shallow pumping wells next. I've got to look over the new geological reports before making a final decision about where to drill them."

Kate turned away, unable to stem the flow of tears from her eyes. She wiped them off her cheeks, wishing he wasn't there to see her cry.

"The broker who bought the leases told me there would be just one well," she said, angry with herself when she couldn't hold back a sob.

Jake stroked her cheek, his expression stormy.

"Are you sure? The drilling permits you signed give us access to any part of your land. And the lease is for the whole three hundred sixty acres. I have trouble believing any land man would have told you we'd be drilling one well on a property where he had to know we'd be putting at least six oil wells. Which land man did you lease to?"

"Jay Harlan. He lives over in Laurel," she said. "I asked him how many wells there might be when I read the papers he brought for me to sign. And he told me just one, if the company who wanted the leases decided to sink a well at all. Jake, this is my home. I want to stay here. How much worse can it be to stay here than it was when they were running that big drilling engine?"

Kate noticed Jake clenching his fists. She could tell from the tight set of his lips that he was furious now. Good thing his fury wasn't directed at her, or she'd be running for cover.

He stood, long legs planted a foot or so apart, and stared down the hill at the well, now quiet as its oil gushed out into the pipeline. When he spoke, the picture he painted sent shivers through her despite the ninety-degree weather.

"You can stay here and put up with twice the noise and twice the dust, because we'll be drilling two wells at once. And after those shallow wells come in, you'll be listening to the drone of diesel pumps that bring the oil to the surface, twenty-four hours a day."

"All the time?" Kate asked.

"All the time, until a pumpjack breaks down. Then the noise will stop for a while. But it will get worse, because we'll have to bring crews in with more engines and equipment to fix the well so it will start pumping out oil again."

"Maybe the noise won't be too bad." After all, Kate thought, she'd lived with the drilling for months.

Jake shook his head. "Even if the noise doesn't bother you, you probably won't like looking at the access roads we'll have to keep cleared so we can get our machinery in and out."

"So to save my home, I've given you the right to make it so I can't live here in peace?" She felt as though she had been run over by a steamroller.

"Don't think of it like that. The land's here. It isn't going anywhere. And with the money you'll be getting in royalties, you can live like a princess anywhere that suits your fancy."

Kate's heart was breaking. Jake's nearness couldn't console her, for his feelings for her were obviously no more than simple lust. "How long will it be like you described?"

"Five, maybe ten years. That's about as long as most shallow wells keep producing enough oil to make it worth our while to keep them in service. Sometimes we sell out marginal producing wells to smaller companies, and they operate them until all the oil runs out. Deep wells, like Number One down there, can keep producing for twenty, even thirty years."

Jake shrugged, as if Kate's distress had hardly fazed him. Suddenly she wanted to lash out at him, although she realized he wasn't the one who had forced her to lease her land. He had just participated in a profitable venture that was about to make her leave the only home she'd ever known.

"I have to think." Getting up slowly from the swing, Kate paced across the wide boards of the porch floor. "Goodnight, Jake," she said sadly.

As much as she needed him to hold her, as badly as she craved the comfort of his touch, she couldn't seek oblivion in his arms tonight. Not when he'd just told her he planned systematically to destroy the place that was all she had left of her father—her family.

She went inside, but it was a long time before she heard the swing stop creaking. Her body tensed. Her heart beat faster.

Was Jake going to ignore her dismissal? Would he come and offer her more of what they'd shared this afternoon? She didn't know whether she was hoping or dreading that he'd come.

But then she recognized the sound of his booted feet as he walked slowly down her front porch steps and out into the summer night.

And she was lonelier than she'd ever been before she knew what she was missing by sleeping alone.

* * * * *

Jake had gone back to the trailer, but he hadn't slept. More than anything, he'd wanted to follow Kate when she'd left him on the porch. To crawl into her bed and fuck her until she forgot everything but how damn good they were together.

To drift off to sleep in the warmth of her sweet embrace. He'd been hard as a rock when he walked away. Hell, he still had a hard-on now.

The hell of it was, if sex had been the only reason he'd wanted to stay, Jake would have stayed.

But he'd wanted more. Goddamn it, he wanted to soothe her mind and heart as well as devour her tempting little body.

He swore loudly and fluently as he dabbed at a nick the razor made on his jaw. No way would he let Kate Black or any other woman get to him, he promised himself with bitter determination.

Concentrating to keep his hand steady, he finished shaving and splashed water across his face. Then he pulled on his jeans and picked up the phone.

"I know damn well what time it is. Six in the morning." Jake held the phone away from his ear to keep Jay Harlan's bellowed curses from deafening him.

"So you were asleep. So what? I want to talk to you, and I intend to do it now." He paused again. "No, by God, it won't wait until you get to the office."

Jake stated his complaint succinctly then listened, his temper moving quickly toward its boiling point, while Harlan tried to weasel his way out of the hot seat.

"Don't try my patience anymore, you son-of-a-bitch. You told Kate Black before she signed that stinking lease that we'd be drilling only one well on the whole damn three-sixty. And you know as well as I do that if the oil is there, any oil company that holds leases on it's gonna sink wells on every section it can get permits for."

Ol' Jacob Green said to get those leases, no matter what I had to do to get 'em.

Harlan's words rang in Jake's ears. He barely heard the land man rambling on, until Harlan assured him that the lease was in order and that GreenTex could drill wherever on Kate's land that it saw fit.

"I know she signed the agreement. And I know goddamn well what it says. I've got a copy in front of me, and I know how to read. What your ass is in a sling about, Harlan, is lying to a landowner. If you know my father, you know he meant for you to up the price as high as you had to, not to get leases signed by telling property owners bald-faced lies."

"What are you gonna do about it?" Harlan's question came through oily and slick, despite the man's heavy drawl. "Back off drilling on Ms. Kate's land and let your company go down the tubes?"

"I'm going to see that you never get another cent of GreenTex money, you cocksucking bastard. We don't deal with liars and thieves. How much did you take off the top of this lease?"

"Wouldn't you like to know?" Harlan asked, his voice dripping sarcasm.

Jake slammed the receiver down onto its cradle. Moments later, he picked it up again when its insistent ringing intruded on his rage.

Chapter Six

"Jake Green," he growled into the offending instrument.

"Jake. Scott. How's everything going?"

Jake let out a deep breath and sat down to take his brother-in-law's call. Briefly, he recounted his conversation with the local land man and got Scott's assurance that Harlan would no longer be representing GreenTex in Calder County, Mississippi or elsewhere. Then he passed along what information he had been able to collect about the fires and the arsonist that they'd caught trying to blow up Black-GreenTex Number One.

"You need to come home for a few days," Scott said when Jake finished talking. "Jacob has to go into the hospital for some tests. He wants you here."

Jake dreaded to hear the rest. His father worked too hard and probably should have retired five years ago, but no one had been able to persuade him of his own mortality. "Is it serious?" he asked.

"Not yet. But his doctors think his heart will start giving him some real trouble if he doesn't have some procedure to unclog the blood vessels. Hell, if you want the details, I'll have Ben give you a call."

Despite his worry, Jake chuckled at the thought of having Ben fill him in. His sister Leah's husband, the cardiologist, no doubt would tell him far more than he wanted to know about the Old Man's heart. "I don't think I'm up to digesting a medical school lecture right now. When do you need me there?"

"Day after tomorrow. Your father won't let them do a thing until all his kids are home. It will take that long for Shana and Bear to get here from *Mina Su'ud*."

Jake thought for a minute while Scott filled him in on the logistics of his sisters' and nieces' expected arrival in Houston. He didn't feel right, leaving Kate here alone, not with the trouble they'd been having. The damn bastards might burn her house next time.

Why not bring Kate with him?

Jake liked that idea, a lot. Too much, he thought as he formed his plans. "I'll drive to New Orleans today and fly home tomorrow," he said when Scott paused. "Are any of the company planes there?"

Jake recalled that GreenTex usually kept at least one plane at the New Orleans hangar to ferry geologists and engineers back and forth between Houston and its Louisiana offshore fields.

"The new Learjet's there. Roy flew three geologists over yesterday in it so they could hop a helicopter out to the offshore platforms. He's spending a few days with his mother in Metairie, but I can get him back if you need a pilot."

Jake thought for a minute. If he brought Kate, he might just try fucking at ten thousand feet. No. It would embarrass Kate half to death to think the pilot might hear sounds of fucking from behind the closed cabin doors. Besides, Jake was certified to fly the Lear himself, and he enjoyed doing it almost as much as he liked having sex.

"Don't spoil Roy's time off. I'll fly myself home. Would you mind having your secretary get somebody to go over and muck out my condo, though? I may bring Kate Black home with me."

"The woman who owns the land where you're having all the trouble?"

"Yeah."

Jake hung up, and he wondered for several minutes whether Kate could take the kind of heat his meddling mother and sisters would undoubtedly dish out.

He was still furious with Harlan. And mad at himself for worrying about how the man had conned Kate into letting GreenTex come and drill on her land. Stomping to the water dispenser, he grabbed a foam cup and dumped in some instant coffee. As he filled the cup with hot water, he wished he could get Kate off his mind.

He'd take her home, show her the pleasures money could buy in the city. Hopefully Kate would forget about wanting to live on this rundown place in Groveland, Mississippi.

Jake thought about his sisters—and Alice. If Kate was anything like them, it shouldn't take more than a week for her to get hooked on city lights, boutiques, fancy dress-up affairs and the like. She'd forget all about her old home place and her objections to it being turned into an oil field.

And he'd exorcise the unwelcome, tender feelings he had for her. He had to. He couldn't risk falling in love.

His aim unerring, he tossed his coffee cup into the wastebasket across the room.

He'd leave Skip to sink seismic holes and deal with the elusive saboteurs. And while he kept vigil at the Old Man's bedside, he'd settle some very personal business with Kate Black.

* * * * *

Kate woke up bleary-eyed. She'd tossed in her bed most of the night, thoughts of Jake, noisy oil wells, and lying land men jumbling together and keeping her from sleep.

Jake had obviously thought she knew all about his drilling plans. Kate would go to Laurel, confront Jay Harlan and make him put the promises he'd made her into writing.

An hour later, she was cooling her heels outside the land man's dingy office above a variety store in the oldest part of downtown Laurel. The sour-faced woman who kept Harlan's books had said he would be off the phone in a few minutes.

Idly, Kate looked at the dog-eared map that decorated the tiny anteroom, trying to locate her land among the highlighted areas Harlan had marked off as properties leased to GreenTex Oil Company.

"You can go on in, Ms. Kate," the woman finally drawled.

"Ms. Kate," Jay Harlan said, a down-home, good ol' boy smile lighting up his florid face when he picked up some papers from a chair beside his desk. With a wave of his hand, he invited her to sit down.

Kate perched on the edge of the dusty chair and looked Harlan in the eye. "You told me when I signed the lease that the oil company probably wouldn't even drill the first well. And you said that if they did, they would just put one well on my land. I'd like for you to put that in writing for me."

"Now I couldn't do that, Ms. Kate. It wouldn't stand up in court anyway, not unless it was part of the lease itself. What's the matter? I heard your number-one well came in big, and I thought you'd be in here thanking old Jay for helping to make you rich."

Harlan bestowed another of his oily grins on Kate before his expression darkened. "You shouldn't have told Jake Green what I said. That was supposed to have been between the two of us."

"Did you know? That GreenTex was going to put a whole bunch of wells on my land? That they were going to make it impossible for me to stay in my home, enjoy the only thing my father left me?"

Kate struggled to keep her voice from rising. How could Jake's company do business with someone who would connive like this?

"Now, lil' lady, with your royalties from Number One alone, you can buy yourself a right nice place anywhere you set your heart on livin'. Have you got any idea how much money you're gonna make from all that oil your precious home is sitting on? You got no call to be upset. You should be down on your knees telling me you're sorry you screwed up my making more deals with GreenTex."

"Did you know?" Kate asked again, but she already knew the answer.

"Not for sure. Nothing's for certain in the oil business. I had a pretty good idea that wily ol' Jacob Green wouldn't go paying no thousand an acre for no five year lease if he wasn't planning to put a bunch of wells on it."

"B-but he didn't pay that. You gave me a hundred eighty thousand. That was only five hundred an acre." Kate had spent all but forty thousand dollars of that money to pay off a balloon note on a mortgage that her father had taken on their home, and she was saving the rest to pay her taxes. The rest of that money would have eased her mind a lot—and made a good-size dent in the bigger mortgage whose balloon note would be coming due next winter.

"Now, listen here, you should know all about making profits. After all, your daddy ran a store. I bought the lease from you for five hundred an acre and sold it to GreenTex for a thousand. That's how I make my living."

Kate watched the sweat form on Harlan's wide forehead. "You don't work for GreenTex?"

"Naw. I work for me. I buy up leases when I get wind of oil companies sniffing round them. Then I sell them to the highest bidder. Sometimes I keep back a piece of the lease and get royalties when wells come in—but I didn't on yours. Old Man

Green wanted the whole thing, lock, stock and barrel. Wish I'd have kept a piece, now, knowing how big your well came in." Harlan looked dejected.

"I'm going to see my lawyer," Kate said, standing up and trying to maintain her dignity.

"Go right ahead. He'll charge you a couple hundred dollars an hour to tell you the same thing I just said. You signed the lease fair and square. I sold it to GreenTex, and they can put wells all over your land, as long as the Oil and Gas Board issues them permits to drill. I'd wondered about Old Jacob's sanity when they filed for all them permits before they even started drilling the first hole, but I guess he knew what he was doin'."

"C'mere," Harlan said, leading Kate to the little anteroom where she'd looked at the map while waiting to see him.

"See here, sugar," he drawled, pointing out the nine forty-acre blocks that represented Kate's land. "That black pin there is Number One. The yellow-headed ones are smack in the middle of each forty where GreenTex has drilling permits. See the land around yours? The pieces I've colored green already belong to GreenTex. The ones in between, they'll get soon enough. I'm working on the owners.

"Anyhow, I was until you went sniveling to Old Jacob's kid about me telling you stuff that wasn't true. Even if they never drill another well on your property, you're gonna be living smack in the middle of an oil field if you stay."

"Why aren't there any yellow pins on the other properties they've leased?" Despite the feeling of desperation that settled in her mind, she was curious.

"'Cause the Oil and Gas Board's giving young Jake Green a helluva time about new permits. Hasn't helped him any that some nut's been sabotaging their number-one well site. Wish they'd hurry and catch him, because I've got a piece of the action on some of these other properties."

Harlan scratched at his chin as if he were pondering something terribly important. "Personally, I think Ol' Man Green should've kept his kid away from the Board. Let his fancy lawyer from Dallas—Tanner's his name if I remember right—take care of getting permits. Or sent Ward, the driller. That ole boy now, he fits right in with those fellas. Green's kid's too much like a foreigner. You know what I mean."

Yes, Kate knew what Harlan meant. She'd lived around here all her life and learned all about subtle prejudice. She was pretty sure that if Harlan hadn't known her heritage, he'd have come right out and said some of the folks on the Oil and Gas Board didn't cotton to dealing with a Jew.

Somehow she couldn't wring out any sympathy for the greedy land man and his investment in the leases where Jake hadn't been able to get drilling permits.

"So they're going to concentrate on putting all the wells on my land?"

"That's my guess, Ms. Kate. At least until Tanner or Old Man Green's kid manages to wheedle more permits out of the Board. Li'l lady, there's nothing you can do about it. Go on. See your lawyer. He'll tell you the same thing."

With that, Harlan waddled back to his desk, leaving Kate to stare at the map that represented money to the land man. It represented horror to her: horror that she had saved her home only to lose the privilege of living there in peace.

Walking out to her father's ancient Lincoln, Kate let hope revive. Before she started the car, she opened all the windows to let the stifling air escape.

As she drove across town to her lawyer's office, her mind wandered to Jake. She'd reveled in the heat they generated when they made love. So different from the overwhelming miasma of this summer day.

Kate refused to dwell on what part, if any, he had played in displacing her from her home.

* * * * *

Her visit to her lawyer had been enlightening, but not as helpful as she hoped. Jay Harlan had been lying. Again. She probably could, her lawyer told her, get the contract set aside for fraud in the inducement. Which, she reflected, might be what Jake was so mad about.

But even so it would be expensive and he couldn't guarantee he could move forward fast enough to stop the next well from being drilled. Every well that was drilled weakened her case. In the end, she might only win monetary damages, and not as much as she'd make from the oil itself.

She couldn't afford the lawsuit. And always scrupulously honest, she had to admit she would have signed the papers even if Harlan had been truthful. Without the money from the lease, she couldn't have paid off that one mortgage, and she'd have lost her home to the bank.

After she left the lawyer's office, though, she had been so upset that she forgot to stop at the supermarket. As a result, she had to make a quick stop at the Groveland crossroads store where Gladys Cahill was holding court with a few neighbors.

While they had all been civil, they'd made Kate feel about as welcome as the plague. Funny. She knew now that most of them had leased their land for oil exploration, too.

Sighing, Kate let her mind wander. She didn't feel like having company. She wished, in fact, that she could just curl up in her bed and escape. She'd like to run from neighbors whose inbred courtesy didn't quite mask the way they viewed her as an aberration—an outsider in their conservative, fundamentalist community.

And she needed to retreat from the feelings Jake evoked in her. Even the thought of seeing Becky made her cringe.

Too bad her friend was coming over. Early this morning, after a restless night spent vacillating between wanting and hating Jake Green, Kate had lacked the words to forestall Becky's visit.

She emptied the two bags of cookies she'd just bought into a ceramic teddy bear jar and set it in the middle of the table. Then she set out plates, napkins, and glasses for cold drinks— milk for the kids, tea for herself and Becky.

When she heard the crunching of tires on her gravel driveway, she pasted on a determined smile and ran outside to help Becky get her toddlers, Rachel and Carey, out of their car seats and into the house. She gave the children some pots and spoons to play with before joining Becky at the kitchen table in front of the window.

"Who's that hunk getting out of the Porsche?"

Kate shifted Rachel's plump little body away from her face so she could look out the window and see who Becky was talking about—as if she didn't already know. How many folks in Groveland, Mississippi tooled around in costly foreign sports cars?

"That's Jake," she said, hoping she sounded more casual than she felt. The other day she'd managed to avoid talking about him after he dropped her off at Becky's house.

"He can park his boots under my bed anytime he feels like it," Becky said with a lascivious grin.

Kate was certain she was joking. Since they were fourteen years old, Becky had been in love with Stan Friedman. Kate and Gilda had set their caps for Stan, too, for a while. The four of them had become inseparable.

Soon, though, Stan had given his heart to pretty, dark-haired Becky. Becky would die, Kate was certain, before she would betray Stan.

"Becky, you're awful."

"Uh-huh. Still, he's a real temptation."

Becky's dark eyes sparkled. Feeling her cheeks warming under her friend's scrutiny, Kate wondered if Becky had already guessed just how far Jake had tempted her.

"Is he coming here?" She didn't want to look out the window again, for fear her composure would shatter.

"No. Darn. I wanted to get a better look. Looks like he's headed down toward the pond."

"I'm not surprised. He has some men down there, drilling more holes."

Kate set Rachel down on the floor and watched as the two-year-old toddled toward the stack of pots and spoons her sister Carey had been playing with. When the baby sank onto her well-padded bottom, Becky turned to Kate.

"Are you just going to stay here and watch oil rigs going up all over your place?"

"I don't know. Jake told me yesterday that they might put in several more wells, and that the noise and dust would probably be so bad I wouldn't want to stay. But this is my home. Where would I go?"

"How about a trip around the world for starters? I wouldn't be sitting here all glum and gloomy if I knew I was going to be filthy rich before too long." Excitement glowed on Becky's expressive face—an emotion Kate wished she shared.

"You'd like that. But you wouldn't be going alone. You've got Stan and the girls."

Kate tried to picture herself gadding about, having meaningless conversations with other women as lonely as she while she tried to enjoy the results of Jake's drilling expertise.

"You could always just latch onto Mr. GreenTex himself."

"Keep dreaming. The last thing on Jake's agenda is getting serious. And even if he was looking for something permanent, I doubt he'd go for a plain, small-town girl like me." The words hurt, but Kate wasn't one to hide from painful truths.

"You need to work on your self-image. You're plenty good enough for any man, including that gorgeous hunk of Texas oil man you're obviously mooning over."

Pausing, Becky got up to rescue Rachel before Carey could finish yanking all her hair out.

"Getting that man to love me would be nothing short of a miracle," Kate murmured, glad she hadn't told her friend just how much she wished for that particular miracle, or how she had settled for one memory-making session in Jake's arms.

Would Becky condemn her for reaching out and touching the kind of joy she'd thought was beyond her reach?

Kate didn't think so.

After she'd sent Jake away last night, she wished so hard that he'd come back. Now all she wanted was for Becky to take her babies and go home so she could be miserable in peace.

She saw speculation in Becky's expression when somebody tapped at the kitchen door. "It must be Jake," she said needlessly as she got up to let him in.

*****

"Becky, this is Jake Green. Jake, Becky Friedman," she said, hoping her cheeks weren't as flushed as they felt. "Oh, and the little girls are Rachel and Carey," she added when he hunkered down to say hello to the dark-haired toddlers who were gleefully slamming spoons onto pans and each other.

"They're Becky's," she said needlessly.

"Looks like they're having fun," Jake observed.

Kate couldn't help but envy the babies. She saw open, uncomplicated joy in his expression when he picked up a spoon Rachel had dropped.

"Here, honey," he said softly as he placed the makeshift drumstick back into the toddler's chubby hand.

"They like coming to Kate's. I think it's because she always finds some new, amusing toys for them to play with." Becky gave Jake a twenty-four-karat smile.

Kate couldn't help the jealousy that tweaked her while her friend flirted with the man she wanted so desperately.

"I like coming to Kate's, too," Jake replied, shooting Kate a look that heated her from head to toe when she finally grasped his double entendre. "Sorry I interrupted your visit, though."

Becky looked first at Jake, who was still crouched down beside her children. Then she picked up her purse and diaper bag. "We'd better be getting along now, Kate. You know how Stan hates to come home and find us gone off somewhere."

Automatically, Kate protested them leaving. Her heart wasn't in it, though.

She hadn't really wanted Becky to come today, and now she wanted…yes, she wanted more of Jake. She wanted him to look at her with the easy affection he gave Rachel and Carey. She wanted him to want her the way she wanted him.

Most of all, she wanted to share more than his passion, more than wild, satisfying sex. More than the fleeting closeness she felt but he denied in the wake of their stormy lovemaking.

She shook off her wistful fantasies and went with Jake to help Becky get her toddlers situated in the car for the short drive home.

"Come home with me," Jake said as they walked back to the house.

He'd thought Kate's talkative friend would never leave. Despite her protests that she must hurry, Becky had chattered a mile a minute while she and Kate buckled the little girls into their matching car seats. Then, she stood outside her car and talked some more. The only word he or Kate had been able to get in was an occasional monosyllabic response to Becky's nonstop commentary.

"Please," he added when Kate didn't respond immediately.

"What?"

"I asked you to come home with me. To Houston." He watched color come to Kate's petal-soft cheeks, and it was all he could do to keep from reaching out and touching her.

"Why?"

"The Old Man wants me home while he has some minor surgery. I thought we might have fun shopping and sightseeing in New Orleans today, then fly to Houston tomorrow afternoon."

"You want to sightsee in New Orleans in the middle of summer?" She sounded incredulous.

"Well, maybe not sightsee. But we could do the mall in air conditioned comfort. Or we could hole up in the St. Charles Hotel and enjoy each other for twenty-four straight hours," he offered with a grin.

Damn. His cock was working on another painful hard-on. "You'd like that, wouldn't you, honey?"

"I'd like for you to quit calling me 'honey,'" Kate snapped. "And why on earth would you want to take me to New Orleans? I'm sure you could find yourself another 'honey' there to...to copulate with."

"For God's sake. You're no starry-eyed little girl. You're a twenty-eight year old woman, Kate, and if you're honest with yourself, you'll admit you want me as much as I want you."

He paused, taking in every nuance of expression in her stormy aqua eyes. "You do want me, don't you?"

"Yes. But sex isn't all I want. I want some tenderness, some caring."

Jake watched her tremble, saw the tears welling up at the corners of her eyes.

"I want to be more than a convenient female body," she insisted.

He shoved his hands deep into his pockets, trying to control the hard-on that clouded his thinking. Damn it, he should be able to squelch the unwelcome emotions that engulfed him.

"You're not just a convenient female body. I'm not a tender man, but if romancing is what you want, I'll do my damnedest to give it to you." He reached out, stroked her cheek. "I want you with me. And I don't want you here without me as long as there are people out there trying to destroy the well." Before he could stop himself, he pulled her to him and had her nestled snugly against his throbbing cock.

Tension flowed from every pore of her skin where it touched his. From the pattern of soft, moist puffs of breath she exhaled against his shoulder, he was able to guess the exact moment when she began to calm down.

He shouldn't be surprised. He'd known from the start that she wasn't the kind of woman to go for a casual fuck.

Understanding that, he gave himself leave to accept Kate's unspoken conditions. For as long as they were together, he would enjoy the softness, the caring, the gentle passion that was Kate Black.

And he would give back as much of himself as was left to give.

"I'd like to go home with you," she whispered against his chest.

Was she a witch who could read his every thought? Had she known he'd give in to her demands?

Without words, he led her into her bedroom and watched while she packed a suitcase with clothes that had seen better days. They'd have to do some shopping, after all.

* * * * *

Four hours later Kate was smiling, but her eyes were unusually bright.

Why should she be fighting tears? Jake set an armload of boxes and bags onto the bed in their hotel room and ambled over to caress her cheek.

She was soft, so soft, and the aqua sun dress he had insisted she wear when she'd picked it out at Macy's made her look young and vulnerable. He had promised her tenderness, and he'd be damned if he didn't actually feel that way toward her.

Almost as much as he wanted to strip her naked and bury his cock in her hot, tight pussy, he wanted to protect her. Damn it, she brought out feelings in him that he'd have sworn had died with his unborn child.

"Kate. What's wrong, lady?" Very gently, he gathered her in his arms.

He heard the softness in his own voice, and he realized he wanted to touch her with words as well as with his body. With gentleness he hadn't realized until now he still possessed, he stroked her back above and below the low scooped neckline of her dress.

"Wrong? Nothing's wrong. Everything is just so... overwhelming I guess would be the word."

Kate toyed with the hair at the nape of his neck, her slender fingers sending shock waves straight down to his cock.

"You mean, knowing you're soon gonna have enough money to buy out the damn stores if it strikes your fancy?" he asked as he lowered his hands to cup her round, tight ass.

"No. I don't know."

"Tell me, Kate."

"It's not the money. I've had money before. Until Pop got sick, I never wanted for anything. Here, with you, everything seems, well, larger than life, for want of a better description."

His cock was feeling larger than life, for sure, but he quashed the thought of tossing her onto the bed and taking care of business right away. He sensed her discomfort from the way her hand trembled when she reached up and touched his face with wide-eyed wonder.

"Honey, we Texans do everything in a big way," he quipped to lighten the tension. "Hey, look. We can see the courtyard from here." He turned her so they both faced French windows framed with curtains so sheer he could see through them.

"Oh, Jake. What are those vines? The ones with the rose-colored flowers?"

She clasped her hands together like a delighted child while he strained his eyes against the afternoon sun to get a better look.

"Bougainvillea. Mom has some out by the pool at home. They grow like weeds, and they've got spines that'll dig in and tear your hide off if you aren't careful."

He grinned when he saw Kate's delighted expression. "Do you like flowers?" he asked, recalling that her yard had been pretty much devoid of blooming things even before the fires.

"I love them. But the yardman was first to go when Pop's money started running out. We never had blooms like those out there, though. Not even when Mother took care of the flower beds."

"I think they need a subtropical climate. They grow in Houston, but I tried to start some at my ranch a hundred miles or so northeast of there, and frost killed them the first winter."

"I guess with the way you travel, you hardly ever get to spend time at home," Kate said sympathetically.

"I usually manage to loaf around the ranch for three or four weeks a year." If he'd had his way, he'd have spent more time there and less in Houston, where Alice had dug in for the duration of their marriage.

Although he'd bought the land soon after marrying Alice, Jake hadn't built a house there until after their divorce. Without the wife and children he'd planned on having when he bought the place, he found the ranch an unbelievably lonely place to be.

Maybe that was why he had grabbed onto the Saudi assignment like a lifeline. Now, with Kate at his side, he yearned for the comforts of home.

That thought disturbed him. Yeah, he'd promised Kate as much tenderness as was in him, but he dared not give this woman the power to hurt him. Better that he keep his mind on pure, hot sex and fuck the troublesome emotions.

Deliberately, he wrapped his arms around her.

"Do you have any idea how much I want to fuck you?" he whispered, but the raw words came out tempered with tenderness. Emotions that scared Jake senseless.

"Jake."

Hearing her murmur his name brought him back to reality. And her exploration of his cock through the rough denim of his jeans helped him bury those unwanted feelings in an ocean of white-hot desire. Groaning at the gentle torture, he grabbed her hand and brought it to his lips.

"Slow, baby. Slow and easy. We've got all the time in the world," he crooned, but her rapt expression of wonder made him wild.

When she cradled his face with both her hands, he reached behind her and unzipped her dress. "Let's get you naked," he said, and he slid the dress over her hips to the carpeted floor.

"Wait. I bought something. Close your eyes," she said excitedly, pulling away and hurrying to search among the bags and boxes on the bed.

"What?"

"You'll see."

He turned around and saw that Kate apparently had located one small bag while dumping the clothes she had just bought onto a chair.

"What's that?" he asked.

"This." She opened the bag and handed him a box of contraceptive sponges. "I read somewhere that men don't like using, uh, condoms. I thought I'd try these."

Her blush was nearly as bright as the hot pink box he held in his hand.

"I haven't had time to go to a doctor and get a prescription for the Pill," she added, twisting a handful of her satin slip nervously between her fingers.

"Do you know how to use these?" he asked, knowing even then that he wouldn't chance riding bareback. But he couldn't help feeling warm inside, knowing she'd done this to heighten his pleasure.

"I can read directions." Obviously Kate wasn't keen on having him explain what to do. "If you'll give them here, I'll take care of it."

"Okay." He handed her the box.

Kate's surprise made him feel too good to let him spoil it. When the time came, he'd just slip on a rubber, too. And he'd tell her, if she asked, that it was a habit he couldn't shake.

Grinning despite himself, he watched her disappear into the bathroom. Then he stripped down and sprawled across the bed—after stashing some protection in the drawer of a bedside table. Anticipating the pleasure that awaited him, he re-opened the drawer and ripped open one of the tiny packages. Carefully he hid it under a fat, soft pillow.

* * * * *

"I—It's done."

Already embarrassed from having handled herself so intimately when she'd wrestled the sponge into place, Kate felt like slipping through the elegant floor beneath her feet.

There was Jake, sprawled naked across the king-size bed, his magnificent body lit by bright sunlight streaming through the open windows.

She was naked, too. Her mouth was dry, but between her legs, moisture was pooling. And her breasts felt tight, as if they were reaching out for the heat of his hands and mouth.

Suddenly she couldn't move. All she could do was stare at him. He seemed totally relaxed, with long-lashed lids concealing his dark, mesmerizing eyes.

In repose his face looked younger, less intimidating, even now, when the stubble of a beard darkened his strong jaw. If she could have moved, she would have gone to him and traced the contours of his thin but sensual lips. She'd have touched the bridge of his shapely nose and the prominent cheekbones beneath deep-set eyes.

Not all of him was relaxed, she realized when she looked lower and saw the hard, swollen evidence of his desire.

Fascinated, she moved to the bed and sat cross-legged beside Jake, who made no move to indicate he was aware of her presence. He was beautiful. And huge.

A sudden gush of moisture bathed her tender cleft.

With her forefinger, she reached out and touched his penis. She grazed rough-soft hair that surrounded the base of him — the heavy sac that shifted against her finger — the silky smooth, pale shaft ridged with distended, blue veins.

Awed, she traced the length of him, caressed the thick, heart-shaped head that was rosier colored and even silkier in texture than the rest of his sex.

From the way her inner muscles clenched, he might have been stroking her, too, even though he hadn't moved a muscle.

She wanted to taste him. And she took his totally passive attitude as tacit permission. Bending over him, she reached out with her tongue and tasted the shiny drop of moisture that had pearled up at the very tip of his penis.

He tasted slightly salty and felt smooth as velvet to her tongue. Totally arousing. She licked him again, this time taking the head of his penis a little way inside her mouth.

"I'll give you about an hour to stop that," Jake growled, and she raised her head to meet his heated gaze.

"Seriously, honey, you'd better get your gorgeous little ass up here before it's all over but the shouting."

With his big, rough hand, he gripped her arm and pulled until she lay on her side beside him. The heat of him, the textures of his satiny skin and crisp body hair, the steady beat of his heart against hers fed her rising passion.

"Tell me what you want." His hot breath seared her neck.

"You. I want you," she gasped when he found her breast and teased the nipple to attention.

She was beyond speech, beyond anything but feeling the pleasure-pain of him rolling her distended nipple between his thumb and forefinger. Beyond caring about anything except that she was slick and wet and desperate to take his hot, hard flesh into her body. To fill the emptiness inside her.

She moaned and rolled on top of him, straddling his hips and rubbing herself provocatively against his throbbing erection. When he rolled to his side, she caught him and tried to bring him back.

"You're going too fast, honey." His back toward her now, he fumbled under the pillow.

Before she could complain, though, he was on top of her, pinning her under the weight of his muscular body.

"You want my cock?" He rubbed himself suggestively against her before he settled into position to make them one.

"You know I do. Oh, Jake. Make love to me."

"My pleasure, honey."

Gently spreading her outer lips and positioning himself at the core of her heat, he thrust forward and filled her.

"God, I love fucking you. You're so tight and hot and wet."

He sank so deep inside her that his penis pressed at the mouth of her womb. Everything went out of focus. All of her feelings centered on his body and the way he stretched and filled her. On the smooth, building rhythm of him thrusting and retreating.

In. He filled her completely. Out. He was slick, too, slick with her juices. In again. Her nostrils flared, full of the scent of him—citrus and male musk.

The smell of sex. Of love.

He nearly withdrew. Her hands went to his hard-muscled thighs, seeking to force his return. But he was teasing her.

Instead of driving back deep inside her, he bent and traced her lips with his tongue. She savored the taste of beignets and café au lait when his tongue plunged inside to mate with hers. Then he thrust forward and filled her once again.

Wanting to capture him forever, she wrapped her legs around his waist and flexed her muscles. Her hands dug into his broad, sweat-slick shoulders. She opened her mouth wider and sucked on his marauding tongue.

And when he rubbed his chest against her and his chest hair abraded her sensitive nipples, her safe world shattered.

He was her world: his rapacious mouth, his hard male body, his earthy taste and smell.

The rasping sounds he made and the heat in her mouth when he shared his breath with her. His hot, hard penis inside her, throbbing out its life, coaxing out the stars and sun and everything she'd ever dreamed of.

Through a haze of sensation, she felt him grow bigger and harder inside her as her muscles constricted around him. Then, as if in a frenzy, he thrust harder and faster into her sensitized flesh. Then he shuddered.

"My God, you can fuck," he rasped out when he buried his face against her neck.

He said more, but her consciousness had deserted her.

When she woke, she half expected to be alone. But she wasn't. She smoothed the tousled sable curls off his sweaty forehead. He lay beside her, his eyes closed, a sated smile hovering at the corners of his perfectly chiseled mouth.

When he opened his eyes and looked at her, his smile broadened. His dark eyes sparkled.

Did she dare hope he'd found more in her than a convenient partner to slake his carnal needs?

For a long moment, they stayed there, their eyes locked in each other's.

Then she remembered the sponge and that she was supposed to take it out. When? She needed to look at the directions again.

She got up and smiled down at Jake. Unable to resist, she glanced at his sex that had just given her so much pleasure. When she did, she wanted to cry. He hadn't trusted her, she realized when she noticed the ballooned-out condom that still sheathed his penis.

Chapter Seven

Jake had some explaining to do.

After all, he'd let Kate think he appreciated her surprise.

And he had. After all, she must have been thinking about them fucking when she'd inserted that sponge.

Otherwise she wouldn't have come to him with that soft, starry-eyed look. And what she had done—the way she'd touched his cock with a curious finger and a flick of her wet, pink tongue—had gotten him hotter than an oil well fire.

Why hadn't he thought to get rid of the goddamn rubber before she saw it?

He stood beside the bed and shook unruly strands of hair out of his eyes. Then he peeled off the condom and tossed it in the trash, skipping his usual ritual of checking for leaks.

He had enough explaining to do without delaying any longer, so he padded to the bathroom after Kate.

"You leave it in awhile," he said when he found her holding a thin paper instruction sheet. It pleased him that she didn't reach for a towel to hide her nudity.

"Why? You used something anyway."

"Yeah. I did."

"Are you afraid of catching something from me?" she asked in a tiny voice.

"Hell no. Don't even think that."

She looked up at him, tears in her eyes. "Then why did you use the condom?"

It would be easy to tell her he'd forgotten in the heat of his passion. That he'd grabbed the condom out of habit. He'd never told anyone why he was obsessed with keeping his lovers from becoming pregnant. Now, though, he found that he wanted to tell Kate.

"I swore after my divorce that I'd never again risk starting a life some woman could destroy," he said gruffly. "And I won't. Not unless I marry again, and my wife and I decide together that we want a family."

"I may be naive, but I know the Pill is the best kind of birth control, and that diaphragms and sponges are better at preventing pregnancy than condoms."

"Birth control pills are better, honey, but only if the woman's actually taking them the way they're supposed to be taken. I'd argue about the diaphragms and sponges. Still, even if they work better, they depend on a woman to use them. I use the best condoms money can buy because it's the only way I can know for sure that I'm protected."

"I'm sorry. I thought—oh, I don't know what I thought. Except that you'd like it better if you weren't wearing one of those things." Her eyes still glistened, and that made Jake feel like shit.

"I would like it better. Believe me. Wearing a condom's like going wading wearing boots. There's nothing I'd like more than putting my cock in your tight, wet little pussy with nothing between us. But I'm not going to take the risk." He paused, wiped away a tear that was making its way down her cheek. "Hey, honey. It's not you. It's me. Me and my hang-ups, left over from a lousy marriage."

"How long were you married?" Kate asked quietly.

"A little over eight years. We got married right after we graduated from college. It was a mistake we probably would have corrected sooner if I hadn't spent so much time out in the oil fields."

The hand she lay on his chest felt gentle. Caring. Jake fought the desire to give his emotions free rein. "I'm sorry," he said.

"So am I."

At that moment, Jake wished he could kill Alice for robbing him of the ability to accept and nourish Kate's sweet, caring concern. "It's finished now."

And so was Jake's capacity to give any woman the kind of love Kate obviously wanted.

"Did you lose a child?" Kate asked, her voice full of concern.

"We never had any."

"But...you said something about destroying—"

"My wife didn't want kids. Oh, she said at first that she'd want some eventually, but eventually never came." Jake inhaled deeply, as if that would cleanse his mind of the horror he was about to relive. "By the time she accidentally got pregnant, our marriage was in pretty bad shape. I'd been spending a lot of time out of the country, probably more than I had to for the job. Anyway, I came home unexpectedly when she'd gotten careless with her pills. She was furious when she found out about the baby, but I was certain she'd get over it."

Kate smiled. "You must have been thrilled."

"Yeah. I was. For about two weeks. That's how long it was between the time she told me she was pregnant and the night she spilled the news that she'd had an abortion and filed for divorce."

He sensed Kate's horrified reaction, and he reached out to wipe away another tear that was making its way down her cheek. When she stood and held her arms out to him, he took a step forward and let her enfold him in a comforting embrace.

"I'd be thrilled to have your baby," she said softly, and her warm breath tickled his naked chest.

"Come here." She led him into the bedroom. Still nude, they curled together on an antique couch. Just being close to her warmed him and soothed the pain—pain that came back with a vengeance every time he let himself think about his son or daughter that Alice had destroyed.

"Why did she do it?" Kate asked softly, her fingers making idle, soothing circles across his stomach.

"Someday, maybe I'll tell you." He dared not risk giving Kate his full trust. Not yet.

And he wasn't about to fall in love with her, no matter how she charged his emotions with her understanding.

Sex. That was all that fueled these tender feelings he needed to suppress.

But he could damn well indulge his cock.

Slowly, lazily, he began to stroke her. She was silky smooth all over, creamy pale against the darkness of his hands. She shuddered when he paid special attention to the sensitive spots behind her knees, the musky dampness of her inner thighs.

He'd never had a woman who responded so quickly to his simplest touch.

His balls drew up, aching as though he hadn't just come an hour earlier. When she moaned his name, his cock turned rock-hard again.

Jake scooped Kate into his arms and lay her across the bed. Within seconds he'd sheathed himself and plunged back inside her welcoming pussy.

He moved in her, sinking slowly into her tight, wet heat then retreating only to slide back deeper when she clamped her legs around his ass and whimpered for more. When he took one hardened nipple into his mouth and sucked it while lightly pinching the other between his thumb and forefinger, she sank her fingers into his hair, pressing his cheek into a satiny breast.

She felt good. Too good. But it was sex. The primal need to lose himself inside a warm, willing body and spurt out his seed. Only sex and nothing more.

Slowly. He felt his climax coming for more long, slow thrusts than he could count. Felt her pussy contracting around his cock, her wetness bathing his balls. Still he held back, wanting to prolong the pleasure, make her scream out again with delight.

Shifting slightly to one side, he slipped a hand between their bodies and tweaked her clit.

"Oh, Jake. Yesss."

He rammed his cock inside her to the hilt and let her pussy milk him dry.

Buried inside her, coming and coming and coming, Jake had no trouble concentrating on sex and sensation, ignoring emotions he wasn't ready to explore. When it was over and he withdrew from her soft, warm haven, however, unwelcome thoughts returned.

As he stood at the vanity watching the water wash away his semen from a condom, long-suppressed dreams flooded his mind. Against his will, he imagined a dark-haired boy. A petite honey-haired girl with Alice's pale, stunning beauty. His baby would have had its second birthday by now. For what had to be the millionth time he cursed the woman who had denied it life.

Stalking back to the bedroom, he stared at Kate. She said she'd love to have his baby. His balls tightened at the memory.

And at the sight of her, so innocent-looking and yet so wanton, with her soft, dark curls askew against a snowy pillowcase.

He focused on her small, high breasts and soft, flat belly. Despite himself, he imagined that belly growing rounder, distended with his seed.

Recalling how his sisters had looked when they'd nursed their babies, he pictured Kate's breasts heavy, blue-veined, the nipples leaking pale fluid to sustain his son or daughter. Jake smiled.

Then he remembered how she'd thought he would have rejected her if he'd known before they fucked that she was a Jew. Conservative, country-born and raised, Kate probably believed folks should stick with their own kind. And that could pose a problem if, as he thought was likely, Kate harbored old-fashioned prejudices.

It would take a hell of a lot of tolerance to accept everybody in his eclectic mixture of a family. And Jake would never marry anybody who didn't.

He'd find out soon. She'd meet Scott and Bear, and when those guileless aqua eyes widened with disbelief, Jake would be able to let her go.

Pushing thoughts about a possible future with Kate to the back of his mind, he picked up the phone and made dinner reservations. Then he started to dress while she napped.

* * * * *

She had to be exhausted. After their afternoon of shopping and bedroom gymnastics, Jake had taken Kate to Antoine's for dinner. Afterward, she'd laughed like a child at the antics of the street musicians and hustlers in the French Quarter.

Seeing her so happy had made him feel good enough to shelve most of his melancholy memories. When he'd held her and they'd swayed to the jazz beat in a Decatur Street tavern, he had more fun than he had in years.

Now, though, they were back in their hotel suite, and he watched her slide nude between the satin sheets. Amazingly since he'd come twice this afternoon, his balls drew up and his cock rose to attention.

Jake willed them to behave. Tonight he wanted to hold her, give her a taste of the tenderness she craved—the emotional involvement that came so hard to him. He shoved his slacks down, stripped off his underwear, and crawled into bed.

Turning on his side, he positioned her pliant body against him and cradled her head on his arm. He nuzzled her cheek and rested one hand against the softness of her breasts.

"G'night, honey."

A sense of peace flowed through him with the sweet scent of the woman in his bed. His half-hard cock rested quietly against her rounded bottom. And he went to sleep.

* * * * *

"Yes. This is Jake Green's room."

Kate's sleepy voice brought Jake to life again. Who the hell could be calling at…what time was it anyway?

He reached over to the bedside table for his watch. "Who the hell is it?"

"Somebody named Scott Carrington. He says he needs to talk to you."

Jake flipped on a lamp and took the phone. Noticing Kate's embarrassed expression, he shot her a quick grin and reached under the covers to tweak her nipples.

"Yeah, Scott. Do you know it's four o'clock in the morning?" Jake paused. "When?" Again, he waited for Scott's reply. While he listened, he pulled Kate closer.

"Okay. Just a minute. Kate, we need to leave for Houston earlier than we planned."

He read confusion in her sleepy aqua eyes. "Why?" she asked.

"My father's had a mild heart attack."

"Oh, no. I'm so sorry. Jake, you go on. I can get myself back home."

"Uh-uh. Honey, I need you with me," he said, confident that this was all she needed to hear to be persuaded to stay.

"If you're certain."

He turned back to the phone, a little taken aback. He really did need Kate at his side, but he damn sure wasn't happy about it. He listened to Scott, interspersing a few terse comments. After he hung up, he noticed that Kate had gotten up and was packing clothes into her suitcase.

"Sorry to change our plans, honey. We've got to get out to New Orleans International as fast as we can. Scott's calling the hangar now and having them get the plane fueled and onto the tarmac. It will be ready to go by the time we get there."

"How bad is your father's condition?"

Her expression mirrored her concern as she stepped into new silk bikini panties and slid a matching half-slip over her hips.

As concerned as Jake was about the Old Man, he couldn't help wanting to nuzzle her enticing bare breasts above the silky lingerie. And it was damn impossible to ignore his raging hard-on.

"According to Scott, he's stable right now. He had the heart attack while they were doing preoperative tests. He's not in any real danger, but his surgeons think they may have to operate before tomorrow. The Old Man's as stubborn as a mule, though. He's refused to go under the knife before he's seen everyone in the family."

Jake frowned. Kate had just fastened the front hook of a wispy lace bra. Though he'd like to stay naked and haul her back to bed, he pulled on a pair of dark briefs.

"Will we be able to get there in time?" she asked, her soft voice full of concern.

"Yeah. It's Shana and Bear who may not make it if the surgeons decide they can't wait. They're in the air now, but they won't arrive in Houston until late tonight. It takes around thirteen hours of flying time to get there from Kuwait City. I'm glad you're coming with me. This will be one of the few occasions when all of us get together. Between company business and my brothers-in-law's interests, something or other always has somebody away from home."

Not taking time to be neat, he dumped his spare clothes in a duffel bag before putting on clean jeans and a knit shirt.

His concern for his father gave way to wondering how Kate would react to the people he loved. No use thinking about it. He'd find out a little sooner than he'd planned.

Jake dug impatiently through the tangled linens on the bed. Where the hell had he put his socks?

"Is this okay?" Kate held up a new khaki blazer and skirt against the yellow and aqua print shirt she'd just put on.

Typical woman, worrying about her clothes. "Sure," he said without looking.

"Really, Jake. You didn't even look."

He gave the outfit a quick glance when he sat on the edge of the bed to put on the socks he'd just found. "I like it."

"Does one of your sisters work in Kuwait?" she asked, and Jake realized that his earlier comment must have just registered in her head. "I didn't know your company had offices there."

"We don't. We've got partial interests in some Kuwaiti oil fields, but no permanent facilities over there. Shana's only involvement in GreenTex is spending the dividend checks she gets every quarter. Her husband's business is in Kuwait." Jake stood up, socks in hand, and zipped his bag.

"Oh. I don't think I'd like living in that part of the world."

"Why?" He waited for her to voice the typical reaction to the Middle East and its people, a reaction that had become especially vehement since the events of September eleventh—distrust mingled with a healthy dose of fear.

She grinned. "As backwoodsy as you think I am, I have watched TV. I wouldn't like having to wear long robes and keep my face covered up all the time. And it must be awful, being isolated in a harem."

"I'm sure Shana wouldn't like that, either. I can't imagine her putting up with most of the old Arab traditions. She and Bear live together with their kids when they're there, same as they do when they're in Houston. No harem for Bear. No multiple wives, either. Shana would kill him."

"Doesn't it bother her, the way women have to dress when they go out?" Kate asked, her expression revealing nothing more than curiosity.

"I'm sure it would if they lived in a country like Saudi Arabia where there are laws about things like that. But Kuwait's pretty modern by comparison. If you looked around on the streets in Kuwait City, you'd see at least as many Kuwaitis wearing western clothes as those in traditional Arab robes."

"Oh. I didn't know."

Kate's nonpolitical, purely feminine reaction pleased Jake, and he couldn't resist pulling her to him and giving her a quick, hard kiss.

"We'd better go," she said breathlessly, stepping back and smiling up at him.

"Yeah. I'll call the desk and have them bring the car around."

* * * * *

Jake kept quiet while he made his way through New Orleans's early morning traffic. Kate reasoned that he must be more worried than he let on about his father's condition. Gripping her hands together to stem their nervous motion, she tried to visualize an older version of Jake holding court from his hospital bed.

Staring down at the outfit she had on, she wondered if it was too simple. Or too dressy, she amended when she realized Jake had on even more casual attire.

"We're here," he announced, breaking the silence.

She looked around and saw a silver metal building and some crisscrossed runways. "Surely this isn't the terminal," she said of the spartan looking structure where Jake had stopped.

"It's the GreenTex hangar, honey. We're going to take the plane that's out on the tarmac." He gestured toward a small, sleek jet that had been painted gleaming white and emblazoned with the oil company's insignia.

When Jake had told her he was going to fly them to Houston in a company plane, Kate had pictured a little two-seater—not a jet she imagined must have cost several million dollars or more. As she tried to recover from the shock of realizing Jake's family must be not just wealthy but mega-rich, she saw a rotund, smiling man emerge from the sleek plane and limp toward them.

"Marty!" Jake's voice boomed out, carrying over the drone of the jet's idling engines.

"Hey, boy! You're ready to go." Marty slapped Jake on the shoulder and turned to stare at Kate. "You gonna introduce me to this pretty lady?" he asked.

Hurriedly, Jake made the introduction and thanked Marty for getting the plane ready. Then he tossed his car keys to the man and stowed their bags in an open compartment at the side of the jet.

"See you later, buddy," he said as they prepared to go on board.

"Tell the Old Man I'm pulling for him," Marty yelled in parting.

Kate read genuine concern in the man's expression before she turned and climbed the stairs to the plane.

* * * * *

"Want to sit up front with me or relax back here?" Jake asked as Kate looked, wide-eyed, around the elegant salon.

"Up front?"

"Yeah. I've got to go up there to fly the plane."

Another surprise. She should have guessed Jake would want to fly himself around instead of relying on a pilot. "Oh," she said, unable to come up with an intelligent response.

"Oh, what? Don't you think I know how to fly?"

"I hadn't thought about it. But I'll sit up there with you if you want me to." She had no desire to spend the flight time in the solitary luxury of the salon.

"Come on then. We're burning jet fuel, standing here talking." He led the way to the cockpit and waited until she settled into the copilot's seat.

"Fasten your seat belt, honey," he said after he sat down and ran through what she guessed must be a preflight checklist. His big, capable hands were as sure and steady on the controls as they were when he used them to stroke her, arouse her desire.

His voice projecting absolute confidence, he asked the control tower for clearance to take off. Though Kate had never been on a small plane before, and she certainly never had gone to the cockpit to see the action on the few commercial flights she'd taken, she wasn't afraid. Jake exuded self-confidence and competence with the airplane, just as he did with everything else.

A wave of excitement ran through her body. Jake was actually taking her home to meet his family. Never mind that the only reason for the trip was his father's illness.

And now they were on their way. He'd taken off so smoothly Kate hadn't realized at first that they were in the air.

From the cockpit, she found she could enjoy the colors of the morning sky from a new and wondrous perspective. Then the view changed. The clouds were below them like a fluffy blanket of white, and they headed into a void of purest blue.

She watched Jake visually scan a green computer screen before pressing one of the many buttons on the mind-boggling control panel. After studying the screen again, he released his seat belt, stood, and strode toward the plane's salon.

"Jake!" she exclaimed, wondering if he expected her to perform whatever mysterious functions were needed to keep the plane in the air.

"I'm getting our breakfast. The plane's on autopilot," he told her with a grin.

"Oh. You should have told me." She felt as if she had been given a reprieve from sudden death, but she made herself smile when he sat back down and handed her a cellophane-wrapped tray.

"Sorry. I forgot you aren't used to flying in small planes."

Small? This plane had room for a dozen or more passengers and a crew of three. Again, the differences between Kate's lifestyle and Jake's hit her hard.

"I'm probably not used to doing lots of things you take for granted," she said, peeling away the wrapping from the tray and looking over the assortment of cut fruit, croissants, cheese and meat. The mouthwatering aroma coming from the two steaming mugs of coffee Jake had set in cup holders filled the cockpit.

"This looks good," she murmured as she picked up a juicy strawberry and popped it in her mouth.

"It is. Want to fix me a sandwich?" he asked, snagging another berry and sinking his teeth into it.

She layered some ham and cheese between two halves of a croissant and handed it to him. "Here you go."

What on earth was she doing here? And why had Jake asked her to come home with him?

Kate's stomach started turning cartwheels when she thought about meeting an entire, globetrotting clan of Texas millionaires—or were they billionaires? "Tell me about your family," she urged Jake, searching for comfort in knowledge.

"I already did, honey, the night we went to Hattiesburg."

He took a bite from his sandwich, and she wondered if he would repeat that offhand chronology. Surely they were too close now for him to be so reticent. Or were they?

For all their lovemaking, for all the smiles they'd shared, did Jake still think of her as a stranger? Had he asked her to come with him only to share his bed?

She couldn't resist prodding him. "Let's see," she said, deliberately keeping her tone light. "You have a mother, a father, and three older sisters. Your mother and sisters are all trying to get you married off. Your father runs GreenTex. Did I leave anything out?"

Jake swallowed the last bite of his sandwich. Then he grinned. Kate loved the way one corner of his mouth lifted just a little off-center and the tanned skin at the corner of his eyes crinkled when he smiled. When he spoke, his voice reminded her of soft, warm velvet.

"I told you more than that, honey." His attention focused on the control panel now, he spoke in a matter-of-fact tone. "There's Mom and Dad. Then there's Debra. Deb's forty-six, but she'd kill me if she knew I'd ever told anybody that. Scott's her husband. He's the one who woke us up this morning."

"Debra and Scott," Kate repeated, trying to fix the names firmly in her mind. "Scott—" She hesitated. "Scott Carrington, isn't it?"

"Yeah. They have three girls. Cat—Catherine—is about twenty. Lenore's sixteen, going on thirty. And Tracy is seven. I imagine she must have been a big surprise to Deb and Scott, but she's a neat kid. You'll meet them soon enough."

"How about your other sisters?"

"You'll like Leah. She was forty-three last week. Damn! I forgot to send her a present, so she's likely to skin me alive. Can I count on you to keep her from clobbering me?"

She couldn't help smiling. "I don't know. How tough is she?"

"Not very. She's pregnant again, hoping that this time she and Ben will have a boy. I guess the baby's due pretty soon."

"Do they have other children?" Kate wondered how Leah felt about being pregnant at such an advanced age.

"Ruthie. She's about a year and a half old. Ben was a widower. He had three teenage daughters when he and Leah got married four years ago. Somehow, I never pictured Leah with kids, but she's good with them. Maybe it comes from her being a psychologist before she decided to become a mom."

"Does Leah's husband work for GreenTex, too?" Kate asked, struggling to catalog all the names firmly in her mind.

"Uh-uh. Ben's a cardiologist. Scott's the only in-law who works for GreenTex."

"What about your sister whose husband has a job in Kuwait?"

"Shana? She's thirty-four, three years older than I am. She and Bear have two girls and a boy. Yasmin's ten, Selena's eight. Their little boy, Jamil, is about six months old."

Jake grinned at Kate. "We'll be landing in another twenty minutes or so," he commented as if he'd said all he intended to say about his siblings.

"Oh."

Setting the empty food tray on the floor beside her seat, she tightened her seat belt and tried to relax. When the sea of white disappeared and she saw the ground beneath them, she realized they'd begun their descent.

As Kate tried to keep Jake's nephew and nieces' names matched with the proper parents, her tension mounted until the plane touched down.

* * * * *

Jake had brought Kate to a world of luxury beyond her wildest imaginings. First, he'd invited her aboard a multimillion dollar airplane as if it he thought that mode of transportation was no more out of the ordinary than climbing into a car and driving to the general store.

At Houston's Hobby Airport, he'd taken the keys to what the terminal manager said was one of his brother-in-law's cars—some exotic foreign job she couldn't even pronounce the brand name of. They'd driven straight to a hospital where a uniformed attendant parked the car.

She looked around the private sitting area outside the room where Jake was visiting with his father. This VIP tower was like no other hospital accommodations she'd ever seen. Since when did hospitals provide suites with original oil paintings and sleek designer furniture for its patients?

As she caressed the glove-soft leather covering on a chair arm, she stared at a massive chrome-and-glass lamp that rested on plush mauve carpeting. Staring down at her simple beige suit, she felt as out of place as she would have if she'd suddenly found herself on Mars.

When the outer door opened, Kate looked up and saw a woman and three girls. And a tall, blond man whose arm was wrapped in a proprietary way around the waist of the striking dark-haired woman. When the woman moved, Kate noticed the diamonds flashing at her throat, on her fingers, around her wrists, and in her ears. A subtly draped jumpsuit of pale gold silk enhanced her well-kept body. Kate felt dowdy and fully intimidated by the time the glamorous family entered the room.

"Is Jake in with Dad?" the woman asked.

Kate realized then that she must be one of Jake's sisters. "Yes."

"I'm Deb. This is Scott. And these are our daughters." She smiled and turned to the girls. "Cat. Lenore. And Tracy." Affectionately, she ruffled the youngest girl's hair with a jewel-laden hand. "You must be Kate Black. Scott said Jake was bringing you with him."

"Yes. I'm glad to meet you." Kate hoped she appeared more at ease than she felt. "Don't let me keep you. I know you must be anxious to see your father. And Jake." She smiled tentatively at the intimidating group.

"Go on, love. I'll wait out here." Scott stepped away from Deb and sat on a couch across from Kate. "Girls, let your mother go in first and see how Grandpa Jacob is feeling."

Then he turned to Kate. "I suppose your first oil well has you bursting with excitement," he said cordially.

The arrival of more people saved Kate from having to make more than a monosyllabic reply. Scott introduced the newcomers, Ben, Leah, and tiny Ruthie Schulberg. While Deb had overwhelmed Kate with her opulent display of wealth, Leah stunned her with pure intensity.

Leah's dark, intelligent eyes focused on her, as though she might be assessing Kate's suitability for Jake.

Kate's cheeks still burned, minutes after Leah had gone in to see her father.

"Will Jake's other sister be here soon?" Kate asked Ben, whose daughter was busy tugging at his horn-rimmed glasses. At least he didn't intimidate her. Maybe that was because of his quiet poise and unassuming manner that reminded her a little of David.

"They'll be in tonight, won't they?" Ben asked Scott. Kate thought she detected a little discomfort on Ben's part.

"About seven o'clock, unless their plane is delayed. Kate, would you like a drink?" Scott asked as he got up and crossed the room. She watched him open the doors of an ebony sideboard to reveal a small refrigerator and a large selection of liquor.

"Something soft, please." Kate turned back to Ben. "May I hold Ruthie?" she asked, sensing that the squirming toddler had just about worn out her daddy's patience.

Ben handed his daughter over. Ruthie was soft and sweet smelling, with fine dark hair she'd obviously inherited from both her parents. It felt good to hold her.

Soon Ruthie tired herself out and rested her little head against Kate's breast. In spite of the noise from Deb's girls chattering and Ben's stiff conversation with Scott, she drifted off to sleep.

After a while Tracy curled up by Kate's feet, and Lenore and Cat stopped their bickering and included Kate in their conversation.

The cozy scene of Kate with his nieces settled around her met Jake when he came out of the Old Man's room. For a minute, he just stood and watched her. Holding Leah's baby, with Tracy at her feet, Kate looked happy and maternal. And she was keeping the older girls occupied with questions about their school and career plans.

Despite the inappropriateness of time and place, Jake wanted to hand Ruthie back to Ben and take Kate in his arms. "Honey, come here," he said instead. "Mom and Dad want to meet you."

Noting how gently she touched his niece's cheek after settling her onto the chair, Jake's wary heart softened a little more. He couldn't keep his hands off Kate any longer, but in deference to the horde of relatives around them, he looped one arm over her shoulder and rested his hand above, not on her breast.

"Their bark's worse than their bite," he whispered when she started to tremble. "Don't tell me you're scared."

"A little."

Once they got inside, Jake introduced her to his parents.

While they exchanged pleasantries, he watched his father's expression. Kate was obviously charming the hell out of the Old Man, though it didn't look to Jake as if she was even trying.

His father's wish, expressed frequently over the years, echoed in Jake's mind.

I want grandchildren who will carry on my name, and I'd like to have them before I'm too old to enjoy them.

Jake would like that, too. But he wasn't about to let the Old Man push him. If he should decide Kate was the woman he wanted to spend the rest of his life with, his father would be the first to know.

Looking at the family members gathered around him, he read the speculative looks that passed between his mother, Deb and Leah. He could almost hear them scheming. It didn't take a genius to figure out that thoughts of rings, showers, flowers, musicians, reception menus, and so on, were running rampant in their heads.

Jake felt as if the walls were closing in on him. As soon as he could politely do so, he extricated Kate from his mother and sisters and wished the Old Man a restful night.

"Tell Shana and Bear to come on over to my place when they leave here," he told his mom as they left.

* * * * *

"No, Mom...not tonight...For God's sake, Dad is having surgery in the morning. Do you really think you ought to be asking us over to dinner tonight?" Jake shifted the portable phone from one ear to the other. "Yeah. I know you want to get to know Kate. Well, now isn't the time."

"But Jake. You're serious about this girl. Finally. After I've despaired of ever seeing you married to a good woman, you've brought one home. Now you won't even let your own mother get to know her."

His mother's tone was petulant, but Jake refused to give in.

"I'll bet you don't even have any food in that tiny apartment of yours. What are you going to eat?" she asked, apparently trying to use reason.

"I'll order pizza. And my condo's not exactly tiny, Mom. It's got seven perfectly good rooms. And a pool, before you tell me I have to bring Kate to the house for a swim."

More than a little annoyed, Jake held the receiver at arm's length and let his mother rave.

"…club. Or would you rather have it at a hotel?" Jake caught those scary words and brought the phone back to his ear. "…could get Debra to help her find a gown that's just perfect…"

"Stop with the matchmaking. If and when I decide to get married again, I'll let you know. You might at least wait 'til I give a woman an engagement ring before you start thinking about flowers and receptions. That way, you'll avoid being disappointed when your schemes fall through. Goodbye. We'll see you in the morning at the hospital."

Jake set the phone back in its cradle and turned to Kate.

Chapter Eight

"Better watch out, honey. If you don't, Deb will be taking you shopping for a wedding gown. Leah will be planning parties. And my precious mother will be arranging the wedding of her dreams. God only knows what Shana will pull to try and get us married off, when she gets here. Do you see now what I meant when I told you they drive me insane?"

"I guess so. They're all so…"

Kate didn't finish her sentence. Jake figured she couldn't find just one word that adequately described his female relatives.

"So what, honey? Pushy? Overbearing? Ostentatious? Hmmm. How about 'downright obnoxious'? Hey, they didn't scare you off, did they?" He shouldn't have left Kate in the clutches of his enthusiastic mother and sisters while he and Scott had gone over some company business with the Old Man.

"No. They were…very friendly. Does Deb always wear so much jewelry?" Kate asked as if she were trying to get the women's effusive welcome off her mind.

"No. Sometimes she wears more. Deb's got a thing about diamonds. And Scott's so crazy about her, he buys her all she wants. I think it must get his blue Boston blood hot to see her flashing rocks as big as spotlights."

"Oh." Kate's soft, sweet face registered confusion.

"We're not very traditional, honey," Jake said casually. "Don't let my sisters get to you."

"What do you mean traditional? There's nothing wrong with liking jewelry or having children late in life. Or even being concerned over your son's or brother's happiness," she said with a twinkle in her eyes.

"They don't put you off?" Jake asked, watching Kate to gauge her reaction.

"No more than you do. I'm not used to riding around in private jets and fast foreign sports cars, and when Pop was hospitalized he stayed in a plain old semi-private room. I admit, when I saw Deb and her girls come into that hospital suite wearing clothes that probably cost more than I've spent on mine during my entire life, I felt out of place. But they were kind, and they welcomed me. They obviously adore you and want you to be happy."

If Jake wanted answers, he was obviously going to have to fish. "How traditional are you?"

"In what way?" Kate asked.

"Religion, for one."

"Not very. It would have been hard to follow Jewish traditions very closely, growing up in a place where the closest temple was fifty miles away. There were only five Jewish kids in my high school when I was there. There were fewer than that when my father was a boy, I imagine."

"Just so you know, Scott's a Christian. So was my former wife, if you apply the term loosely. Shana's husband is a gentile, too, as is the Old Man's stepmother whom we all adore."

"You think this should bother me?"

"It could. I hope it doesn't."

"It doesn't. Jake, why are you angry?"

When he looked at Kate, Jake's body began to stir. "I'm not angry," he said, but that was a lie because he was furious with himself.

One by one, this soft, gentle woman was tearing down the barriers to a relationship he still wanted to fight with all his strength. His cock seemed determined to defeat his resolve, he thought as he tried to quell its unruly demands.

"That must be the pizza," he said as he went to answer the door, grateful for the intrusion.

* * * * *

Jake's condo looked spartan despite its plush beige carpeting and comfortable looking leather upholstered furniture. Kate stared at the only object in the living room that marked the room as his.

It was a massive painting above the stone fireplace. Stark metal derricks dwarfed twisted mesquite bushes. They rose, as if against all odds, out of harsh looking desert land into a magnificent sky whose tones of rose and gray and brilliant blue warmed the scene and gave life to the room.

"Like that? It's a painting of the west Texas field my grandfather opened up back in the thirties," Jake said as he set the pizza down on a glass-and-chrome cocktail table. Sitting on a low leather hassock, he stretched out his long muscular legs. "I thought we might as well eat in here."

"It's beautiful," Kate said, moving close to the table and sitting cross-legged on the floor at Jake's feet. There was something about that scene, something powerful that kept her from looking away.

The scene reminded her of Jake. Hard, sometimes stark, yet imbued with softer, gentler qualities that shone through the tough outer shell like the rosy hues of the setting sun softened the bleak desert scene. Finally she turned to Jake and met his gaze.

"I've always thought so. I rescued the picture from Mom's attic. Her taste runs more toward abstract stuff."

Kate watched him pick up a slice of pizza. Silently she followed suit, and they didn't speak further until it was gone.

There was no need for words. She felt the pull of his powerful body, and somehow she sensed he felt that same magnetic attraction toward her.

Finally he shoved away the pizza box and took her in his arms. The kiss he began was endless, and it fueled her need to a painful, fever pitch.

"Jake, let me make love to you," she said softly when he broke the kiss, and he saw unshed tears in eyes darkened with passion to the tone of a stormy azure sea.

He nodded. Didn't trust himself to speak.

Her hand moved. He heard a snap opening, the rasp of a zipper being pulled down. She freed his throbbing cock and caressed it with a slow, smooth rhythm.

He took it for as long as he dared. Minutes, maybe. Probably just seconds. Then he stilled her hand.

"Stop."

"You don't like this?"

"Oh, yeah. I like it way too much. Maybe after a while I'll be able to enjoy it longer without losing it. But I can't now."

But she didn't release him. Instead, she rose to her knees. Her hands scorched his flesh when she slid his jeans and underwear down.

Then she cradled his balls in both hands. Weighed and measured them while she stared, awestruck, into his eyes.He couldn't look down. If he did, he knew damn well he'd embarrass himself. But he had to see as well as feel her loving torture.

Struggling for control, he focused on her rosy, pebbled tongue as it darted out between her soft pink lips to flick the tip of his cock again and again.

She bathed him there like he'd once seen a mother cat lave her kitten. It struck him again how pale and small her hands were. And soft. Silky soft against his own dark, straining flesh.

The pointed tip of her tongue still teasing the blunt head of his cock, she looked up at him. His balls tightened painfully in her gentle embrace.

God, she was killing him with her sensual torment. He was going to die if he didn't scoop her up and drag her to his bed, sheath himself first with a goddamn condom and then with her tight wet pussy.

But he couldn't move. His strength was in her hands. And in her mouth. Her sweet, soft lips slid down his cock, and the wet, hot cavern of her mouth devoured him.

Her hands rocked gently, rolling his balls against her palms. Her swallowing motions against the head of his cock were driving him out of his mind.

She took more of him than he dreamed was possible. Now she wrapped one hand around the base of his cock. Sucking and swallowing. Squeezing and releasing her hand. Rocking his balls gently against her other palm.

He should stop her. Hold onto the thread of control that was slipping away in an erotic haze.

But he couldn't. Giving up, he closed his eyes and let her carry him over the edge.

"Yes," he cried out as he spurted out hot semen into her mouth for what seemed like hours.

Later, when his sanity returned, Jake watched Kate use a linen towel to wipe him clean. Then he pulled up his pants, scooped her up, and took her to his bedroom.

"I'm gonna fuck you as thoroughly as you just loved me," he growled as he tore off both their clothes and dragged her into the shower.

* * * * *

Water sluiced over his darkly tanned skin when he re-joined her in the shower a few minutes later, a condom sheathing his erection. The hard muscles in his shoulders and chest rippled when he splayed his hands over her buttocks, lifted her as though she weighed no more than a feather, and pressed her back against the shower wall.

"Wrap your legs around my waist," he said gruffly.

Could they make love that way? Kate wondered, but she did as he asked. She held onto his shoulders, too, although she had no doubt that Jake could still support her weight if she let go.

Truth was, she just wanted to touch him everywhere she could, feel those hard, lean muscles flexing beneath his supple skin. She loved the way the silky hair on his chest teased her nipples into rigid points while his penis throbbed against her mound.

He took her mouth and coaxed it open, but he nibbled instead of gobbling. Light nips of his teeth and a slow, lazy exploration with his tongue primed her for him. And when he thrust his tongue deep in her mouth it made her want to take his big, hot penis into her body and ease the now-familiar feeling of heat and fullness that suddenly was too much to bear.

"I want you to love me now," she told him when he came up for air.

Warm water slithered between their bodies, and the lingering scent of the liquid soap they'd rubbed into each other's skin filled her nostrils. When she nibbled at his shoulder, she tasted coconut and something else tropical and erotic. With her tongue, she lapped up water off his body, and between her legs she felt him swell and pulsate against the opening to her vagina.

"Feel my cock? It wants inside you, too. Loosen up your legs and let me slide you down."

Slowly he lowered her, not stopping until she was fully impaled. He throbbed inside her, the broad, blunt tip of his steely sex doing wicked and wonderful things deep where it pressed against the mouth of her womb. In this position she was fully open to him, and the sensation of his pubic hair tickling her already swollen clitoris each time he partially withdrew and sank back inside her soon had her screaming out in ecstasy.

"Hold on, honey. You've got me coming again."

The jerky spasms of his climax set off another series of tremors in her pussy that soon spread through her body.

Just as he lifted her off him and set her down, the doorbell rang.

"Damn. That must be Shana and Bear."

Kate looked through the cascading stream of water at Jake, sorry their romantic interlude had to end for now.

"I didn't think they'd be coming for another hour," Jake said, his tone reflecting annoyance when he turned off the water and handed her a thick, soft towel. "Hold onto those feelings, honey."

Hurriedly blotting herself dry, she couldn't take her eyes off him. God, how she loved everything about him, from his darkly handsome face to the bottom of his well-shaped feet.

As she was admiring his long, muscular body, he dropped the towel, and her mouth watered at the sight of his sex, impressive even now, when it was only half erect in its nest of soft, dark hair. Her nipples hardened, and her pussy rained moisture onto her thighs.

"You'd better put on some clothes," she said inanely, as conscious of his rapacious gaze on her as she was of her desire for him.

"Yeah."

Striding into the bedroom, Jake opened a drawer and pulled out a soft, old Texas A&M sweatshirt. "Here, honey, this ought to cover you up enough to be decent," he said, tossing it to her as he stared lasciviously at her taut, tingling breasts. He pulled on some gray sweatpants and padded barefoot toward the door, his sable hair still glistening wet from the shower.

They'll know what we were doing.

Alone in the bedroom, Kate rummaged through her suitcase. She pulled on panties and an old pair of running shorts. Setting down the bra she'd selected, she put on Jake's sweatshirt instead. Her nipples ached, but for his touch, not the restraint of lace and nylon.

Somehow wearing his shirt made her feel closer to him. As she hurried to run a brush through her damp hair, she wondered if the sex could be any better if Jake loved her. The way she loved him.

Setting her dreams aside, Kate went to meet the last of Jake's sisters.

"Shana couldn't wait. She had to see her favorite brother before we went to the hospital, or the house, or anything. Looks as though we may have come at a bad time, though," a man was saying as he crushed Jake in a fierce bear hug.

He was huge, about Jake's height but thicker than Jake through the chest and shoulders.

"That's okay. By the way, I'm your wife's only brother. How was your flight?" That was Jake, sounding out of breath after the other man's greeting.

"Bear! I haven't hugged my brother yet," a beautiful brunette complained, her arms full with a plump, dark-haired infant. "Here, you take Jamil." She thrust the baby into the man's big hands.

Then Kate watched her practically leap into Jake's arms.

The man knelt with the baby, bringing his face level with those of two pretty, quiet little girls. "Uncle Jake will get to you, too, my little princesses," he told them in a deep, slightly accented voice that made Kate wonder if he'd been educated in England. His tailor-made dark gray suit contrasted vividly with the pristine white cloth that covered his head and rested against his massive shoulders.

Kate smiled. The larger of the girls looked like a feminine version of her father, while the other one was the image of the beauty in Jake's warm embrace.

This was Shana. The sister nearest Jake's age, the one he'd grown up with. The one who made his cynical expression soften whenever he spoke of her.

"Jake. Are you going to introduce Kate?" Shana asked, freeing herself from her brother's embrace and turning to smile at Kate.

Kate felt out of place in the loving group until Jake joined her and wrapped his arm around her waist. "We weren't expecting you for a while," he said with a wicked grin.

"I can see that, little brother. Come on. Where have your manners run off to?"

Jake made the introductions, leaving Bear for last. "And this is Sheikh Dahoud el Rashid, better known around here as Bear."

Sheikh? Jake had told Kate his sister lived in Kuwait, but she didn't remember him saying Bear was Kuwaiti. She'd certainly not visualized the man as this big, dark, absolutely gorgeous specimen who looked so good that women must fight each other for the chance to join his harem. Kate hoped she managed to hide her shock. "Bear. What an unusual nickname."

"My teammates gave it to me," Bear said with a grin.

Shana shot her husband a loving look. "Bear was an all-American linebacker for the Longhorns, but he's really a teddy bear. Jake, did you tell Kate how I met Bear?"

"No. But I guess I'll have to, now. Shana was staying with me at the hospital after I had a run-in with Bear on the football field. Nice guy that he is, he came to see how much damage he'd done to a poor, unsuspecting freshman second-stringer for his team's biggest rival. Of course, this was after the game was over and the Longhorns had trounced the Aggies. From then on, he and Shana were inseparable. They both had been on the UT campus for three years by then, but that was the first time they'd run into each other."

"I didn't know you played football." There was a lot Kate didn't know about Jake, she thought as she tried to school her expression into one of neutral friendliness.

"Jake! I can't believe that. From the time you were ten years old, all you talked about was drilling for oil and being a first string quarterback in college. Jake still holds the Texas A&M record for most yards passing in a single game." Shana's dark eyes sparkled, and Kate realized how proud she must be of her brother.

"Yeah. Well, it's been a long time since college. Probably if it was football season, I'd have mentioned it." Jake's voice sounded strained, and Kate wondered what was bothering him.

"We need to get to the hospital and see Dad. I just couldn't wait to see you," Shana said breathlessly, her dark eyes sparkling with apparent curiosity when she watched Jake lay his hand on Kate's hip.

Jake turned to Bear. "Better lose the *ghutra*. No need to get the Old Man's blood pressure up before his operation. Since when have you started keeping Kuwaiti traditions in Texas?"

"Since I didn't have time to get a haircut before we rushed out and flew halfway around the world," Bear replied, reaching up and removing the white cloth and the woven cord that had secured it to his head. Laughing, he shook his head and almost shoulder-length jet-black hair flowed from beneath what looked a lot like a loosely woven yarmulke.

"Shana, you let him go around like that, shaggy as a dog?" Jake asked.

"I like his hair long. Gives me more to run my fingers through, doesn't it, darlin'? Besides, yours was almost as bad when you came up to see us last month before you left Riyadh."

They teased and visited for a few more minutes before Bear herded Shana and their children out the door.

* * * * *

"Go ahead. Spit it out, honey." Jake handed Kate a glass of soda and took a long sip from his bottle of beer. "Tell me what you're thinking."

"Bear's an Arab."

"That he is. He's Muslim, too, before you ask. He's also heir to some of the richest oil fields in Kuwait. And he's one helluva good friend."

"I'm sure he is. It just surprised me because I'd had him pictured as being an American," she replied reasonably.

"Not half as much as it surprised Mom and Dad when Shana told them she was going to marry him. And not one tenth as much as I understand the news shocked Bear's family back in Kuwait."

"But it didn't shock you?"

He shook his head. "People are people. Some are good, some are bad. But they're people. They're who they are, not where they're from or how they worship or how much money they've got, or who their ancestors were a thousand years ago. I liked Bear from the start. He's one of the good guys. And he's been good for Shana."

"They seem very much in love," Kate said, her voice soft and giving.

"They are. Mom and Dad realized that right away and dropped the objections they'd had at the beginning. I don't imagine it took a whole lot longer for Shana to wrap Bear's father around her little finger. Now, since they've been married eleven years, no one in either family thinks twice about the ethnic differences."

"Except maybe Ben. Bear was quite a jolt to him when they met at Leah's wedding. Of course, to give Ben credit, he had just recently reconciled himself to joining a family that didn't keep Kosher and had two Christian in-laws at the time." Jake chuckled as he described Ben's initial shock at meeting his other brother-in-law to be at the rehearsal.

"Your family's a regular melting pot, isn't it?"

"Yeah. And I'm the only one so far whose judgment in selecting a partner turned out to be bad." As much as the failure of his marriage to Alice had hurt Jake, he knew it had devastated his parents more.

"What went wrong?" Kate asked, her aqua eyes soft with compassion.

"Her killing my child was the final straw. If she hadn't already filed for divorce, I'd have left her over that. But she'd already made her decision and picked out her next victim before I realized our problems were too complex to solve."

"Did your religious differences cause the problems?"

"No. That was one of the few things we never argued about."

He noticed Kate's questioning look. "We fought about me working in the oil fields. About where and how we were going to live. We hated each other's friends and argued over how we'd spend our leisure time. You name it, Alice and I most likely fought about it at one time or another. Except for the sex. That was good until the end."

"Oh."

That one word conveyed a lot of understanding. And hurt, too. "Even that wasn't better than it is with you," he told Kate.

He paused until her frown turned to a smile. "Alice hated everything about my work. At first, she resented the time I had to spend out in the fields more than anything else. But after awhile, my being away didn't bother her as much as the fact that I wouldn't even consider taking the suit-and-tie job she thought I should have." He rubbed a hand across his aching forehead.

"I'm sorry." Kate took his hand and stroked it gently.

"Yeah. Pity Alice didn't realize her feelings sooner—for instance before she agreed to marry me."

"Your home must have been a battlefield," she said, the faint lines beside her soft, sweet mouth deepening when she frowned.

"A silent one most of the time. At least for the first few years, before I started bugging her about having kids. Then the war between us heated up. I wanted a family badly. I even promised I'd take an office job with the company if she'd agree to have a baby. When she balked, I should have walked out and given her grounds for divorce."

If he had, it would have saved him a hell of a lot more pain than it would have cost in the huge divorce settlement Alice could have hit him for if she hadn't had another fish on the hook.

"Why didn't you?"

"I didn't want to admit I'd been a fool to marry her in the first place. I'd grown up seeing and believing that marriage is for keeps. Hell. I didn't leave Alice then because I still wanted her more than any other woman I'd ever fucked."

Almost as much as he wanted Kate now.

"Jake. Don't tell me any more." Kate's voice was hoarse, as if she was having trouble choking out the words.

A tear made its way down her soft, pale cheek. Jake realized then that she was valiantly trying not to weep.

Her emotional reaction humbled him, for he had used up his own deeper feelings long ago—those months when he'd grieved for his lost child and his broken marriage.

When she stood and took his hand, he followed her silently back to bed and let her nurture and comfort him. He was too tired, too battered inside, to fight his need for tenderness tonight.

"Shana knew we'd been making love before they got here," she said much later as they lay together on his king-size bed.

He rolled over and grinned. "Yeah. She knew. So did Bear. So what? Do you think they got their kids out of a Cheerios box?"

"What we've been doing won't make babies," Kate commented, looking pointedly at the supply of condom packets strewn on top of the bedside table.

"Don't worry about Shana, honey. She'd be the last one of my sisters to deny me my pleasures. Or to think badly of the woman who provides them."

Jake didn't want to think. He wanted to start all over again, taste every inch of Kate's soft, sweet body. Rolling over, he grabbed another condom from his stash before settling himself on his knees and elbows above her.

"Speaking of pleasures…"

"Jake, stop it. You won't take anything seriously. Your sister has to think I'm hardly better than a two-bit whore."

"Hush. If I know Shana, she'll keep Bear up all night satisfying their sexual appetites. Someday I'll tell you the whole story about how they got together because she wanted him to satisfy a fantasy she had about being a houri in a sheikh's harem."

"Really?"

"Yes, really. But right now we need to sleep so we can be with Dad tomorrow. But my cock's cold. It wants to be inside you."

He fumbled to sheath himself, then buried himself in her tight, wet pussy.

"Hold on now, honey," he said as he rolled to his side, taking her with him.

And soon they slept.

* * * * *

Across town Jake's prediction was coming to pass.

In the master suite of the luxury condo they kept for their visits to Houston, Bear and Shana relaxed after they'd visited her dad and checked on the kids whose nanny had tucked them into their beds.

"They were fucking when we got there."

Bear laughed. "I surmised as much. Apparently Jake's as hot-blooded as his big sister. And as brazen."

"Kate was blushing like a virgin. You don't suppose—"

"No. I doubt very seriously that she's untouched. Not with the way Jake was looking at her."

Shana smiled. "And how was that?"

"This way. The way I still look at you. Dance for me?"

Her still-lithe body swayed to the muted rhythm of a *tabla* that they'd captured on tape long ago. "Did it make you hot, knowing we'd walked in on them?"

Bear's dark eyes glittered as he watched the jewels on her fingers and in her ears and navel, winking at him in the dimmed light. His cock rose, tenting the white *dishdasha* he'd slipped on after the shower they had just shared. "You make me hot, *houri*."

She'd counted on it. Nothing turned Bear on more than reliving the fantasy she'd whispered to him eleven years ago, when they'd first met.

I want to be your love slave. I want to live in your harem and compete for the attention of your big, beautiful cock.

She swayed to the beat of the drum and tambourine. Slowly, undulating while she worked the fastener on her jeweled belt, she tossed it away. Now her silky pussy was shielded only by the strings of smoothly flowing beads that hung from a brief, glittering half-bra that revealed nipples she'd recently had pierced so she could display sapphire-studded nipple shields Bear had brought back to her from a trip to Egypt.

"Come to me, slave." Bear rose, cast away his robe, and lay back against jewel-toned cushions that heightened the olive tones of his muscular, hairless body.

Unsnapping the front clasp of the bra, Shana dropped to her knees and bent her head to swirl her tongue around his huge, engorged cock.

How she loved it! How she loved him!

Reverently she cupped his balls and rolled them between her palms as she sucked the head of his cock inside until it filled her mouth, then licked around the sensitive ridge where he'd been circumcised. God, but he still tasted as good as he had that first time, years ago.

Bear knew the game, recognized the intensity of the orgasms that wracked her body when they played their sexual games. And he wanted to oblige his beautiful wife before she coaxed out his climax with her talented tongue and the finger she'd begun to insinuate gently up his ass.

"Put the rings on me, and then come here and let me drink your honey," he ordered.

The bite of smooth, cold metal against his gonads and the sound of the mechanism locking into place never failed to heighten his arousal, no matter how often she clamped the familiar rings around the base of his cock and balls.

And the swipe of her tongue along his shaft had his cock bucking against the pressure of the rings. "Cease, *houri*," he growled as he dragged her up his body by tugging on the ponytail she'd secured with a sapphire-studded barrette.

She straddled his face and lowered her pussy to his mouth for his pleasure and her own.

Her clit was already hard, and it trembled against his tongue when he burrowed between her satiny labia and settled in to feast. Her firm, round ass cheeks filled his hands, though he didn't need to use them to hold her there.

Shana loved being eaten, almost as much as she loved having him fuck her. Bear slid a hand between her legs, found her dripping pussy, and inserted three fingers inside. Allah, but in spite of having given him three beautiful children, she was as tight now as she'd been that first time he'd sunk his cock into her welcoming sheath.

He wanted to roll her off him, remove the constricting rings, mount her, and fuck her until his climax relieved the throbbing in his cock and balls.

But he wanted to love her this way, too. To taste the clean musk of her and listen to her little moans of pleasure when he brought her to a shuddering climax with his hands and mouth.

Watching the flickering candlelight play off the huge sapphire and a smaller diamond that twinkled in and above her navel like his own private mark of ownership aroused him almost as much as feeling her warm wet mouth on his cock, her breath tickling the sensitive skin of his scrotum.

And the musk of her and him that mingled with the spicy incense that burned in a brazier on the table was headier than any aphrodisiac. A smell he'd always associate with Shana and sex.

How he loved feeling her labia pressing against his chin, as smooth and satiny as their baby's bottom! Slowly, sensually, he sucked her clit while he moved his fingers in and out of her pussy.

With a finger of his other hand, Bear circled her puckered anus while he sucked harder on her clit. When she bucked, as though asking for some anal play, he dipped his fingers into the bowl of warm, clove-scented oil that she'd placed next to the brazier.

One knuckle at a time, he worked his oiled middle finger past her anal sphincter until his palm rested in the crack of her butt cheeks. Her pussy clenched around the fingers of his other hand, and her clit stabbed into his seeking tongue.

His genitals were ready to explode.

"Yesss." Her pussy rained creamy honey over his face and hands.

He increased the pressure on her clit, sucking and licking and swallowing her copious cream, ramming his fingers into her pussy and her ass while she came and came and came.

When she collapsed against him, he rolled her over onto her belly, released the ring from his tortured cock and balls, and sank into her wet, hot pussy from behind. Wanting her with him, he reached around and cupped her satiny mound, finding her still-engorged little clit and scissoring it with two fingers before grasping his ball sac and rubbing his balls over her most sensitive flesh.

God! Shana braced herself on her hands and knees, raring back to take all of Bear's big, beautiful cock. The pressure it put on her g-spot had her practically screaming with pleasure-pain.

Her newly pierced nipples ached for his touch—a touch that was to be denied her for another ten days, until the piercings fully healed and she could thread the plain gold barbells through the openings in her beautifully crafted nipple shields. Shields that would ring the sensitive tips, make them stand out for her sheikh's avid tongue and teeth.

"Come with me, *houri*. Now." His speech dissolved into a guttural moan when his cock bucked inside her and started spurting against the mouth of her womb. At his first yell of triumph, she began to come again, her vaginal muscles convulsing around the thick, hard length of his cock even harder than they had moments ago when he'd fucked her with his hands and mouth.

* * * * *

"I hope my little brother got half as good a fucking as you gave me last night," Shana said early the next morning, her fingers caught in Bear's shoulder-length sable hair as they lay together on a sleeping couch draped in jewel-toned silk. "Don't get this cut too short. I like it like this."

"Your wish is my command. Roll over now. Get more sleep. I shall return before we need to go to your father's bedside."

On his way out, Bear stopped by the nursery and dropped a kiss on baby Jamil's plump cheek. His son resembled his namesake—or maybe that was merely Bear's imagination. On the way to the salon and while a chatty woman styled his hair, he wondered whether he'd ever see his good friend and cousin, Jamil al Hassan, again.

* * * * *

Jake woke quickly when the alarm went off. Kate's soft, sweet body warmed him.

He had to get up. If he stayed, they'd be going at it again, and it was time they dressed and joined his family at the hospital.

Hurriedly he shaved. Then, he pulled on clean underwear and jeans before waking Kate.

"We need to hurry," he said as he shook her gently. "The Old Man's surgery is at ten."

"Oh. You should have gotten me up earlier," Kate protested as she sleepily eyed his state of partial dress.

"I thought you could catch a few more minutes' sleep while I shaved." He grinned at the belated modesty she displayed, draping the top sheet around her like a toga.

"I can still see those pert, pink nipples beading up under that armor," he said. "And I feel something else getting hard."

162

She glanced down at his crotch, then drew the sheet tighter as though it was medieval armor. "Oh."

When she looked at him, she blushed. She wanted him, too. And his cock didn't give a damn that they had to be at the hospital in an hour.

"Better hurry or we won't have time to stop for breakfast." Especially if she enticed him back into bed.

"Will everyone be at the hospital this morning?" Kate asked a few minutes later as she slipped on a clingy dress that matched her eyes over mouth-watering scraps of lace that passed for underwear.

"What? Oh, yeah."

It was hard as hell to think when they were alone in his bedroom, within spitting distance of a mighty inviting looking bed.

His mouth watered and his cock was hard as stone. And he hadn't even touched her. All he'd done was ogle the lacy garter belt that ringed her tiny waist, its thin suspenders framing pale, translucent silk that barely veiled her pussy. He couldn't help drooling over her ass, either. It was plump and enticingly bare, with a skinny line disappearing between her cheeks and pointing right at where he wanted to be.

Somebody ought to outlaw those g-string panties. And tight jeans, too, he decided when his began to strangle his balls. Damn it, he'd be thinking about getting in her pussy all day long now, and he wouldn't be able to do a thing about it.

That was a goddamn painful prospect. Jake swore under his breath.

"What's wrong?"

"This." He unzipped his jeans and shoved them down far enough to free his throbbing cock. "It hurts, and it's all your fault. Come here and help me fix it," he ordered as he grabbed a rubber and rolled it on.

When she did, he lifted her. "Wrap your arms and legs around me and let me fuck you," he whispered, bunching her skirt up out of the way and nudging her G-string to the side with his cock head before slamming her hot dripping hole onto him all the way to his aching balls.

He had her backed against a wall, her legs spread wide and locked around his narrow waist. Impaled on his huge, hot penis, she couldn't move.

She was helpless but not afraid. Helplessly enthralled with the way he rammed her like a piston, hard and deep, over and over. Each upward thrust opened her further, brushed her swollen clitoris, and made her grip him harder.

His lips came down on her mouth, forced it open for his marauding tongue.

"Come for me, honey," he gasped when he broke the kiss, throwing his head back and fucking her harder, faster than before. "Oh, God. I can't—"

She felt it coming, that sensation that started in her clit and made her vaginal muscles contract around his pulsating sex. "Don't stop. Jake…"

"Yesss." His head braced next to hers against the wall, he held her there for a long time before lifting her off his still-rigid penis and setting her down on her own wobbly legs.

"How was that for a quickie?" he asked, tossing away the condom and stuffing himself back into his jeans.

"Good. Really good." Her cheeks burned when she met his hot gaze.

"Yeah. Slam-bam, thank you, ma'am, but I'm glad it was good for you, too. We'll take care of the preliminaries later, when we've got more time. Meanwhile, we'd better get going."

Jake handed Kate her purse and practically dragged her out of his condo.

Chapter Nine

Jake's family had gathered in the sitting room of his father's hospital suite. They were lucky to have each other for support at a time like this, Kate thought as she recalled her lonely vigil by Pop's deathbed. She and Jake stood in the doorway for a moment before joining them.

"Is Jacob ready for his ordeal?" Bear asked.

Closing the door to the sickroom, Deb turned to Bear and nodded. "Mother's sitting with him, but he's already asleep. The nurse gave him a shot about half an hour ago. You all may as well make yourselves comfortable, since there's nothing any of us can do now but wait."

"Jake will be disappointed. I know he wanted to talk with Daddy before they put him to sleep," Shana commented. "Here, sit with me," she invited her husband huskily.

"And just how will Jake be disappointed?" Jake asked when he and Kate came in. He looked around the room, where his sisters and Bear had apparently settled in to wait for the Old Man to have his operation. "Can I go in and see Dad?"

"Daddy's already asleep," Deb said quietly, standing and walking into Jake's embrace. "Mother's with him."

Extricating himself from his eldest sister's arms, Jake bent to brush his lips briefly across Leah's cheek. "You gonna forgive me for forgetting your birthday last week?" he asked, obviously teasing.

"Of course not." Leah smiled, but her voice sounded strained.

"Hey, I'll send out for something now if it'll make you smile. How about a pound of your favorite chocolates?"

Jake was a totally different person around his sisters than he was with her, teasing and cajoling and free at showing his affection. Kate wondered if he would ever act so at ease with her — or any other woman who might be sharing his bed.

Her heart ached. Jake's family might want him to find a woman to love, but he made it very clear that his heart would stay under lock and key. She forced sadness aside when Jake stepped back to her and wrapped a muscular arm around her waist.

When they sat on the other sofa and he held onto her as if she were his lifeline, she did her best to ease his worries.

* * * * *

Kate looked around the room. Over two hours ago, the orderlies had taken Jake's father off to surgery. For a while, everyone had chatted aimlessly, as if to ward off feelings of unease. Then Jake and Scott had gone into a huddle at a desk in the corner of the room, where they were still going over some papers Scott had brought with him.

Ben had joined them a few minutes ago, and his tentative smile and slightly aloof demeanor reminded Kate again of the man she had almost married. She watched him greet Leah, his manner exuding gentle concern.

Jake's mother had opted to wait with them rather than in a crowded surgical waiting room. Obviously nervous, the older woman smiled as she twisted a lace handkerchief around in her well-manicured hands. Shana sat beside her, obviously offering what comfort she could.

Kate's heart went out to Adele, for she could imagine how helpless she'd feel if it were Jake lying helpless under a surgeon's knife.

"What did you say?" Kate asked, brought out of her thoughts by a deep, quiet voice. She looked up and saw Bear standing in front of her, two crystal glasses in his hand.

"Would you like a drink?" he repeated, holding out one of the icy glasses.

"Nothing alcoholic, thank you." She'd already turned down offers of various alcoholic beverages from Deb and Ben.

"Jake said you wouldn't want hard liquor, so I fixed fruit drinks for us. I don't drink alcohol, either."

Kate realized when Bear smiled how easily a woman could fall in love with him.

"Thank you," she said as she took the drink from his large, nicely shaped hand. "It's not that I don't drink. It's that I can't drink much and still function."

"Don't let me make you nervous, little one. Shana would kill me if she thought I'd scared you off from her baby brother."

Kate's cheeks burned. She hadn't realized her surprise at meeting Bear had been so obvious. "You won't. Jake hadn't told me…"

"Don't be embarrassed. Shock is a natural reaction, one I encounter here often outside the haven of Shana's family. When people's reactions are especially vehement, I remind myself that Shana faces the same age-old prejudice when we are with my people."

Bear's hawk-like features gave him a fierce look, but they didn't negate Kate's feeling that this was a kind, caring man. She saw decency and compassion in his eyes and in the softly upturned corners of his lips. Not to mention that he obviously was one sexy sheikh, at least to his beautiful wife.

He wasn't wearing the *ghutra* today, and his hair had been cut into a style that was definitely western. In boots and indigo jeans, with a plaid western shirt he'd left open at the neck, Bear looked a lot like Jake.

She glanced over toward Jake and Scott, then smiled at Ben, who had taken Ruthie from Leah and was patiently lulling the toddler to sleep in his arms. It didn't escape her attention that Scott glanced Deb's way frequently, apparently concerned about how she was holding up under the strain of waiting.

In their own very different ways, Kate decided, each of Jake's brothers-in-law demonstrated deep love for their wives.

She turned back to Bear. "Thank you for the drink. Bear, I'm sorry if I was rude last night. It just surprised me to see Jake's sister with…"

"With an Arab? It surprised my father more to see me with Shana when I first brought her home. Over the years, though, he has come to love her as much as I do." Bear grinned. "He has even accepted that I will take no other wives, and that Shana is more than enough woman to keep me happy."

"J-Jake said you don't keep a harem."

"No. I don't. This is not entirely because of Shana. Before I married her—before I even knew her, I had decided that one woman would be enough for me. Not many Muslim men keep harems or take more than one wife anymore. When Jake brings you to visit us in Kuwait, you'll learn that most of us are actually quite modern and Western in our outlook."

Kate smiled. Bear and Shana were way off-base if they thought his being an Arab would scare her away from Jake. She loved him desperately. She wanted nothing more than to be his wife, make a home for him and bear his children.

He could have a relative who was a convicted ax murderer, and it wouldn't change the way she felt. If only Jake would return her love.

Too bad that was such a big "if only."

Ruthie stirred in Ben's arms, making Kate think about Bear and Kate's children and wonder where they were today. "You're the only ones who left your children home," she commented.

"Yasmin and Selena were tired from the long trip, and Jamil has an annoying tendency to bellow when he doesn't get his way. My daughters argued with each other and my son howled the entire time we were here with Jacob last night, so we decided it would be less stressful on everybody if we left all of them at the condo with their nanny." Bear shrugged, but Kate saw the love and pride shining in his eyes.

"What beautiful names for your beautiful children. I've never heard the name Jamil before. What does it mean?"

"Handsome." Bear shook his head as if admitting that embarrassed him. "But we didn't name him that because we thought he was a pretty baby. He bears the name of my cousin, Jamil al Hassan, whose plane went down in Iraq during the Gulf War. Though we have expended every possible effort, we have not been able to learn whether he is alive or dead."

"That must be awful, not knowing."

"Yes. It is. We pray daily for his safe return, though hope dims every day when we receive no word from him."

They chatted easily, as though they'd known each other for years. Kate had no trouble seeing why Shana had fallen in love with her sheikh, or why Jake considered Bear his friend as well as his brother.

"The doctor is here," Bear said suddenly, leaving Kate and hurrying to Shana's side.

Kate stayed in the background, moving into the crowd of anxious relatives only when Jake came over and growled that he wanted her with him. Massaging his sweaty palm with her thumb, she stood with the others and listened to the surgeon's verdict.

* * * * *

"What did the doctor mean?" Adele looked first toward Jake, then turned to Ben when Jake told her he didn't know.

Kate watched Leah's husband. It seemed he hesitated, as though choosing his words carefully. Jake's palm was damp in hers, and from the almost painful way he gripped her hand, she sensed his anxiety.

"Dr. Cohen meant the surgery went well, but that Jacob will have to retire. His heart can't stand the kind of stress that running a company like GreenTex must create. Will Jacob's retirement be such a tragedy?" Ben asked. "He's years beyond the age when men usually want to sit back and relax."

Kate watched him put his arm protectively around Leah's distended waist.

"Scott. Jake. What will happen with the company?" Adele's troubled gaze shifted from her blond son-in-law to her youngest child.

"GreenTex will go on as it always has," Jake assured his mother. "Let's worry for now about getting Dad well."

"Will you finally stay home and take your rightful place in the company now, the way Jacob has always wanted you to?" Adele asked, her expression intense.

"Mother. It's neither the time nor the place for this discussion." Jake's fingers tightened against Kate's hand. "Scott. We'll need to talk later," he added, looking his brother-in-law in the eye.

"Someone needs to let Mama Anna know how the surgery went," Deb said.

"We will. Kate?" Jake held out a hand to Kate, then pulled her gently out of the family circle toward the door.

Leah shot him a puzzled look. "Aren't you staying?"

Leah was the one Kate thought should leave. She looked drained, pale beneath her olive skin and her cap of short, dark curls. From the lines that radiated from her trembling lips and the way she clutched her swollen belly, Kate guessed she must be uncomfortable.

"No," Jake said, giving his sister a pat on the shoulder. "There's nothing I can do here. You should go home, too. You look tired. I'll go give Mama Anna the news about Dad and introduce her to Kate all in one trip. Mom can call me on my cell phone if she needs me."

If Kate hadn't guessed Jake wanted more to avoid discussing his future role at GreenTex with his mother than to whisk her away to meet his grandmother, she'd have taken the gesture as a sign he was getting serious about her. As it was, she read nothing of significance in his action. She did, however, share Jake's obvious need to escape from what she imagined could become a civilized clash of wills with no easily acceptable compromise.

Scott kissed Deb, then joined Jake and Kate at the door. "I'm going to the office. I'll let everyone there know Jacob came through the surgery," he told Jake as they walked together to the hospital parking lot.

"When do you want to get together?" Jake asked.

"I'll come over to your place late this afternoon." Scott climbed into a silver Jaguar and drove away.

Though Kate had looked for evidence of rivalry and competition between the two, she hadn't seen any. When she stripped away the glittering trappings of their wealth and looked at the people beneath the props, she realized that Jake and his family had been blessed with a huge amount of love and camaraderie.

"You'll like Mama Anna," Jake said as he steered Scott's sleek Lamborghini along a curving, tree-lined street in one of the older sections of Houston.

"She's your father's mother?"

"Stepmother. But she's the only grandmother I've ever known. Mom's parents were killed in an accident before I was born. Mama Anna doesn't go out much because she's crippled with arthritis, but her mind's as sharp as a teenager's."

"What about your grandfather?" From earlier conversations, Kate knew he'd been dead for some time.

"He was a great old guy—took me everywhere with him when I was a little kid. He died when I was ten. For a long time, I kept looking for him to come back and take me out to ride his horses."

"What did he do?"

"He was a geologist. He founded GreenTex before this country got involved in World War II. Before that, he had hired out to some of the South African mining companies to locate diamonds."

"That sounds exciting."

"When I was a kid, I lived to hear about his adventures. He made me want to go out and find treasures under the ground, just like he had." Jake pulled up at the curb in front of a big, old-fashioned bungalow. "Ready to meet my grandmother?" he asked as he opened the gull-wing door for Kate.

Kate took his outstretched hand and walked with him up the winding pathway.

* * * * *

"I love her," Kate exclaimed after Jake crawled back in the car.

"Mama Anna's something, isn't she?" Jake turned the key and brought the car's powerful engine to life. "For a ninety-year-old lady, she's got a hell of a sense of humor."

For the last hour he'd watched Kate while his grandmother captivated her with stories of his childhood, his father's teen years, and his grandfather's uncanny ability to ferret out oil deposits hidden under west Texas scrub land.

Jake's resolve had strengthened. No one—not the Old Man and not his mother—would be able to persuade him to leave the oil fields and assume the presidency of his family's company. Scott wanted the job. He had worked hard for it and by God, he would have it.

"When is Leah's baby due?" Kate asked while they were driving back to Jake's condo.

"Any day now."

"She and Ben must be anxious for the baby to be born."

"I'm sure they are." Leah had looked awfully tired, and Jake doubted her exhaustion had as much to do with their father's illness as with her being nearly nine months pregnant.

Kate reached over and squeezed his thigh, something he doubted she'd have had the nerve to do before they'd spent the past two nights and days together. He liked having her touch him.

Her soft voice and gentle smile warmed and reassured him, made him feel content even now, when his future was in turmoil. Maybe, he thought, after the hassles about the saboteurs and the Old Man's retirement were done with, he'd deal with the emotional attachment to her that seemed to be growing every day.

It had been a long time since a woman had made him want to share more with her than a few hours in bed. And that made him damn uneasy.

* * * * *

He'd worn her out.

Watching Kate sleep made Jake want to take care of her. Slowly he padded across the carpeted floor to the bathroom.

While hot needles of water pounded his body, he tried to think of anything but her and how she made him feel.

What he needed to focus on was how to get his father to accept that he could never tolerate being cooped up in an office, assigning other engineers the exhilarating task of searching for oil.

The Old Man had known Jake's feelings about running GreenTex for years.

Still, the stubborn man hung onto the hope that eventually his son would tire of fieldwork and accept what Jacob considered his birthright. Sighing, Jake toweled himself dry and put on a pair of jeans. He padded barefoot through the bedroom, tucking the covers around Kate as he passed the bed.

Scott arrived while Jake was paying for the sandwiches he'd sent out for from a nearby deli. Handing his brother-in-law a Reuben and a beer, Jake followed him into the living room and watched Scott stare out the window.

"I don't want to run GreenTex," Jake said flatly.

Turning to face him, Scott smiled. "I know. And I do. But my last name isn't Green. The Old Man wants his son to take over his company."

He took a sip of beer and sank onto a chair. "What do we need to talk about?"

"How to persuade the Old Man he should put you in charge, and be satisfied knowing I'm out in the field finding oil and making us all richer." Jake took a seat on the other leather lounge chair and stared at his own sandwich that still lay untouched on the cocktail table.

"You could be CEO, make me executive VP, and we could keep on doing what we've always done—except that you'd be making the final decisions the way Jacob has always done." Scott's tone was light, but Jake was certain that this wasn't what his brother-in-law really wanted.

"Or, you could be president, I could placate the Old Man by taking a seat on the Board of Directors, and we could keep on doing as you said—as we've always done, except that you'd be the one making the business decisions." Jake downed half a beer while he waited for Scott to respond.

"That might work. Jacob knows your value to us out in the field. Still, you're his son. I'm not."

"You are by everything but birth. Hell, Scott, you've been a member of this family since I was back in grade school."

"I know. And all of you have always made me feel like I belong. But Jacob has this special feeling for his only son. I'd feel that way about my son, too, if I had one. There's something about one's own flesh and blood."

"And male flesh and blood's more important than female? That's goddamn unfair." Jake had always felt tremendous pressure to achieve, to fit a mold the Old Man had designed for him. As far as he knew, no such pressure had been put on any of his sisters. He'd always envied them for their parents' unqualified approval of anything they wanted to do.

"To carry on a name...tradition...yes, it is. I love my daughters dearly, but it still hurts that Deb and I lost our son."

Guilt washed over Jake. He'd almost forgotten that, early in their marriage, Scott and Deb had lost a baby boy who had been born with some rare, congenital heart disorder. "I'm sorry, man. I'd almost forgotten."

"You were just a boy. I didn't expect you to remember. Damn it, Jake, I know how hard Jacob has pushed you to follow directly in his footsteps. But as much as I've sympathized with you, watching you get pushed toward a career you don't want, I understand how Jacob feels, too."

"After I told him I'd come back and take care of the problems in the Groveland field, Dad said I was more like his father than I was like him. You never met Gramps, did you?" Jake picked up his sandwich and took a bite.

"Just once, before Debra and I married. He died not too long after that. From all Deb has told me about her grandfather, I get the feeling that you probably are a throwback."

"Gramps would never have tolerated working up in a steel and glass cage. The Old Man should understand I can't live with that kind of restriction, either."

"Maybe."

"We have to try. I'd be the lousiest goddamn executive anyone could imagine. Six months with me running things, and the company would be down the tubes."

Scott rested his chin on his hands. "Not so. You could delegate. I'd be there for you just like I've been there for your father all these years."

"Damn it, I don't want to run GreenTex. Can't you and the Old Man get that through your skulls? I'd crumble up and die if I couldn't be out in the middle of the action. And I don't want to be a figurehead, either, getting the credit for your executive genius. What do I have to do to convince you?"

"You don't have to convince me. But we don't want your father to have another heart attack. Look. I've got four hours' worth of work piled up on my desk. I'll give it some thought and see if I can come up with a solution."

Scott unfolded his long, lean body from the chair and handed Jake his empty beer bottle.

* * * * *

"You had company."

Kate's eyes were still droopy from her nap, and she stretched like a sleepy kitten, loosening her green silk robe and offering Jake a tantalizing view of her soft, rounded breasts.

"Yeah. Scott left a little while ago. Come here," he ordered gruffly, patting his thighs as he raised the recliner to an upright position. When she sat on his lap and rested her head against his shoulder, the tension inside him began to dissipate.

"How's your father?"

"Still pretty out of it, but doing as well as the doctors expected. I spoke to Mom a few minutes ago."

"Are your sisters still at the hospital?"

"Shana and Bear stayed. Mom said she'd persuaded Deb and Leah to go home a couple of hours ago. She wants us all to come to the house for lunch tomorrow, after we visit with Dad."

"How can she be at the hospital and still fix lunch for everybody?" Kate asked, her fingertips making a circular pattern on his bare chest and sending blood surging to his groin.

"Mom doesn't fix meals. She has a housekeeper to take care of details like that."

Jake trailed his fingers through Kate's silky hair, breathed in the clean, fresh smell of her shampoo. She felt so good. So sexy, especially when she purred and smiled when he touched and petted her.

Kate leaned her head into his hand, brushed her open lips across his palm. "I don't know how I'd keep busy if I had servants to cook and clean," Kate said, her voice pensive. "What do your mother and sisters do to keep themselves busy?"

Jake nibbled at her neck. "What all self-respecting idle rich women do. They belong to social and charitable organizations, play golf and tennis, hang out at the country club. Mom spends half her life planning fund-raisers for one good cause or another. Leah volunteers as a psychologist at a half-dozen shelters for abused children. Deb and Shana just play with their kids, shop, and hang out at the country club unless Mother shanghais them to work on one of her committees. Here, anyhow. In Kuwait, Shana's put together a volunteer organization to raise money for war orphans all over the Middle East. She shrugs off the importance of what she's doing, though, says she may as well use the talent for wheedling that she developed as a kid and fine-tuned on Bear."

"I can't imagine myself playing golf or tennis every day. Or coaxing money out of reluctant donors, even if it was for a good cause. I'd rather mess around with you," Kate said, laughing.

"Me, too. But I've got to put in some time at work, or you won't be getting the GreenTex royalties that will soon have you richer than God. So you'd better get some ideas about other ways to spend your idle time." He nibbled her breast through the thin silk robe, breathing in the familiar flowery scent that always seemed to surround her.

"I'm pretty sure I wouldn't like planning parties, not even if they're for a good cause." She wriggled in his lap like a playful kitten.

What her moving like that did to Jake made him feel anything but playful. His cock was about to burst already, and the additional stimulation damn near sent him over the edge. "Stop it, already."

"You don't really want me to."

Hell no, he didn't want her to stop. But he wanted to carry on a conversation with her, and to talk he needed a functioning brain.

"So will you spend your days lolling around in bed, waiting for your lover?" he asked, figuring that if he could ignore his hard-on, eventually it would subside. He knew damn well how he wanted Kate to spend her nights, at least for the foreseeable future.

"I don't know. That's what scares me. This oil well has changed my whole future, and I don't have the vaguest idea what's going to happen to me. Before Pop died, I thought I'd stay at home, teach, and preserve the heritage he left to me. That maybe some man would come along, we'd fall in love and marry, and raise children to carry on after us. But all that has changed."

Because she sounded forlorn, Jake wrapped his arms around her to give her comfort. "You could teach anywhere," he pointed out gently. "And marry. Groveland isn't the only place in the world where you can raise a family. There must be hundreds of places where you'd feel more at home than there."

"That's my home. Except for when I was in college and the year I spent teaching in Jackson, I've lived there all my life. I have my friends. Becky and Stan. And Gilda. They all live in Laurel, but we get together nearly every week. Until I leased my place to you, my neighbors had been good to me. Did you know Ms. Cahill came and helped me get things ready for the funeral after Pop died? And that everybody from miles around brought food and sent flowers to the cemetery? They're angry now about me leasing my land, but they'd be there for me if I needed them." She looked up at him, tears in her eyes.

Kate has never known real acceptance. Or tolerance. She excuses her neighbors' meanness because they bring her a truckload of fucking cakes and pies when their social consciences require it.

Jake recalled the barbed words he'd heard Gladys Cahill spew out at Kate, and his blood began to boil. "Honey, you're a lot more charitable than I am," he finally said.

"Not everybody's as tough as you."

Her soft drawl flowed around him like sweet honey, and the way she tangled her fingers in his chest hair and stroked his nipples was driving him insane.

He tried to ignore her sensual assault, but his cock wasn't listening to his brain. "I'm just realistic. I can't see anybody wanting to stay someplace just because their family lived there for a hundred years or more."

"You've lived here all your life," Kate pointed out gently.

Jake chose to interpret Kate's comment literally. "No I haven't. I bought this place about a year ago, for when I'm in town and don't want to commute back and forth from the ranch." I doubt if I've spent a total of a month in this place."

"You know what I mean. Houston has always been your home, your family's home."

"Wrong again. Dad brought Mom here from Dallas after they got married. And he came from a hell of a long way away from here. He was born in a little town in southern Germany. After Gramps brought him to Texas, they lived in Midland until after World War II was over and Gramps decided his company ought to be based here, where he'd be in the thick of things with other Texas oil men."

Her eyes widened. "I didn't know. I thought your family was Texan from way, way back."

"Yeah. I guess you would think that. We are, on Mom's side. And the Old Man's done a pretty good job, melting into good old American ways. Of course he's had more than sixty years to do it." Jake caught her hands.

"He must have been very young when he first came here."

"He was seven when Gramps moved them here in 1936." Jake stood, cradling Kate in his arms for a minute before setting her on her feet.

"Let's go out to the kitchen and see what we can find to snack on. We've hardly eaten anything all day," he said, figuring he might forget about sex for at least as long as it took to stuff his stomach with food. "Later, if you're really interested, I'll tell you about Gramps and how he came to be an American oil man." He stalked off toward the kitchen, leaving her to follow.

Chapter Ten

"Here. Hold this while I climb down." Jake handed Kate a heavy album bound in burgundy leather before backing down the library ladder in the den. He took back the album and put it on a glass-topped cocktail table, then sat in the center of a beige leather sofa and patted the place beside him.

When she'd settled in, he set the album on her lap. She ran her fingers over his name, embossed deeply and engraved in gold on the cover. "What's in here?" she asked when he reached over and flipped it open to the first page.

"Mementos and pictures. You wanted to know what makes my family tick. Mama Anna had a different one made for me and each of my sisters after Gramps died. Might as well let the album tell the story. I haven't looked at it for years."

He flipped open the cover to reveal a portrait Kate thought could be of Jake, if not for the man's old-fashioned attire and the faded sepia tone of the photo.

"That's Gramps in 1937. He'd just found oil on a desolate piece of West Texas land when he had this picture taken. Here's one of Dad that was taken around the same time." He turned the brittle page.

"That's your father?" The pale, thin boy with the sad eyes looked nothing like the dynamic man she'd met at the hospital.

"Yeah. He'd gone through a lot the year Gramps took that picture. Shows, doesn't it?"

"Yes. What does this letter say?" Careful not to damage it, Kate touched a wrinkled, dog-eared letter written in a language she didn't immediately recognize.

"Dad's mother wrote it to Gramps just before she died. I can't read it either, but Gramps used to say that letter made him hurry back from Capetown to get Dad and move him out of Germany."

"Before the Holocaust. How did he know?"

"He didn't. I remember him saying he must have been the luckiest man alive. Gramps came back, got Dad, and brought him here."

"How?" Kate looked at the letter, trying to make out some of the words.

"By getting passports and tourist visas, and buying passage on a ship. I guess that must have been before Hitler started restricting travel. When they got here, Gramps applied for their permanent visas. Because he was a well-known geologist, he had no trouble getting them."

Jake turned the page and pointed out his grandfather in a group picture of men posed at the base of a wooden derrick.

"There's the first GreenTex well," Jake told her proudly. "Between 1937 and the end of World War II, Gramps brought in over a hundred wells in that field. They didn't have pipelines then. They used trucks like the one you see in the background to haul crude to the refineries in Midland."

Kate looked at the picture, touched by the starkness of the rig against sandy, arid flatlands. "Drilling for oil back then must have been hard, dirty work."

"It's still hard, dirty work, honey. But it gets in your blood, and you don't want to do anything else."

She thought she saw pain in his expression as he flipped the page.

"These are pictures of Gramps and Mama Anna's wedding."

The black-and-white photos had faded over the years, giving her a blurred image of Jake's tall, rugged grandfather and a petite, blond lady who bore a vague resemblance to the elderly woman she met earlier. Her gaze settled on young Jacob's smiling face. "Your father looks happier there."

"Yeah. Mama Anna was good for him. The Old Man's always telling us how he owes her for loving him, helping him forget being scared and alone after his mother died. Turn the page," he urged.

Kate found herself looking at an eight by ten studio portrait of a young man in the uniform of the U. S. Army Air Corps. She stared at the earnest face, the sergeant's stripes on his shoulders.

"Dad joined up in forty-six, as soon as he turned seventeen. He worked for U.S. intelligence in London. Because he was fluent in German, they assigned him to piecing together information of all kinds—particularly to ferreting out the truth about what had happened in the concentration camps."

"Oh, Jake. That must have been terrible."

"I imagine his duty of going in to inspect the camps after Germany surrendered was a lot worse," he commented as he flipped over several pages in the album. "He doesn't talk about it—at least he never has, to me."

"I'd think experiencing horrors firsthand like that would have made your father bitter." Kate shuddered as she recalled TV documentaries about the Holocaust and its aftermath.

"It could have. But what it showed Dad was the absolute extremes to which bigotry could go. He talked about that a lot. The worst damn caning I ever got at school was for calling an Oriental kid in my class a chink. And that punishment was nothing compared to the talking to the Old Man put on me when I got home. I must have been about seven years old at the time. I learned young that I'd better not judge folks by the color of their skin or the way they worship."

That had been one of many lessons Jake had taken to heart. Thinking of his father now, with his fragile heart and tired-out body, he was sorry he couldn't be the man who'd take over the far-flung business Gramps had started and his father had nurtured. Needing distraction from those troubling thoughts, he reached for Kate's hand and rubbed his thumb across her small, soft palm.

"That's the well Gramps drilled in Saudi Arabia," he said when he showed her a faded color photo of a derrick rising proudly out of desert sand. "And there he is." He pointed to a man standing beside the rig, apparently deep in conversation with a robed Bedouin worker. A broad-brimmed hat obscured his grandfather's face.

"He drilled just one well over there?"

"Just that one. That photo was taken in 1977, the year before he died. It was one of the first free-flowing wells over there. It's kind of ironic. Gramps brought that well in over twenty-five years ago. When I was over there last month, I shut it down for the last time."

"So you don't have a well there anymore?"

"Not that one. But we had twenty-three producing wells in the western Saudi Arabian desert as of this morning." He frowned. "Dad negotiated with the Saudis to get drilling rights over there. Those wells have kept us going, while our domestic fields have been going dry over the years."

"You go there often, don't you?"

"For the past three years I've put in more time in Riyadh than Shana and Bear have spent in Kuwait City. Now, with Dad needing to retire, I'll probably stick closer to home, concentrate my efforts on getting maximum production out of the Groveland field."

"Out of my land." She trembled, and when he tried to cradle her against his chest she pulled away.

"Your land's only a small part of the Groveland field. As soon as we catch whoever is trying to sabotage our drilling sites, the Oil and Gas Board will cut loose with permits for us to put wells in on the other properties we've leased. For God's sake, honey, you act like having oil wells on your land's the worst thing that could happen."

"Can't you understand? That place is my home. It's all I have left of Pop, all he was able to leave me. I'm the last of my family. I was born there, and I expected to die there."

Tears rolled down her cheeks, and Jake saw she was trying valiantly to hold back the ones that were welling in her eyes.

"You said you used to be engaged. Did you expect your fiancé to come to Groveland and live with you on your ancestral land after you got married?"

She didn't answer right away. The pensive look in her eyes gave Jake a guilty twinge.

"No," she finally said. "We were going to live in Jackson. David told me we could keep the place and go there for weekends and vacations and such. I'd wanted him to set up his medical practice in Laurel, but he wouldn't. He told me there wasn't enough call for a urologist there, and that when country people who could afford a specialist needed one, they'd drive to Jackson instead of relying on the local talent."

"He was probably right. Anyhow, you were willing to leave your home for him. What was he going to give you in return? What in hell did he do to make you want his kind of life?"

This David character had given Jake no reason to be jealous, at least as far as his physical relationship with Kate went. And since he didn't love her he had no reason to care that she'd once loved somebody else enough to plan a life with him. Still it burned Jake to think she'd been willing to leave her precious home for the doctor—but that she was furious now because his company's drilling was driving her away from it.

"David would have given me everything I always wanted," she snapped.

"Now why do I doubt you were ever starry-eyed, head-over-heels in love with the guy when you never even let him in your bed?"

She scowled. "David was gentle and thoughtful. Since I was a little girl, I wanted nothing more than to be a wife and mother, to make a home for my own family. He'd have been a good husband, a wonderful father. A good provider."

"Do you still love him?" he asked.

If Kate did, that shouldn't bother Jake. Unless he was starting to feel more for her than was safe. And he wasn't. He only felt possessive—no, more like territorial—because he was the only man who'd ever fucked her.

And if he kept reminding himself of that, maybe he'd keep on believing it was true.

"No. I don't know now if I ever really loved him. You've made your point. I would have left home if I had married David. And I probably would have slept with him if I'd been head over heels in love, as you put it."

"Then for God's sake, quit agonizing over what our drilling is doing to that piece of ground. It's only a place. Not some sacred legacy you've got to sacrifice your life to protect."

He paused, searching for words to comfort her as he rubbed his thumb gently over her palm.

"Hey, I know it hurts to let go of a place that meant everything to you when you were a kid. I nearly lost it when I had to go to Midland ten years ago and shut down the last of the wells in that field Gramps opened long before I was born. That was where the Old Man sent me to learn the oil business from the bottom up. It hurt to shut that well down, but I realized that nothing stays the same forever. We all have to face that fact, sooner or later."

"I know. It's so damn hard, though." When she spoke, she looked up at him, a tremulous smile on her soft, inviting lips.

For a moment, Jake wished he could love his gentle Kate. Then Alice stepped between them in his mind, reminding him that with love came pain so fierce that he couldn't bear to risk suffering that way again. Forcibly he closed the door to his heart.

The hopeful look in her eyes faded, and she turned away. Jake wished he could banish her sadness. How could he, though, when he was barely able to cope with the emotional turmoil she caused in him?

"Yeah, honey. I know," he said, reaching out to touch her shoulder. "Life's a bitch. Come on to bed. I'll give you a rubdown so you can get some sleep. Tomorrow morning I'll have to leave you to Deb and Shana's mercies while I go to the office for a meeting."

"Should I be afraid?"

He laughed. "Unless you want to find yourself being fitted for a wedding dress, you'd better have all your wits about you. They're in full matchmaking mode."

Jake couldn't muster his usual quota of horror when he thought of his sisters ganging up to get him married off.

* * * * *

I'd like to wake up every morning to the feel of your warm, soft ass snuggled up against me.

Jake shook his head, as if that action would rid him of unwelcome urges that had begun to come over him at the most inconvenient times.

Why couldn't he stifle them? Now was not the time—if indeed there was a time—for tender feelings to rear their inane heads. Not when he had to find a way to satisfy the Old Man without letting himself be swept up into a position he neither wanted nor considered himself qualified to handle.

Abruptly, he rolled off the bed and pulled on dark brown briefs. They hardly hid his insistent erection, but maybe the light pressure from the cotton knit material would remind him he had more important things to do this morning than mess around with Kate.

Shaking her gently, he told her she had less than half an hour to dress before Shana would get here to pick her up.

When in hell had his condo shrunk? Jake tried to ignore Kate's sweet, enticing body while they washed and dressed in what seemed to be ever-tightening confines of his bedroom suite.

The doorbell rang, and Jake thanked his sister silently for making it on time. Zipping his pants as he went, he hurried to let Shana in.

"I like Kate—a lot," Shana said, her dark eyes sparkling with mischief.

"Good morning to you, too," Jake growled. "Go to the kitchen and pour yourself some coffee. Kate will be right out."

With that, he stalked away to hurry Kate up. Maybe when she was gone, he would be able to focus on how he could make his father happy without giving up the work he loved.

"Shana's here," he said curtly, determined to keep his fingers out of the mass of dark-brown curls Kate had brushed away from her face and anchored high on her head with some kind of scrunchy looking ribbon.

It was yellow, a little darker than her crisp-looking, butter-colored suit but lighter than the bright, silky shirt that showed under the open jacket. Other than enameled earrings that looked like white daisies, the ribbon was Kate's only adornment.

She looked adorable.

"I'm ready." She picked up a handbag that matched her high-heeled sandals. "I hope your meeting goes well."

Putting her hands on his shoulders, she stretched up on tiptoes for his kiss.

"I hope so, too. Go on. Shana's in the kitchen. Tell her I'll see you both at lunch." He pulled her close and gave her one last long, wet kiss.

God, he had to get a hold on his libido or he'd have blue balls by the end of the day. Worse, he had to rein in the treacherous emotions that threatened to burst loose.

Instead of telling Shana to cool her heels while he hauled Kate back to bed, Jake picked up the starched white shirt he'd set out earlier and started to put it on.

When Kate was gone, her scent stayed with him, torturing, tantalizing and distracting him. Would he ever be able to get her off his mind?

For a long time, Jake stood and stared out the window, his fingers working the buttons through stiff, little used buttonholes down the front of his dress shirt.

Why the hell was it taking him so long to dress? Jake hated ties, but he'd never been so awkward at putting one on before. The beige and brown number he'd snatched from the rack in the closet kept resisting his efforts to form it into a presentable knot.

The tight, scratchy collar of his shirt was damn near strangling him. Finally he managed to knot the tie. After giving himself a cursory once-over in the full-length mirror, he shrugged into the jacket of his khaki suit and headed for the downtown Houston skyscraper that housed GreenTex Oil Company's main headquarters.

* * * * *

Of everything that made up his family's business, Jake liked this steel and glass cage in downtown Houston least. To him, the vertical beams between panels of gray smoked glass resembled bars in a prison cell. He saw the elegant decor as an ostentatious waste of the black gold that the real GreenTex Oil Company wrested from a reluctant earth.

Yeah, the facade was necessary. The banks and brokers expected to see trappings of the company's success. And the analysts, accountants and legal people that the company employed had to have somewhere to work.

Still, the place gave Jake the creeps.

"Good morning, Mr. Green," a perky receptionist chirped as he passed her desk on the way to the bank of elevators against the back wall.

Jake nodded and smiled. Because he couldn't recall the woman's name, if indeed he'd ever met her, he didn't bother to speak.

He stepped inside the elevator and fumbled for the key card that would tell the computerized machine to take him to the restricted, executive floor. As the door closed behind him, he reached up to loosen the collar that was threatening him with asphyxiation.

When it opened again and he stepped out into a spacious foyer, he breathed deeply and headed for the plush corner office whose door had a discreet brass plate that bore his name.

"What the hell is this?" he asked when he looked at the stack of papers on the desk he seldom used.

No one ever put anything on his desk, but stuff was sure as hell here now—a neatly arranged stack about ten inches high in the center of the massive, dark-wood status symbol. Not getting a reply to his shouted query annoyed Jake, and he strode through the connecting door to the Old Man's office in search of a secretary—and some answers.

"Ellen, what are all these papers doing on my desk?"

"Why, those are the reports I get for your daddy to review every morning when he comes to work."

Ellen Drake had been his father's secretary for as long as he could remember, but Jake had never cared for the prissy woman who'd always seemed to view him as being about as useful to the company as tits on a boar.

"Why are they on my desk? For all you know, you might have kept piling them up to the ceiling before I wandered in to take a look at them. Take them to Scott."

"Mr. Carrington gets copies, too. I thought, since Mr. Green is ill, that you would be taking over for him." Ellen's expression soured, reminding Jake that he had never been one of her favorite people, either. "Since he isn't here, I can do your correspondence, so I didn't call downstairs to get you a secretary from the pool."

"All right. I don't have any letters to write, but you can get Skip Ward on the phone for me. I'll take the call in my office."

Jake stalked back the way he'd come, pausing at his office door to study Ellen's board-straight back. "Tell Scott I'm here," he added curtly.

Ellen turned to face him. "Mr. Carrington will be in later. Mr. Green asked him to come to the hospital on his way to the office. I'll have the receptionist let him know you need to see him."

Jake nodded. Settling onto the glove-soft leather chair behind his desk, he flipped through the reports until he found one he could understand—a summary of chief geologist Bob Fishman's scientific findings about land parcels the company had leased in the Groveland field.

A smile played at the corners of his lips. Fish's sophisticated studies confirmed his own gut feeling that they'd stumbled onto the biggest domestic oil discovery in years.

"Mr. Green. I have Mr. Ward on the line for you."

Ellen couldn't have sounded any more self-important if she'd been announcing the President. Jake grinned as he punched a button that would allow him to talk with Skip without picking up the receiver.

"Hey, Skip."

"Jake. I was shaking in my boots. Thought it was the Old Man calling me. Since when does Ms. Ellen give you the kid gloves treatment up there in the office?"

"Since she heard Dad's going to have to retire, I guess. I wish she'd spare me. So far, the woman has stuck me with about three hundred reports here to wade through, at least two-thirds of which I won't know any more about after reading them than I do now. What's going on there?"

"We caught the other arsonist. He tried again last night, after everybody but me and the security guys had left. We holed up in the trailer with the lights off, and let the bastard get clear onto the well platform before we stormed out there and dragged him down."

"Shit." Jake leaned closer to the speaker. "What about proof? Or did you just have him arrested for trespassing?"

"Hell, no. He was trying to set the gas lifting apparatus on fire when we caught him. Could have blown himself as well as all of us to kingdom come. Sheriff Jones charged him with arson and tossed him in jail."

"Is the guy talking?"

"Not yet, but the DA says he's laying on the heat."

"Good. We've got to find out who's behind this and stop them for good. I want to get those new permits issued and send in two more drilling crews. We're sitting on a pool of oil like nothing either of us have ever seen in this country."

"You sure?"

"Fish is. I've got his report right here in my hand. Hell, I'm certain, too. We're smack in the middle of a sea of black gold.

You've sensed it, and so have I." Jake started to jerk the knot out of his tie, but stopped his hands in mid-air.

"When will you be back?"

"Next week, if the Old Man keeps improving. At least I'll come back long enough to bring Kate home. Dad has to retire. I may have to start spending more time here, unless Scott and I can talk sense into him."

"Okay. Look, I have to go. Fish is here now with his computers. The truck with the rest of his seismographic gear can't be far behind. I'll call and let you know about the new seismic readings."

Jake heard a click and knew Skip was gone before he pressed a button and silenced the loud dial tone that filled the room. Restless, he got up and paced.

What were his sisters doing with Kate? He doubted that she was enjoying her morning much more than he was enjoying his.

* * * * *

She wasn't. Perched on the edge of a damask-covered chair in the bright, cheery room Leah called her conservatory, Kate felt like a captured insect, held in place with pins for its captors to prod and examine under a microscope.

In their husbands' company, Jake's sisters had been politely inquisitive. Left to their own devices, they appeared obsessed with ferreting out her intentions toward their grown-up baby brother. And pitching the qualities that made him top-flight material in the marriage market.

Belatedly she tuned in on what Deb was saying.

"…every girl he'd gone to school with was absolutely bereft when he came home from college married to that woman," Deb concluded, her tone scathing.

"And Kate, you're just the type of woman Jake should marry. You grew up out in the country. I know you'll just love his ranch. It's only an hour away from Houston when he takes the Cessna." That was Shana.

"Jake isn't serious about me," Kate protested again, but it seemed that nobody was paying her the slightest attention.

"Nonsense. That woman hurt Jake. He's understandably reluctant to admit he's fallen in love again. Kate, he needs you. All you have to do is love him, and he'll eventually come out of that brittle, cynical shell he wrapped around himself as protection from her." Leah spoke in a soft but compelling tone.

I do love him.

Kate stared out the window when Deb started in on her again.

"He needs a little push. I know. Since Dad's coming along so well, I'll give a party next week. Kate! Tomorrow, I'll take you shopping. You'll need something out of this world to wear when we announce your engagement." She reached for the portable phone and began to dial a number.

Not about to let Deb make a fool of her, Kate snatched the phone away and fumbled with it until the sound of a dial tone let her know she'd managed to hang up on whoever Deb had been trying to call.

"I think we should wait to plan an engagement party until after Jake asks me to marry him," she said firmly. *As if he ever will.*

Kate listened helplessly to the buzzing conversation around her until, mercifully, Shana reminded them it was time for them to go to their parents' home for lunch. Settled on the passenger seat of Shana's bright red Mercedes convertible, Kate braced herself for another barrage of questions.

She was grateful that Deb was bringing Leah in another car, since that would give her a few minutes' respite from the women's three-way assault.

"You love Jake, don't you?"

"Is it so obvious?" Kate's cheeks burned. She'd known that sooner or later Shana was bound to mention the disheveled state she and Jake had been in two nights ago when she and Bear had dropped by Jake's condo. To cover her embarrassment, Kate focused her attention on well-kept homes that got bigger and more opulent the farther Shana drove down winding roads in the elite Houston residential district called River Oaks.

Shana laughed. "Yes, it's obvious. Women who blush like you did the other night when somebody walks in on their sex games don't play those games at all unless there are some pretty heavy feelings involved. Besides, every time you look at my little brother, you've got stars in your eyes."

"Please don't." Tears welled up behind Kate's eyelids, and she fought to regain her composure.

"Don't let us get to you, hon. We like you and want you to be happy. And we believe you can help make Jake happy, too. He hasn't been for years, you know. Not since he realized Alice wouldn't opt in for the kind of life he wanted. Her running off with that worm, Durwood Yates, was just the final straw."

"I want Jake to be happy, too."

"Then marry him. Let him get you pregnant if that's what it takes. Jake loves kids. It was that woman who refused to have them."

Kate laughed. It was either that, or cry. "I wouldn't trap him," she said, wondering if she might resort to that ploy if Jake himself weren't so obsessed with preventing an unplanned pregnancy. She couldn't picture herself poking holes through the packages of condoms he kept in the drawer of his bedside table.

"That was just the product of a desperate mind," Shana replied. "I know Jake, and I know what he really wants is a loving wife and family. Here we are," she added as she pulled onto a winding driveway that led to the biggest house Kate had ever seen.

When Shana parked behind Scott's Jaguar, Kate realized this was a co-ed affair and assumed that Jake would soon arrive. That eased her mind. She wasn't looking forward to facing his mother alone.

Chapter Eleven

It was time for his mom's lunch ordeal, but Jake wasn't at his parents' River Oaks estate yet. Instead, he stood, practically squirming with discomfort, beside the Old Man's hospital bed. When Scott had finally come to the office, he'd said Jake's father wanted to see him right away.

Jake had waited around the office all morning, pretending deep concentration on those incomprehensible reports, while the Old Man had kept Scott here discussing who-knew-what. Now more than ever Jake knew he couldn't take over the reins of the family business.

"You don't want me to manage the company," he told his father flatly, forcing himself to stare the Old Man down.

"You're my only son. GreenTex Oil is your heritage." Jacob Senior's voice was strong, belying his frail, tired appearance.

Jake frowned. "It's my heritage, yes. It's also Shana's, Leah's and Deb's. I want it maintained for my children and theirs, as much as you do. That's why I want you to put Scott in charge. I'll do more for the company out in the field than I ever could, sitting in your office and trying to be what I'm not."

His father let out an exasperated sigh. "Your children, Jake? You're thirty-one years old, and you haven't given me the first grandchild. This Kate Black is the first woman you've given the slightest hint that you might be serious about since you left the witch your mother insists did all she could to destroy you."

"Damn it. You can't force me to produce your grandchildren the way a rancher sets his prize stud to the mares he wants bred. No more than you can make me follow in your footsteps and run the business end of the company. I'm me. Not some puppet whose strings you can pull and make dance to your tune."

As pissed as he was, Jake forced himself to shut up. Not soon enough, probably, because the Old Man's face was beet-red and a vein in his neck was throbbing. Maybe he should call in the nurse.

"Is there some reason you can't father a child, son?" Jacob asked suddenly, his voice a feeble croak.

"No." He had fathered a child, but the bitch he'd married had killed it before it had a chance to live. "Would you have wanted a grandchild of yours to be torn apart inside when I divorced its mother?" Jake asked gently.

"I want you to be happy, as I've been with your mother all these years." The Old Man paused, as if his mind was somewhere far away. "Marry again. Have a son who'll follow in my footsteps the way you follow in your grandfather's. Do that, and I can rest easily, knowing Scott will hold my legacy for the next generation of Greens."

It was extortion, pure and simple, done by a master of the art.

Settle down and start a family again, and you can keep doing the work you love. Don't, and you'll be stuck in that jail cell of an executive suite, making decisions that may very well destroy your family's business.

"What are you saying, Dad?" Jake asked, demanding confirmation of his suspicion.

"I'm saying you can take a seat on the Board and the title of vice president, and keep on managing the GreenTex fields…" The Old Man's words trailed off, but his eyes remained steadily on Jake.

"If?" Jake prompted.

"If you marry again and assure me you will make an effort to provide me with a grandson as soon as possible."

Subtlety was an alien trait in his father, Jake thought. Frustrated, he slammed his fist onto the table beside the bed. "Have you picked out my bride, or do you plan to leave that insignificant detail up to me?" he asked.

"I leave the choice of a woman up to you."

"Gee, thanks." Jake thought of a lot more things he could say, most of them profane, but he held them back in deference to his father's condition. After a long pause, he spoke again.

"Damn it. I'm a petroleum engineer, pure and simple. Even if I had a burning interest in the financial and legal details of our business, it would take me years to learn enough to be able to make informed decisions about them. By that time, I'd probably run the company into the ground and make paupers of us all.

"I won't risk our livelihood. But I won't be a figurehead, either, and sit behind a desk looking important while Scott makes all the decisions."

"So you plan to remarry soon?" the Old Man asked, his words barely audible.

Jake paused. Would Kate marry him if he asked her? He thought she would. And he wouldn't mind having her warm his bed every night.

Yeah, he might as well make the Old Man happy, if marriage and fatherhood was all it would take.

He pasted a grin on his face. "I expect you to be well enough to dance at my wedding, say in about eight weeks or so," he told his dad with all the grace he could muster.

"So it will be Miss Black."

The Old Man's satisfied expression galled Jake to no end. He wished he could give Kate the degree of trust his father apparently bestowed so easily.

"If she'll have me. I'll let you know. It would seem I have some proposing to do," Jake said curtly as he turned and stared out the window at the lush, landscaped grounds around the hospital.

Kate. His bride-to-be. The idea of marrying her didn't seem half-bad. Being faithful to her wouldn't be a hardship, the way she kept him with a constant hard-on. He'd offer her a home and children, and all the material things she might ever want. Surely she wouldn't demand his heart as well.

"Jake?"

"What?" He turned and looked back at his father.

"Are you certain this is what you want?"

"Hell no. All I'm sure of is that I don't want to take on a job I'm not qualified for, and that I'd die after a month being stuck in that prison of an office building that you and Scott seem to like so much."

"You want to marry again, don't you?"

"Sure. I want kids. For that, I need a wife. I'd even been thinking that Kate might suit me as well as anybody else I know." Jake rubbed his hand across his brow.

"Do me a favor. Let everybody else think I'm getting married entirely because I want to. There's no way I want Kate to hear about your blackmail. If this marriage happens, I want it to last."

"This conversation will remain between us." The Old Man closed his eyes. This confrontation had to have exhausted him.

His father had kept working, carrying a load that would have crippled many a younger man while he held onto the hope that Jake would someday want to take his place as head of the oil company his own father had founded.

Now, when most of his friends had long since retired to sunny Florida beaches, the Old Man was very reluctantly giving up part of his lifelong plan. Jake vowed to do his best to make the rest of his father's dream come true.

"All right, Dad. Rest. I'm going to find Kate and get this over with. I'll spring the news on everyone as soon as she says yes."

In three long strides, Jake reached the door and turned the knob.

* * * * *

"Kate. Come with me for a few minutes," Jake said when he cornered her in his mother's living room. He'd taken off his jacket and loosened his tie, but he was still dressed up more than she'd ever seen him.

His grin looked forced, as if he wasn't anxious to do whatever it was he had in mind. Curious, she excused herself and followed him to his mother's beautifully landscaped garden. He stopped in a secluded gazebo a few yards away from the large, free form swimming pool and turned to face her.

"Sit," he said gruffly.

She did, and he joined her on the wrought iron bench. Creamy gardenias and orchids of many colors gave off exotic fragrances that hung in the hot, humid air. Dense dark green foliage fluttered around the latticed enclosure, giving evidence of a light breeze she could hardly feel.

What did Jake want? Had she done or said something to offend his mother or one of his sisters? She guessed she hadn't when he sandwiched her hand between his rough, work-hardened palms.

"I think we should get married," he said casually.

Kate looked into his dark, inscrutable eyes. Was he serious?

He certainly acted it. His feelings, whatever they might be, were hidden beneath the deliberately bland expression on his handsome face.

"Why?" Her mouth opened and the question came out involuntarily.

"Why not?" His lips curved upward in a semblance of a smile.

"Are you serious?"

"Dead serious, honey."

As if he was trying to convey some deeper feelings he couldn't put into words, he massaged the top of her hand absently with his thumb.

"Then, yes. I'll marry you. Oh, Jake, I love you so much."

"Good. Let's go inside and tell my family," he said abruptly, standing and pulling her up beside him.

"Now?" He should be taking her in his arms, echoing her words of love here in this spot she thought Adele must have had specially designed for such romantic declarations.

"It's hot as hell out here. And Mom will be holding lunch for us. Come on."

"Jake. Don't you want to tell me something first?"

"No, baby. Not what you're expecting to hear. Love is for kids and fools. I went that route before and got nothing but grief."

He put his arms around her, as if to remind her of the chemistry that flowed between them. When he spoke again, the softness of his voice didn't quite mask his bitterness.

"I'll tell you this much. I want you. I want to come home and mess around with you every night, and wake up fucking you again each morning. I want us to have kids together. But I don't love you. I don't think I'm capable of loving anyone the way you want to be loved. Not any more."

Kate batted back tears. His honesty hurt.

But he'd been hurt, too. Tightening her arms around his waist, she told herself she loved him enough for both of them. Jake wanted her, and that would have to be enough.

"It's all right," she said as she ran her hands up and down the hard, muscled length of his back and buttocks.

"You're still willing to marry me?"

"Yes."

"You won't be sorry," he promised, bending to seal their promise with a quick, deep kiss. Then, he wrapped a hard-muscled arm around her waist and herded her back through the garden to his childhood home.

* * * * *

"We'll tell them after we eat," Jake told Kate as he led her into the dining room, to a mahogany Victorian sideboard that groaned with a staggering selection of food.

"The roast beef and ham's always good," he told her as he speared several paper-thin slices of each and put them on her plate.

Marriage to Jake had sounded so simple just moments ago, when he'd casually invited her to be his wife. Now, looking at the variety of elaborately prepared dishes set out for a supposedly informal family meal, Kate began to have second thoughts.

Not only was she blithely planning to marry a man who admitted he didn't love her, she was also opting to join his globetrotting, wealthy family. The thought sobered her.

"Come on, honey, get yourself some food and let's go over to the table."

"I'm sorry. I was just thinking." She helped herself to some of the beautifully arranged fresh fruit sections, a small serving of green beans, and some lobster salad before she followed Jake over to the table.

Smiling bravely, she looked around the table at the familiar faces. She'd survive. She had to. Just having Jake at her side and feeling his hand at the small of her back bolstered her confidence, made her push aside her trepidation. She might not have his love, but she had him as a lover and protector, and that worked, at least for now.

Jake's father's place at the head of the mahogany table with its lemon yellow linen cloth remained empty. Adele sat like a queen at the foot of the table, and her children and their mates had taken places along the sides. A maid hovered unobtrusively in the doorway.

"May I have Maria bring you something?" Adele asked, apparently noticing Kate's scarcely touched plate of food.

"Oh, no, ma'am. Everything's delicious. And so pretty," Kate murmured. She felt Jake grinning—even before she sneaked a glance his way.

He took the fork from her hand and held it there, next to her plate where everyone could see. Kate trembled a little when she looked around the table.

"Mom. Everybody. Listen." Jake's deep voice boomed out, causing his mother, sisters and brothers-in-law to focus their attention on him and Kate. "This morning Kate and I decided to get married."

"Wonderful."

"When?"

"Where will the wedding be?"

"It's about time, Jake!"

"Congratulations!"

Everyone spoke at once. Jake sat there grinning while Kate looked about helplessly, trying to voice an appropriate reply but unable to think amid the cacophony of congratulations and questions.

"Give 'em a few minutes, honey. They're always like this." Jake let go of her hand and put his arm around her shoulders. "You'll get used to it. Maybe."

"When do you want to get married?" she asked, remembering having heard that question more than once while everybody had been talking at the same time.

"As soon as possible. Could you do it in a couple of months?"

That depended on just what kind of wedding Jake had in mind. "A real wedding?"

He shrugged. "Sure, if you want one."

Kate hadn't had time to consider how they'd get married, so she paused for a moment. Yes, she decided, she'd like a wedding to remember, but she'd assumed Jake would rather find a justice of the peace and get the legalities over and done with. After all, he came right out and said he didn't love her.

"Do you?" she asked.

He shrugged. "It's up to you, honey. You haven't gone through it all before. Weddings are mostly women's doing, anyhow. My only request is that whatever kind of shindig you want, you set the date as soon as possible—and that we do it here in Houston. The Old Man won't be in shape to do any traveling for a while. We can fly in your family and friends."

Jake looked away from her to eye his squawking family members. "I'm tired of listening to them chatter like magpies," he said, and he tapped on his glass with the handle of a spoon.

"Would you all shut up long enough for us to get a word or two in edgewise?" he asked when the dining room was finally quiet. "Thank you for your good wishes. We haven't talked about any details yet. No, Deb, I haven't bought Kate a ring, but I'll do that this afternoon. Yes, I know Dad will want to be at the wedding. Kate and I would like to tell him ourselves, so we'll appreciate it if you give us the rest of the day to do so before you spring the news."

"Will your mother want to help you with your wedding plans?" Adele asked with what seemed to be serious concern.

"My mother died when I was twelve, and Pop passed away this spring. I really don't have any relatives, unless you count some distant cousins I hardly know."

Pop would have liked Jake. Eventually. Jake would have put him off at first with his tough outer veneer and commanding physical presence, but they'd eventually have gotten along. Kate wished they'd had a chance to meet.

She smiled at Jake, then turned back to his mother. "I'd like for us to get married quietly here in Houston, and have a small dinner afterward at some nice restaurant. I shouldn't need a lot of help to arrange a simple affair."

"Nonsense, child." Adele's dark eyes sparkled with excitement. "Just pick a day and leave the rest to me. It will be my pleasure to arrange a wedding you and Jake will never forget."

"Mom. It's Kate's wedding you're trying to take over." Jake sounded as if he had climbed onto a roller coaster that wouldn't stop.

Kate certainly felt that way.

"Well, maybe she'll have to do a bit more than just tell me what day you want to get married. Let's see." Adele lifted her eyebrows and stared out the window for a minute. "Kate. You'll have to pick out your wedding gown, of course, and decide who you want to be your attendants. Shana, can you think of anything else you had to do before your wedding? After all, you'd insisted on going with Bear when he took those flying lessons in San Antonio, so you weren't here to do for yourself."

Shana grinned at Kate and Jake. "I had to make up a list of people I wanted to invite who weren't already on your list. And help Bear get together the names and addresses of his friends and family. And oh, yes, I picked out my bridesmaids' dresses and added a couple of special dishes to the menu for the reception. And I did most of it over the phone."

Jake cleared his throat. "Look, Mom," he said affectionately. "We've just decided to get married. I'm sure Kate will want your help in planning whatever kind of wedding we want. When we decide, you'll be the first to know. We're going now to look at rings. Then we'll stop by the hospital and visit Dad."

* * * * *

Jake watched Kate fiddle with the huge, round-cut stone in the ring he'd insisted on buying for her at a friend's jewelry showroom. Wearing the frankly ostentatious diamond seemed to make her nervous.

She'd wanted a smaller stone. There was no way, though, he'd have bought her anything smaller than the gaudy marquise-cut rock Alice had selected so many years ago.

Kate would soon get used to the weight of the ten-carat solitaire, he told himself as they waited for the elevator to his father's hospital suite.

"Will your father be pleased?" she asked, straightening the ring so the stone was centered on her finger. She looked embarrassed when she glanced away from the sparkling diamond that nearly hid the first knuckle of her ring finger.

"He'll be ecstatic." And that was no exaggeration. "We won't stay long. His doctors told Mom everyone should limit their visits to fifteen minutes or so."

Jake wouldn't be surprised if the Old Man was unusually tired after their earlier conversation and the long talk he'd had earlier with Scott. He paused and laced his fingers through Kate's when he saw a nurse hurrying out of his father's suite.

"Is he up to having company?" he asked the woman when she stopped and gave him a stern once-over.

"Not if you plan on upsetting him the way you did this morning. We had to call the doctor to come in and give him something to settle his heart down."

"I think our news will do more to perk Dad up than any medicine." Jake grinned, and the nurse moved away from the doorway after a momentary pause.

"See that you don't disturb him," she warned them. "And don't stay more than a few minutes."

With that warning, she strode toward the nurses' station, her starched skirts swishing noisily. Jake put an arm around Kate and let her precede him into the Old Man's room.

* * * * *

Later, Kate realized how tired she was. Between her morning with Jake's sisters, Jake's surprise proposal and his family's enthusiastic reaction, and an afternoon of selecting a ring and breaking the news of their coming marriage to his father, she hadn't had a moment to think.

Now, while Jake conferred with Skip on the phone, she lay back in the swirling water of the hot tub and tried to collect her thoughts.

Everybody in Jake's family wanted her to marry him.

She stared at the immense diamond Jake had put on her finger hours earlier. Sick as he was, his father had seemed thrilled at the news of their impending marriage. She'd nearly cried when he'd hugged her and welcomed "another daughter" into the family.

And Jake's mother and sisters had overwhelmed her, even before Jake told them she was to be his bride. She'd be hard pressed not to let Adele get carried away with her plans to make the wedding Houston's social event of the year.

Kate had trouble believing it. She was going to have a husband she adored. And a family. Children of her own.

Just one cloud hung over her happiness. Yes, she understood Jake's reluctance to commit himself emotionally. He'd been terribly hurt.

Understanding, though, didn't cure the pain of knowing he didn't love her.

She hated Alice. That woman, Jake's sisters had called her. For eight years, Alice had possessed his love. But she'd betrayed Jake, left him bitter and distrustful. Damn the woman and the power she'd once had to make Jake love her. Damn the cruel sword she'd wielded to destroy that love. And double damn the power she apparently still possessed to keep Jake's heart frozen, make him afraid to love someone else.

Pulling her left hand out of the water, Kate looked at the ring that weighed so heavily on her mind. It had cost Jake a fortune, many times as much as the smaller, more delicate one she'd liked.

He'd laughed and said he didn't want folks thinking he was a piker as he slid this ring on her finger and closed his fist over her hand. Had that been true? Jake didn't strike Kate as being the kind of man to give much of a damn about what folks thought of him.

Kate thought it was more likely that Alice had insisted that he buy her expensive tokens of his love. Or that she'd spurned his simpler offerings.

Jake wanted the world to think he valued her more than he ever prized his faithless ex-wife, Kate decided. She hoped the day would come when he'd actually feel that way.

"You'll get used to wearing it, honey."

She looked up at the sound of Jake's deep voice. Clearly, her reservations about the ring amused him. His grin—and the sight of his powerful, naked body framed in the open doorway—took her breath away.

"It's so big, Jake. But it's beautiful." *Like you*, she thought, her mouth watering at the way his long, thick penis stood at attention against the muscular ridges of his belly. She wanted to take it in her mouth, tease him until he lost his iron control.

"Come here." She moved over to make room for him on the sunken bench at the edge of the tub.

He moved like a predator, smoothly and quickly. Every well-honed muscle rippled under deeply tanned skin that was only a shade lighter across his lean, powerful hips. As she watched, his penis grew bigger, harder. His testicles tightened.

Her mouth went dry, and her body turned liquid inside when he sank down beside her in the swirling water.

"Skip caught the other guy who torched your barn," he said as he traced a path of fire with his hands from her cheek to her aching breasts.

His tension showed in the almost imperceptible tremor of the hand that was plucking at her left nipple.

"Is the trouble over now?" Kate asked.

"It will be, assuming your sheriff can make one or both of the bastards rat out whoever hired them."

Kate shuddered, setting off a chain reaction of tiny ripples on the water's swirling surface. "Surely they won't keep quiet. Not now." She couldn't fathom the kind of sick mind that would want to destroy a company enough to risk human lives.

"I'm beginning to think the trouble will never stop. Seems that no one we've caught so far knows who hired them to do their dirty work."

"Jake, I'm so sorry."

"Don't mind me, honey. What I do know is that we've got to get back to Groveland. Skip has enough to do without keeping on the district attorney's back, just to be sure he goes for these guys' throats—and the balls of whoever in hell hired them." His expression softened. "Hey, let's forget about this right now. I'm thinking we've got more important things to do."

Taking her hand, he dragged it down his body, and when she curled her fingers around his rigid erection, he covered her hand with his own and coached her in the motions that drove him wild.

"Milk my cock, honey. Like this."

When she held the pulsing life of him in her hand and looked into dark eyes full of hot, wild passion, Kate turned to mush inside. His willing slave, she did all he asked.

She loved Jake with all her heart. And right now, every cell in her body demanded to join him in a carnal feast.

"We'll go back day after tomorrow. You can spend tomorrow with Mom and whoever's available of the terrible threesome, so you can let them know anything special you want for the wedding."

Then he kissed her. His tongue plunged deep in her mouth the way Kate knew he'd soon thrust his rock-hard penis inside her body. With callused hands, he played a symphony on all her erotic places. Her nipples. The sensitive spots behind her knees. Her thighs. Her clitoris. Finally he dipped two fingers inside her and brought her to a gentle little climax.

Kate wanted more. Wanted to see stars, experience the mind-blowing orgasm she got whenever she took all of him into her body. She climbed on his lap and kissed him hard...but he shoved her away as though she'd suddenly gotten the plague.

Swearing viciously, Jake climbed out of the tub and stalked into the bedroom. She fought back tears, wondered what she'd done wrong.

"Stay there, honey. I'll be right back." Dripping water onto the carpet, he padded into the bedroom and opened the nightstand drawer.

He ripped open a condom wrapper and sheathed himself, the thought registering that soon this wouldn't be necessary.

The prospect of riding Kate bareback, feeling the rush of her wet, fragrant heat and spurting his semen into her body, made him swell almost to bursting.

"Okay, buddy, you're gonna get yours now," he muttered to his cock. He strode back to the bathroom and stepped into the hot tub.

Kate's eyes were wide, darkened almost to the color of a raging sea. Her tongue darted out when she raked her gaze over his body as though she wanted to taste every inch of him.

He lifted her, letting the smell of flowers and hot, wet woman surround him. "I love it when you get turned on. Bend over and hold on to the rim of the tub."

Silky soft, hot, and wet, her ass cheeks glistened above the swirling water. His cock jerked, more than ready to get inside her. But he wanted this to last, so he rubbed his cock head slowly between her parted legs with one hand while plucking and tugging her hard little nipples with the other.

Her pussy muscles contracted against his cock, as if she was trying to coax him in.

Her tits swelled in his hands the way a woman's should, and her ass nestled trustingly against his groin.

"Want this?" he asked, pulling back and nudging her pussy playfully with his cock.

The sudden pressure of her small hand on his erection did in his resolve to wait. Shifting slightly, he let her position his cock head at the hot, tight opening to her pussy. Then he sank inside.

Chapter Twelve

He filled her so completely that her body wept around him.

She'd never get enough of Jake's hot, wild loving. Kate clasped the rounded edge of the hot tub and watched the sparkling reflection of fiery rays from the diamond in her ring.

When he stroked her from behind, his hips moving with the same rhythm his fingers played on her aching nipples, she realized that in this way if in no other, he gave her of himself.

"Oh, Jake, this feels so good."

"Yeah, honey. Damn good. " His hot breath tickled the back of her neck. "Come on. Come for me. I'm about to…oh, God."

Shuddering, he slammed into her twice more, sliding his hands down her body and rubbing her swollen clitoris.

The pressure built inside her. Feelings bubbled over— passion, lust, and love. When the dam burst and she tumbled over the edge into a climax that took her breath away, she closed her eyes and enjoyed the fall.

Wrung out, she lay against the Jacuzzi wall enjoying the afterglow, until he came in one last mighty thrust and they both went up again in a burst of flame.

* * * * *

Later Kate watched Jake sleep. Sprawled out over snowy sheets, his hard-muscled body still awed her with its beauty and power. But his face looked younger in repose, more approachable.

With luck this kinder Jake might someday come to love her. She sighed and curled up against his side, drifting off to sleep with his scent in her nostrils and hope in her heart.

When she woke the next morning, he was already up. The smell of fresh coffee beckoned, and she followed it to the kitchen.

Jake sat at the table, frowning at some notes he'd made on the pad in front of him. Veins stood out in the hand he was using to hold the portable phone to his ear.

"Excuse me." Kate turned to leave so Jake would have his privacy.

He held out his hand. "Don't go."

When she looked back at him, his hand was over the mouthpiece.

"There's nothing I've got to say that you can't hear," he said. "Sit down and have some coffee."

When she did as he asked, he resumed his conversation. At least she assumed he was conversing, for she heard him make occasional monosyllabic, profane replies while he doodled on the pad.

"I'll be there tomorrow afternoon," he finally said before he shut off the phone and set it down beside the note pad.

Kate fiddled with her coffee mug. "I didn't want to intrude."

"You weren't. We're going to be busy today, getting ready to go back to Groveland. That was Skip. One of our arsonists has fingered the man who hired him. As we speak, the sheriff should be picking him up." His frown deepened, but he didn't enlighten her further.

"What do you want me to do?" she asked, a little put off when he shot her a hard, cynical look.

"Make up your mind real fast what you don't want for a wedding. Mom and Deb are on their way here now to go over plans with you. Their plans, not ours." Jake grinned, but stress was evident in his eyes.

"What don't you want?"

"I don't care. Like I said before, weddings are mostly women's doings. Just remind Mom that I own two tuxes and that I have no intention of wearing anything any fancier than one of them. Bear can be my best man. I'll ask Skip and Scott to stand up with me, too. She can pick out anybody else you women think I need to fill out the wedding party."

He ripped away the paper he'd been using and scribbled some names on a fresh sheet. "Here," he said. "Tell Mom to make sure she invites these folks. Aside from them, she can ask whoever she wants."

"You're not going to be here?" The idea of discussing their wedding with his mother and sister but without him scared Kate silly. She slipped the paper into the pocket of her slacks and tried to still her trembling hands.

"Sorry, honey. I can't spare the time. If we're leaving in the morning, I've got to spend the day at the office, checking out what's going on in our other fields. It's easier to do from here than from the site in Groveland."

"But Jake. I don't know what you want. Would you like dinner? Dancing? A religious or civil ceremony? All you've said is that you don't want to wear anything fancier than a tuxedo. That doesn't tell me much."

Kate panicked. What if he hated everything about the wedding his mother was dead set on arranging?

"It tells you there's no way Mom is getting me into tails again. Every male in the wedding party had to wear them for Shana's wedding. Leah's, too, but I was fortunate enough not to have to stand up with Ben." Jake paused and raked his hand through his dark, thick hair. "A sit-down dinner and dancing are givens, unless you can dissuade my mother a hell of a lot better than I can."

"Do you want a religious ceremony?"

"Your choice, honey. We'll be just as married either way."

"You don't care?"

"No."

She hesitated. "Jake, I don't want this to remind you of your other wedding. Tell me about it."

His expression turned fierce. "It doesn't matter."

She looked into his eyes, silently pleading for him to open up, at least a little, and let go of some of the hurt she sensed was still festering inside him. "It matters to me," she said.

Suddenly, he stood up. "All right. I said it doesn't matter. There's no way any wedding Mom has anything to do with planning will remind me of my first one. But you obviously want to know, so I'll tell you."

Kate cringed at the pain she saw in his dark eyes. "It's all right," she said, contrite. "You don't have to. I know it must be painful to talk about."

"Damn it. Don't credit me with having a bunch of stupid sentimental emotions. Shut up and listen." He looked as if he was daring her to interrupt.

"We got married in her hometown, in the little country church she had gone to all her life. The reception was there, too, on the picnic grounds outside, with cake and peanuts and little sandwiches with pastel-colored fillings. Her mother made the cake and punch, some green stuff that almost matched the bridesmaids' dresses. It had big blocks of lime sherbet floating around in it."

He'd loved Alice so much that he'd married her in her world instead of his own.

"Sounds like some of the weddings I've been to back home," Kate said lightly, trying to smile and hide her pain. She realized now how much he must have loved the wife who had betrayed him.

"Yeah. It was a country shindig, all right. There was no dancing and no booze. The whole thing, reception and all, didn't take two hours. No way would Mom plan anything remotely like that."

"We'll have a civil ceremony then," Kate said quietly.

"Whatever you want. I need to get to the office."

Today Jake had on jeans rather than a suit like the one he'd worn yesterday. He looked good enough to eat, either way.

"That must be Mom and Deb now," he told her, practically running to answer the doorbell.

After greeting them perfunctorily, he gave Kate a hasty kiss and deserted them, looking like a man who couldn't wait to escape.

* * * * *

"I'm going to nail that bastard to the wall this time," Jake spat out the minute he set foot in his brother-in-law's office.

"What bastard? Back up and tell me what you're talking about." Scott looked up from the report he'd been studying. "Sit down. Want some coffee?"

"Thanks." Jake poured a cup from the silver carafe on the corner table, then sat and stretched his legs in front of him. For a minute, he stared at the toes of his boots before meeting Scott's curious gaze.

"Durwood Yates." The son-of-a-bitch had been his nemesis even before he took up with Alice. "Skip called me at the condo this morning. One of our arsonists in Groveland has fingered Yates as being the man who hired them."

Scott's grin was feral. Jake imagined he was recounting the money Yates had cost GreenTex over the years. "You mean the arsonist pointed the finger at one of Yates's minions, don't you?"

"No. He fingered Yates personally. As we speak, a couple of Houston's finest should be picking Durwood up. Unless he fights extradition he should be in a Mississippi jail by this time tomorrow. We've finally got him by the balls." Jake tried to tamp down his personal hatred for Yates and focus instead on the damage he had done to the company.

"Do you want me to go to Groveland and make sure some country DA doesn't let Yates off the hook?"

Jake appreciated Scott's offer and thought he understood his reasons for making it. There was no way, though, that he was going to relinquish the pleasure of twisting the figurative knife into the bastard responsible for Dale's death and millions of dollars' damages to GreenTex property.

"I've got to be there anyhow. Now that we don't have to worry about sabotage any more, the Oil and Gas Board should be issuing us new drilling permits. I'll need to get two more drilling crews out there if we expect to get production going fast enough to bail us out of debt."

"But you've got a wedding to get ready for," Scott pointed out.

"I'm sure Mom and Deb already have their plans laid out for that. They're at my condo now, conning Kate into agreeing to whatever kind of three-ring circus they've conjured up. You can't leave here now, anyway. Not with the Old Man out of commission."

"What about Kate?"

"What about her? I'm taking her with me. She'll have to pack up whatever she has in her house that she wants to ship out to the ranch."

"How's she going to feel, seeing you take out your anger at your ex-wife on her present husband? I'd hate to try convincing Deb I didn't still care for a woman who could fuel that much hatred in me." Scott leaned back and regarded him seriously.

Kate would understand. Jake was certain of it. She'd already agreed to marry him knowing he didn't love her and probably never would. "Kate's a lot more easygoing than Deb," he said noncommittally.

"Okay. You know your lady better than I do. What can I do here?"

"Get our legal department to put all the pressure they can on Yates Petroleum. The more the lawyers who work for Yates are tied up here, the less they can do to help their boss with his problems over in Mississippi."

"What good will that do? The creep will be out on bail and back in Houston, as soon as they get him indicted." Scott picked up a pen and shifted it from one hand to the other.

"Maybe not. The whole town of Groveland could have turned to soot and ashes if Yates's hirelings had managed to set that well on fire, and the district attorney is counting on press coverage to help him push his own statewide political agenda. Skip says he's asking the judge to deny bail."

Scott nodded. "I'll have our legal department file civil suits against Yates for the damages at the west Texas fields as well as the one in Groveland. That should keep his lawyers hopping. In any case, the criminal investigation out in Lubbock will heat up now that Yates has been linked to the Groveland sabotage." He pushed his gold-framed reading glasses up onto his forehead and looked at Jake. "You're positive you don't want me to handle this?"

"Yeah." Maybe by putting Yates away, Jake could lay Alice's betrayal to rest once and for all. "I'll check out what's going on in our other fields before I leave. Before I go, I'll leave next month's production estimates on your desk."

"All right. Let me know how the drilling is going on that new offshore rig, too."

When Scott frowned, Jake recalled how opposed his brother-in-law had been to buying those leases in the Gulf of Mexico and sinking hundreds of millions of dollars into specialized offshore drilling equipment.

"I will." Giving Scott a farewell nod and forcing thoughts of Alice and Durwood Yates to a corner of his mind, Jake headed back to his office. While he waited for Ellen to place calls to the GreenTex field supervisors, he wondered how Kate was faring with Deb and his mother.

* * * * *

Kate's head was spinning.

How could Adele and Deb have done so much so fast? And what had she agreed to in the past two hours? She stared blindly at the array of advertising materials spread out on Jake's oversize cocktail table.

With numb fingers, she picked up hotel brochures and tried again to focus on the slick, four-color photos of ballrooms where she and Jake might have their wedding. They all looked opulent, and each of them looked as if a thousand guests could get lost within their confines. She couldn't imagine herself getting married in any of them.

But she thought she'd just been gently badgered into choosing a downtown Houston hotel whose restoration had made it functionally modern while maintaining an aura of old-world grandeur. At least, that was what Deb had said.

The wedding was to be on Sunday evening. The sixth of September. A federal judge who Adele said was an old family friend would perform the civil ceremony.

There would be a sit-down dinner with dancing afterward, for what Deb had called an "intimate gathering." Personally, Kate wouldn't call a party for six hundred people intimate, but then what did she know?

Vaguely, she recalled suggesting that they get Jake's friend Mel Harrison to provide the music.

She couldn't believe she'd just agreed on a menu that included lobster appetizers, prime rib, baked potatoes, and two vegetables to be chosen by the chef. Whatever happened to finger sandwiches and frilled cups full of salted nuts?

Deb had talked her into choosing a huge, four-tier cake with raspberry filling and pedestals between each tier. But Kate drew the line at having a personalized statuette of her and Jake made to sit atop of the ornate confection. She wanted her cake topped with a simple spray of sugared violets, her favorite flower.

That decision set the color scheme. Kate's bridesmaids would wear gowns in different shades of violet. Fortunately the various hues flattered Jake's dark-haired, olive-skinned sisters as well as Deb's blond daughters. And Becky, who would be Kate's matron of honor, liked violet, too. Kate wasn't sure about Gilda, who said her carrot-red hair and freckles clashed with nearly every color that wasn't neutral.

Kate's gown had to be ivory, she was told. Jake's younger nieces, as flower girls, would wear ivory trimmed in violet, and his mother and Mama Anna would carry through the color scheme by wearing deep purple.

Kate blinked to try to bring everything into perspective.

"Maybe I should call Becky and Gilda to be certain they can come," she suggested to Deb, who had already written her friends' names on a list of people who'd need gowns fitted.

"Of course they will. You can talk to them when you go home tomorrow. We're due at the boutique in twenty minutes to pick out gowns." Glancing at her diamond-studded watch, Deb put her notebook away. "Mother, will you join us?"

"You girls go ahead. I promised your father I'd have lunch with him at the hospital. Kate, did Jake give you a key?" Adele rose and collected her tapestry briefcase.

Kate shook her head. "He told me just to lock the door. Deb is going to drop me off at his office later."

Since she and Jake were leaving Houston tomorrow, she'd better pick out a dress today. She could just imagine herself getting married in that fancy hotel, wearing the sort of wedding gown she might find in Laurel or Hattiesburg.

She squared her shoulders. Tomorrow she could collapse. She was certain that by then she'd be sitting back, shaking with terror at the prospect of being on display at her wedding for hundreds of Jake's friends and employees.

She could even torture herself tomorrow with self-pity because Jake didn't love her the way she loved him. Today, though, she'd choose her wedding gown and pretend theirs was the greatest love match that ever was.

* * * * *

"Yes?" Jake looked up at Ellen from the scattered stack of papers on his desk.

"I understand congratulations are in order," the Old Man's secretary said stiffly.

For a moment, Jake didn't understand what the woman was talking about. Then he forced a grin. "Thanks. Kate will be coming by this afternoon."

"I'll look forward to meeting her. I wish you happiness," she added, her usually grim expression softening a little.

"Thanks. Would you get Skip on the phone now?" he asked, uncomfortable with the role of happy prospective bridegroom.

"Surely."

Jake thought he detected a smile as she turned to leave. Apparently everybody loved lovers. Even sour-faced Ellen.

Staring at her back, Jake kicked himself mentally for not having realized immediately why Ellen was congratulating him. Hell, he'd better put on a better act than that.

No way did he want a soul in Houston—not one who knew about the disastrous end of his marriage, anyhow—to get the idea he was anything but head over heels in love with the woman he was about to marry.

Not only would that hurt Kate, it would give his bitch ex-wife more grounds for vicious satisfaction. He got Ellen on the intercom quickly, before she could make the call to Skip.

"Forget about Skip. I'll get hold of him myself. I forgot to get Kate an engagement present. Call Sol Weintraub for me. There's an aquamarine pendant I saw in his display case yesterday. Have him send it over."

Jake paused, picturing how the cool, blue-green gem would look nestled in the hollow between Kate's pale, soft breasts.

His cock twitched when he thought of nuzzling that pendant out of the way and nibbling at the ivory flesh between her breasts.

"Is that all?" Ellen asked.

"For now."

"There's someone here to see you," Ellen said in an ominous tone.

"Do I want to see him?" he asked, wondering who could have arrived to make the woman sound so grim.

"Her. Mrs. Green."

"Mother?"

"No. Your former wife."

"Her name is Yates now." Jake shut off the computer on his credenza and faced his desk.

He should have figured Alice would come slithering around, now that he had her crazy husband in a position to destroy him. For a minute, he considered refusing to see her.

"Let her in. But leave the door open," he finally said.

"Jake."

"Alice." Jake didn't do his ex-wife the courtesy of rising. Instead, he insolently swept the length of her long, model-sleek body with his gaze before saying more. "I could say I'm surprised to see you, but somehow I knew you'd come."

"May I sit down?" Her voice was still husky and compelling, and she still looked a lot like the Aggies cheerleader he'd married.

"Suit yourself." He leaned back in his chair and waited for her to make her pitch.

"Thank you." Alice arranged herself gracefully on the sofa and patted the cushion next to her. "Join me? It's hard to talk when there's so much distance between us."

His cock didn't rise to attention the way it used to when she smiled that way at him. And desire didn't slam into him the way it did whenever Kate walked into a room. That was good. "We're close enough. What do you want?"

"What? What happened to your manners? No 'how are you, what have you been doing?' Your mother would be horrified."

"Maybe I used to give a damn how you were and what you'd been doing. Right now, I'm busy. Your bastard of a husband and his henchmen have taken up most of my time for the past few weeks. You've got five minutes," he said flatly, glancing at the grandfather clock against the wall.

Alice frowned. The expression emphasized faint lines around her china-blue eyes and at the corners of the full, soft lips that used to feel so good when she'd closed them around his cock.

"I'm sorry, Jake. I didn't mean to hurt you. Truly, I wish you well."

"I don't see any point in rehashing the past. My guess is that you're here because Durwood's in jail for trying to blow up one of my oil wells. And you believe I can do something to get him out. What amazes me is that you think I'd lift a finger to help you — or him."

She stood up and paced around the room. "That judge in Mississippi is refusing to set bail for Durwood even though he waived extradition and is probably halfway to some backwoods country jail by now. Unless the judge changes his mind, my husband's going to rot in jail until his trial. Your buddy Skip apparently painted a nasty, gory picture for him of what might have happened if that oil well had caught on fire. I want you to ask the judge to reconsider."

"You're nuts. I would be, too, if I asked anybody to let Durwood loose so he can find someone else to do his dirty work around my drilling sites. The bastard's going to be where he belongs — under lock and key. If you don't think so, you damn well belong there with him."

Jake stood. Icy fury was the only emotion that flowed through him now when he grasped the elbow of the woman he once loved and ushered her to the door.

"Goodbye," he said, his voice as cold as his heart.

"Jake. Please. For the sake of all we shared." Her voice broke, signaling that she was about to turn on the tears.

"Don't do this to yourself. What we had together was obviously not all that great. And it belongs in the past. You made your bed with Yates. Crawl back and lie in it."

Dropping his hand from Alice's arm, Jake stepped back inside his office and closed the door. For a long time, he stood at the window and stared out at the cloudy summer sky.

He was going to make sure Yates got put away where he couldn't hurt GreenTex with his vicious attacks, and that meant that he could expect more painful encounters with Alice. Visits that would remind him of her betrayal and his stupidity for having trusted her or anyone of the female persuasion.

It was a long time before he turned back to his desk and noticed the blue velvet box Ellen must have set down there. Opening it, Jake stared at the stone that matched Kate's eyes. And the icy brilliance of the diamonds that surrounded it. He snapped the box closed and forced himself to get back to work on production projections.

Kate would be joining him soon, and he didn't want to keep her waiting.

* * * * *

"You don't want that gown," Deb said sharply when Kate eyed a full-skirted creation of taffeta and beaded lace at Cecilia's Bridal Boutique.

"Why?" Kate didn't expect perfection. The choice of ready-made gowns Cecilia had brought out for their inspection was limited, and she didn't care at all for the others.

One was an all-over beaded sheath, and the other an ornate creation of ruffled organza. She couldn't imagine herself being able to carry off wearing the highly sophisticated sheath, and she was beyond the age for wearing the ruffled number that looked as if it had been designed for a teenage bride.

"It's almost exactly the same as the dress that woman wore." Deb frowned and paused before she directed her attention to Cecilia. "You'll have to make Kate a gown from scratch. Bridesmaids' dresses, too."

Cecilia sat down at the worktable and began to sketch. An hour later, Kate and Deb left. Kate wondered how the woman could possibly make all those dresses before the wedding, but Deb assured her that Cecilia would come through for them.

"I don't want anything about this wedding to remind Jake of his first one," Kate said as they drove to downtown Houston.

"God. Neither do we. I hope you hadn't set your heart on having a gown like the one you almost picked out."

"No. The one Cecilia sketched will suit me much better." She pictured the dress with its deep v-shaped neckline and softly draped skirt. "What about the colors? And the flowers?"

"They're fine. Nothing like what she chose." Deb maneuvered through the heavy late afternoon traffic.

"That woman insisted that we all wear pale green dresses. And she made us carry bunches of white carnations and red roses."

"That sounds…Christmasy."

Deb laughed. "The wedding was in June." Then her expression sobered. "So was the divorce."

As Kate walked into the GreenTex office building, she hoped she never did anything to earn Deb's ire. Unlike her gentle parents whose emotions had been muted and mild, the Greens apparently loved and hated strongly.

Now she had their approval. She almost pitied Alice for having earned their hatred.

Chapter Thirteen

Sorry to bother you, Jake, but your fiancée is downstairs."

He looked up at Ellen and blinked. The amber numbers on the screen had been starting to blur together anyway. "That's okay. I'm about finished here. Have the girl bring her on up."

He pressed a key to save the projections he'd been working on. Then, recalling that he had a role to play, he gave the Old Man's secretary what he hoped she'd interpret as a besotted grin.

"I'll meet Kate at the elevator," he added, demonstrating considerably more enthusiasm than he had shown before.

"Shall I ask everyone to come to your office to meet Ms. Black?" Ellen asked, following Jake toward the elevator doors.

"Give us a few minutes. I haven't seen her since early this morning."

That sounded good. Besides, he needed some steamy foreplay to fire him up for the Academy Award quality performance he was determined to give his fellow executives and their assistants.

"Honey," he said, wrapping an arm around her when she stepped through the elevator doors. "I've missed you."

In full view of Ellen and the girl who was manning the desk in the reception area by the elevator, he bent and kissed Kate thoroughly enough to tighten his balls and send blood rushing to his cock.

"Come on in and I'll fix you a drink."

Kate looked up at him from the long leather couch when he handed her a flute of champagne. Her eyes had a glazed look, one he imagined Mom and Deb had put there with their relentless shopping and maneuvering.

"Tired?" He lifted her soft dark curls off her shoulders and started to massage her neck.

"A little. I hope your mother and Deb know what you want for the wedding." Her tone implied a lot of doubt.

Jake shrugged. "Like I told you, honey, the wedding's for you—and them. Whatever you all want is fine with me."

The obscenely expensive, ostentatious production he could count on Mom and Deb to orchestrate would cement the impression to everyone in Houston, including Alice, that his and Kate's was the ultimate love match.

"They're talking about having six hundred guests." Kate sounded distressed.

"It's okay. Mom wouldn't want to step on anybody's toes by not inviting them." Jake moved his hand lower, tracing her spine over the silky-soft material of her blouse. "Come here," he ground out hoarsely, taking her glass and setting it on the table.

Burying his other hand in her hair, he kissed her deeply. His cock got painfully hard when she darted her tongue out to tangle with his.

He might have to feign loving her, but there wasn't anything fake about what she did to his cock when she was near.

When she pulled away, Jake grinned at the pretty blush on her cheeks. He wanted nothing more than to lay her back against the cushions on that couch, strip off whatever silky scrap of panties she had on, and fuck her until she begged for mercy.

But that would have to wait. Any minute Ellen would be herding in department managers to meet the boss's future daughter-in-law.

Jake strode to his desk and picked up the blue velvet jewelry box he had left in the same place Ellen put it earlier.

"I thought this would look pretty tucked in here," he said, stroking the hollow between her breasts with one finger. "Go on, take a look."

Her fingers trembled as she pried the box open. Her eyes widened. "Oh, my. This is too much," she whispered, and she pressed the open box back into his hands. "I...you didn't have to do this." She twisted her engagement ring back into place on her slender finger.

"Yeah. I did. I haven't been able to stop picturing this pendant around your pretty neck since I saw it at Sol's yesterday." He picked up the necklace and dangled it so she could see its aqua fire.

"Let me." He draped the chain around her neck and lifted her hair while he secured the clasp and safety chain. When he finished, he turned her around and pressed a quick, hard kiss on her open lips.

"I've never had anything this beautiful," she said, her small hand going to touch the large, perfect aquamarine surrounded by blazing diamonds.

He'd give her lots of pretty things. And get pleasure doing it. "Get used to it. You're going to be Mrs. Jake Green. If I feel like it, I'll drape you with as much glitter as Deb wears."

Kate watched Jake's adoring expression when they accepted congratulations from the last of the GreenTex employees who flocked to his office a few minutes later.

Then she realized he was playing a role.

The heat of his erection scorched her back, and his arms were like a tightening vice, draped as they were around her waist. His heart beat out a steady rhythm against the base of her neck.

"Let's get out of here," he murmured, his warm, damp breath tickling her ear.

His subtle aftershave tickled her nose and made her want to taste him the way he was nibbling at her ear and neck.

"Why?" she asked a few minutes later when he'd settled behind the wheel and gunned the car's powerful motor.

"Why, what?"

"Why did you want everybody in your office to think you're madly in love with me?" As she fastened her seat belt, Kate focused on Jake's big, rough hands. He was holding the steering wheel in a death grip.

"For you, honey. Besides, I like touching you and holding you, and I don't want anyone to doubt that you're my woman."

He frowned. "You don't mind me touching you when we're alone," he reminded her in that deep, seductive drawl he used when they made love to tell her explicitly and succinctly what he wanted.

"No. I don't mind. It's just that for a minute there in your office, I thought..." Kate stopped mid-sentence. She couldn't say it, not now. Maybe not ever.

"You thought what? That you'd managed to draw out some deep emotional commitment out of me? Baby, that just isn't going to happen. I thought you accepted that I don't have that to give."

She trembled. "I did. But why did you pretend the way you did? You should have warned me."

"Warned you? Hell, Kate, what did you expect me to do? Tell my co-workers we made some kind of fucking business arrangement?" Jake shifted gears and maneuvered the sleek sports car onto an exit ramp. "Do you want that? Seems you'd want folks to believe we're getting married because we can't keep our hands off each other."

He paused. "Come to think of it, that's pretty much the truth. At least for me. When we get inside, I'll show you again why I want to keep you in my bed."

He pulled into the garage. His eagerness seemed forced, though, when he hustled her upstairs and into the bedroom.

When he stripped her and then ripped off his own clothes, he acted like a man possessed.

Covering her immediately with his powerful body, he kissed away her doubts. As if he needed her, needed to reassure himself of her presence and her desire, he parted her legs and tested her readiness with tempered strokes of his hand. Wet and unbelievably ready for him, she arched her hips so he'd have easier access.

"God, honey," he moaned, pulling away from her to open the drawer of the bedside table. She watched the play of small muscles in his back as he ripped open the package and rolled a condom over his rigid sex.

God, how she loved this man! She longed to say the words she knew he didn't want to hear.

What he wanted was inside her pussy. Now.

Roughly, he knelt and draped her silky legs around his shoulders. Grasping her hips, he positioned her and buried his cock to the hilt in one smooth thrust.

It felt like heaven and like hell. Her tight, wet pussy clasped him with rippling motions and made him want to lose himself inside her.

His cock pressed against the tip of her womb.

Jake wanted this fuck to last forever. He also wanted to move hard and fast, to explode in a carnal conflagration.

"Jake. Oh, Jake." She clenched down on him hard, arching her back and taking him even deeper. "Love me."

She slid her hands down his back and cupped his ass, urging him to move. He wrenched them away and held them at her sides, stroking her hard and fast until her moans crescendoed and she screamed his name.

One more thrust was all it took. His cock felt like it was exploding when he shot his load. Drained, he barely had the strength to roll onto his side before he collapsed.

She lay there facing him, her face flushed. Her rapid heartbeat made her beautiful tits move rhythmically against her chest.

Kate gave him more pleasure than any other woman ever had, and Jake took satisfaction in knowing he had brought her again to sensual oblivion.

He reached out and smoothed a wayward curl off her sweaty forehead. Then he peeled off the condom and tossed it into the wastebasket before pulling up the sheet and closing his eyes.

Kate wasn't Alice.

Jake kept telling himself that. Staring at the ceiling while the room kept getting darker, he imagined the sun outside disappearing into the western sky.

Painful memories still assailed him. Memories of another woman and love turned to hate, grief for a child that never had a chance at life. The stinging ego-buster of knowing Alice had left him for Durwood Yates.

Yates had to be insane. And his madness must have festered over the years and finally come to a head in his decision to destroy GreenTex.

Despite the warmth of the bed and the woman who slept beside him, Jake shivered.

He didn't love Kate or even completely trust her, but he needed her desperately. He turned back on his side and pressed his body to hers. With one arm, he held her close. She warmed him as nobody ever had before, and he went to sleep.

When he woke, the morning sun was shining. Kate snuggled closer when he moved, and no force on earth was going to keep him from tightening his arms around her and holding her. When they finally got up and headed back to Groveland, Jake began to relax.

That inner contentment vanished when he thought of Yates and his hirelings, and of the vengeance he was going to take on the man for the misery he'd caused.

* * * * *

"You've been awfully quiet," Jake commented as he made the turn off I-10 onto the secondary highway that would take them back to Groveland.

He hadn't said much, either. He hadn't wanted to inflict his bitterness on Kate.

"I've been thinking about what I need to do. I don't even know what you have at your ranch, or how much room you have for my things."

She sounded sad. Jake hoped she wasn't having second thoughts about packing up and leaving the home that obviously meant so much to her.

"You can redecorate the place from top to bottom if you want to, honey." That was the least he could offer. And he was offering damn little, compared with the wholehearted love he'd once given Alice. "You'll like the ranch."

"I'm sure I will."

Jake winced. He had built the house there after his divorce, thinking he would retreat from Houston and the bitter memories. "It's got five bedrooms and six baths. And half a dozen rooms downstairs. There's plenty of space to put whatever you want. I didn't bother furnishing a lot of the rooms."

"Oh. I assumed you'd have hired a decorator."

"It seemed crazy to have the whole place fixed up just for me, since I'm away most of the time."

"I see. Will you be spending much time there after we're married?" When she twisted her ring around on her finger, he noticed her hands were shaking.

"Weekends, mostly. This field will keep me pretty busy for the next year or so, but at least it's close enough so I can fly back and forth."

When he saw her shocked expression, he grinned. "Not in the Lear. I have a twin-engine Cessna I keep out at the ranch. There has to be someplace close to Groveland where I can land it."

Kate smiled. "There's a little airstrip about two miles from my house. Mike Thomas might be willing for you to use it. He has a couple of old airplanes he uses to do crop dusting."

"That would be good." Suddenly Jake realized he didn't want to be away from Kate five days a week. Not as long as his cock was demanding regular attention from her pussy.

"You know," he said, "if the noise doesn't bother you too much, you could come back and forth with me. We could stay at your place. I'd like that."

"So would I. Are you sure I wouldn't get in your way?"

Kate was pretty, but when she smiled at him the way she was doing now, Jake thought she was downright gorgeous.

"You wouldn't be in the oil fields with me while I work. And I like to have you getting in my way at night." Jake paused.

It wasn't just that he wanted Kate around to fuck. He liked waking up and finding her curled up next to him. And he enjoyed the easy companionship they shared sometimes when they both let down their guard.

He could handle those feelings, he told himself. As long as he could hold back the deep, tender emotions that would give her the power to hurt him.

"Would you like that, honey?" he asked, and he reached out and took her hand. With one finger, he nudged the big diamond in her ring.

She was going to be his wife. He recalled the other promise he'd made to the Old Man before he proposed — that he'd start a family without delay.

Keeping her with him made sense. He'd have a better shot at getting her pregnant if the sex wasn't limited to weekends when he made it home. His balls tightened painfully when he imagined fucking Kate every day without a condom between his cock and her tight, wet pussy.

"I'd like to stay with you." Her slender fingers tightened around his hand, as if she shared the sudden sexual tension that just washed over him. "You said you'd like children. Did you mean you want them right away?"

"Yeah, if you don't mind. It's time. I'm thirty-one years old, honey. You're...hell, I don't know how old you are, do I?"

There were a lot of little things he didn't know about Kate. That bothered him. There would be plenty of time to learn, though, he told himself as he stopped the car in front of her house.

Kate unfastened her seat belt. "I'm twenty-eight. My birthday is November twenty-eighth. I guess it's past time for me to start a family, too," she said as he walked around the car to open her door.

"Our birthdays are close together. Mine's the third of December." He got Kate's suitcase and followed her into the house.

"We can celebrate together," he said, setting the bag in the hallway.

"I'll like that. Are you going somewhere?"

Should he listen to his cock or his brain? Stay here and fuck her until they were both exhausted or go check out the drilling situation with Skip? His brain won out, but it was a damn close call.

"I'll be back. I told Skip I'd go over the seismic readings with him and Fish as soon as we got back. Besides, I need to drop my stuff off at the trailer."

Her soft curves tempted him, though, and he wrapped his arms around her and rested his cheek against her silky hair.

"You aren't going to stay here with me?" she asked as she snuggled up closer.

"Not all night. Your neighbors wouldn't much like me moving in before the wedding." And he didn't want to give sanctimonious biddies like Gladys Cahill another stick to beat over Kate's head. "I'll sneak out of your bed and sleep in the company trailer until we're legal."

"But—"

"This isn't Houston, baby, and we're gonna be spending time together around here for a good long time to come." He tweaked her nipples, grinned with satisfaction when they beaded up against his fingertips. "Don't take that to mean we're not gonna have our fun."

"All right. But Jake, I'll miss waking up with you."

No more than he'd miss sleeping with her soft and warm in his arms.

"Give me a kiss," he said as he tunneled a hand into her hair. When he finally broke the contact and stepped back, his cock was so hard he thought it might burst.

"I'll be back for dinner," he said, and then he left while he still could. For a long time, he suffered with a painful hard-on.

* * * * *

Kate wandered around the house, looking at pictures, glassware and furniture she'd lived with all her life. Her feelings were jumbled. She loved Jake dearly and was anxious to marry him and start their family.

But a small voice kept reminding her he didn't return her love. And the thought of taking family treasures out of the home they had graced for generations tore at her heartstrings.

Sighing, she sank down onto a battered recliner that had been Pop's favorite spot to rest. Without Jake, she was at loose ends. How quickly she'd become accustomed to the comfort of his presence.

She'd called Becky and put a chicken casserole into the oven. Now, Kate knew she should start sorting through boxes that held more than a hundred years of family memories. Even though Jake said she could send it all to his ranch, she couldn't take everything. She should pack what she couldn't bear to part with and make arrangements to discard the rest.

She'd start that job tomorrow.

Now she leaned back in Pop's old chair and began to revisit memories she'd leave behind when she moved with Jake to Texas.

Pop used to hold her on his lap in this chair, reading Dr. Seuss books and telling her stories about her several times great grandfather who came to Groveland and built this house. While they'd taken their time together each evening, her mother had sewed or knitted, her slight body curled in a corner of the sofa by the window. Whenever Pop had said something interesting or funny, Mom had set down whatever she was doing and joined in the laughter. Even though Kate was the only one left now, she had a strong sense of family.

Pop had instilled it in her. From his stories, she'd come to know each of the long-dead family members whose pictures hung in nearly every room of the house.

Jake's home soon would be her home.

Keeping that in mind, Kate decided she needed to move everything she wanted to keep, now. She wouldn't send much furniture—only a few pieces that had special meaning to her—so they'd have enough left to use here while his job demanded he be near the Groveland oil field.

The sound of the back door opening startled her.

"Jake?" she called out as she levered herself out of the chair.

"I'm in here, honey. What smells so good?"

She smiled when she caught him sneaking a peek inside the oven. "Chicken casserole. And green beans."

"I'm starved. How about a kiss?"

When she moved close to him, his arms came around her like a vise. He deepened her kiss with a deep, hard thrust of his tongue. When he broke the contact and set her away from him, she saw him shudder.

"Is that about ready?" He looked tired. From the look of his stained jeans and dusty boots, he'd been busy out at a well site.

"Give me five minutes. Do you want to wash up?"

Jake frowned. "Yeah, I want to clean up. You'd better get used to this, though. I work, I get dirty. I won't be coming home squeaky clean after I've been out in the fields."

"I don't expect you to. I have seen you dirty before, you know. Remember when the well came in and you came running up here and kissed me? You might as well have taken a bath in crude. But I loved it. You don't need to clean up on my account." She glanced his way, wondering why he suddenly had gotten moody.

"Sorry. It's been one helluva long day. I'll feel better once I wash off some of this Mississippi mud."

Jake didn't much like the surly guy staring back at him a few minutes later from the wavy old mirror above a sink that sat precariously on a shaky pedestal in the downstairs bathroom.

Kate hadn't done anything to deserve his sarcasm. And he had no business taking out his anger at Alice on her. Frowning, Jake scrubbed the worst of the grime off his hands and forearms.

His ex-wife had no sense.

Alice must have lit out from Houston the minute she'd left his office yesterday, because by the time he'd arrived at the well site, she was already there, working on Skip to let the pressure off her precious insane husband.

It had pissed Jake royally that he had to spend the time he'd set aside for studying new seismic readings, persuading his friend to pay no attention to Alice's drivel that she'd get his drilling company blackballed by all the Texas independents— and that by the time GreenTex got through with Yates, the other company's credibility in the industry would be zero.

Now, instead of spending most of the night pleasurably occupied in bed with Kate, he was going to have to devote that time to reconciling his gut feelings about where they should sink the next wells with Fish's scientific projections.

Skip had a crew here, idle, and another on its way from west Texas. Every day Jake delayed deciding where to drill, he was pouring money out for nothing. Thanks to Yates and his sabotage, GreenTex was operating too close to the edge to waste thin resources.

Knowing Alice was close by unnerved him, too. He didn't put anything past her. In fact, he'd been relieved not to have heard from Kate that his ex-wife had paid her a visit while he was gone.

Unfortunately she could always show up tomorrow.

How would Kate feel if Alice asked her to intercede on behalf of her present husband? More important, at least to Jake, was the question of how Kate would react when he refused to let up on Yates. He didn't know.

Not knowing had him as surly as a rattlesnake who hadn't caught a mouse for weeks. He toweled his hands and face dry and tried to wipe the sour expression off his face.

When he joined Kate, she had set dinner out on the kitchen table. The coffee bubbling on the back of the old gas stove put out a pleasant, stimulating smell. And the fragrant steam coming off that chicken thing made his mouth water.

There was something calming about the look and smell of home-cooked food, Jake decided as he sat down and began to eat.

He knew one thing. He'd do whatever he had to, to keep Alice and her desperate efforts to free her bastard of a husband from disturbing the peace he'd found with Kate.

"I've got to work tonight," he said, hating to break the comfortable silence. "Skip needs to start setting up rigs tomorrow for two new wells."

"So soon?" She looked disappointed.

Hell, she couldn't be any more disappointed than he was that they'd miss out on sex for the first time in nearly a week. "Yates and his hirelings have already put us off schedule. You're gonna be family, so you've got the right to know I have to get big production out of this field, fast. If I don't, GreenTex just might go belly up."

"But you've got millions of dollars' worth of equipment, Jake. And what about the planes and that office building you dislike so much?"

"All that costs a bundle to keep running. This field will put us back on top or bust us, depending on how fast we can get it into full production. The sabotage here and out near Lubbock has us months behind schedule. Now I have the added job of seeing that Yates gets the punishment that's coming to him."

"Who is this person? And why did he target your company for his dirty work?"

"A rival oil man." Jake wished he could leave it at that. "And my ex-wife's husband."

Kate's eyes widened. "What?"

"Yates Oil and GreenTex have been competitors since long before I was born. From what I know, the competition was friendly until about fifteen years ago, when my father and Durwood's bid on the same offshore leases. Yates got the properties, but when they ended up being worthless, Durwood started spreading rumors that Dad and Scott had bid up the price, knowing that they would drop out and leave Yates with expensive drilling sites that had no value."

"But that's not justification for this man to blow up oil wells."

"Durwood was always a hothead. When he took over Yates Oil after his father died a few years back, he swore he would get even with us about that offshore deal. He left his wife and started sniffing around Alice every chance he got. She resisted him for a good long while," he said, giving his former wife credit for remaining faithful for most of the years when he'd spent so much time far away from home.

Jake rubbed the back of his hand across his head, which suddenly ached unbearably. "Alice is here. She's doing everything she can to get the bastard out of jail."

"I'm so sorry."

"So am I. I wouldn't have mentioned her, except that she may come skulking around here, trying to get to me through you. She already tried to get Skip not to testify about the seriousness of the charges."

With his thumb, Jake massaged the soft, dry palm of Kate's hand. "I thought I'd made it clear when she came to me in Houston, that I'm going to take great pleasure in seeing Durwood Yates rot in a Mississippi prison for as long as I can manage."

"Because Alice left you for him?"

He let go of her hand and clutched her shoulders in a vice-like grip.

"No," he spat out. "I'm damn tired of hearing Scott, and Skip, and now you, wondering if I place more importance on Yates having married my ex-wife than on him doing his best to put my company out of business. Because you're going to marry me, and because you didn't have to stand and watch them bury a good man and a loyal employee who died in one of the explosions Yates orchestrated, I'm answering your question. Once. But don't ever ask me again."

"I'm sorry."

She shook so hard, her tremors traveled up his arms into his own body. Guilt slammed into him, because the last thing she deserved was having him take out his anger on her. Deliberately he loosened his grip and softened his voice.

"As far as I'm concerned, taking Alice off my hands was the only favor Yates ever did for me. They deserve each other. I want to see Durwood in prison because he and his hirelings have killed one man and risked the lives of a lot of others. And because they've damn near put GreenTex out of business."

"All for revenge? How horrible." Kate shuddered.

Jake guessed that it would take her time to digest the extent of Durwood Yates's hatred. He pulled her in his arms and fueled another kind of flame, the kind he hoped would burn away his bitterness and pain.

Chapter Fourteen

The next few weeks passed quickly. Every day, Kate expected Jake's ex-wife to seek her out, but so far Alice hadn't come around.

She'd packed the remnants of her family's history, and yesterday movers had come to haul them to Jake's ranch. Tomorrow, the junk man would come get the discards— a hundred and fifty years' accumulation of belongings Kate didn't want to keep.

The house looked bare now, emptied of all the furniture except for a few worn pieces she would keep as long as Jake's work kept him coming to the Groveland oil field.

She'd miss her home. Maybe Jake wouldn't mind if she kept it. She'd like to bring their children here someday to show them her roots.

Kate visualized dark-eyed boys that looked like Jake, perched precariously on a fat limb of the old chinaberry tree down by the barn. Suddenly her smile faded.

She had no idea what Jake's long-range plans might be. He'd been so busy, they hardly had been able to snatch a minute to talk. Every day since they'd been back, he'd come to the house after spending twelve to fourteen hours at the new drilling rigs. They'd eaten and made love—that is, they'd made love when he didn't have to rush back to the trailer to do paperwork he hadn't found time for during the day.

Would it always be like this, or would he find more time for her after the trials of Yates and his cohorts were over?

Kate was frustrated. She'd talked more with Adele and Deb than with Jake. Every day, one or both of them called with questions about the wedding. And every night at dinner, Jake shrugged off her concerns that their wedding was getting out of hand.

The pond beckoned her, tempting her to go there, relax, and enjoy her favorite spot beside the cooling, greenish water. But she couldn't leave the house. Becky was coming, eager to see pictures of her bridesmaid's gown and hear the latest about the wedding.

This whole business was getting to Kate. Half of the time she wished she and Jake had just gone somewhere, found a judge, and said their vows. Deep down, she guessed, she was afraid he'd change his mind and decide he didn't want her after all.

She forced away her worries and sat down on the window seat where her mother had often curled up to read or embroider. Idly, she flipped through the pages of a notebook Adele sent, knowing Becky would expect a detailed recounting of the preparations going on in Houston.

With her finger, she traced tiny violets and leaves beaded in shades of pale lavender and green on the small sample of ivory silk Adele had sent to show her the design Cecilia was working on for her wedding gown. Kate couldn't help being excited.

She was going to feel like a princess in that dress.

If only Jake loved her, she'd be the happiest woman alive.

* * * * *

Jake dared not name his feelings love, but he cared for Kate. Every day, he felt a stronger emotional pull toward her.

Guilt ate at him. Getting permits and coordinating the efforts of three drilling teams left them precious little time together.

Now he was wasting some of that time in the Calder County district attorney's office, summoned because Alice had fed the man a pile of crap about him framing Yates to get revenge.

"I don't have all day," he snapped to the bored-looking, forty-ish receptionist who had been staring at the same magazine since he'd walked through the door.

"Mr. Randall will see you soon," she replied, returning her attention immediately to her reading material.

Jake rose and headed for the inner door. "Randall will see me now or not at all. He set this appointment for two o'clock. I didn't."

"All right. I'll go tell him you're in a hurry."

Jake watched her disappear through a scarred doorway. When she came back, she motioned for him to come on in. Randall greeted him with a politician's smile and a crushing handshake.

Jake paced, too angry to sit still while the lawyer recounted Alice's story. When Randall paused, he stopped and made eye contact with him.

"I'll admit on the stand to having been stupid enough to marry Alice. But you're way off base if you believe the reason I want Yates behind bars has anything to do with him having married her after we divorced. Hell, you have my statements, and plenty of witnesses to back them up, about the trouble the man has made for GreenTex over the years."

"Look, Mr. Green. I want Yates convicted on every count. I'm running for the state senate next year, and winning this case will put me head and shoulders above the guy who's planning to run against me.

"Not to mention, of course, that my primary goal is to uphold the law," Randall added with another down-home grin.

"Can you tell me honestly you'd be pushing this so hard if the man hadn't stolen your wife?"

"Damn it! If anything, I'd give the bastard a medal for that." Jake slammed his fist down on Randall's cluttered desk.

"You're not still smarting about her leaving you?"

"I'm smarting so much that I'm marrying Kate Black in five weeks. But I thought you knew that."

"I'd heard you and Kate were gonna get married," Randall said. "Still, I'm worried about your ex-wife getting on the stand, persuading the jury you're lying about Yates to get back at him or her. She's one hell of a looker."

Jake shrugged. "If you're going to stew over it, I can't stop you. Personally, in your place I'd be jumping up and down with glee. Durwood Yates gave you an ironclad case against him when he hired his arsonists. You'd damn well better convict him, if you don't want a lot of GreenTex money going to your opponent's campaign for that senate seat next year. Kate and I will be at the trial. I'll make sure it's obvious to the jury and everyone else that I'm not pining over Alice."

Randall ran a pudgy finger under the collar of his shirt. "Y'all do that. Sorry to have called you away from your work. But I had to see you saying your feelings about Yates's wife aren't tied up with your statements about what he has done to your company."

"They aren't. I'll see you at the trial." Jake turned to leave.

"Don't forget now. Bring Kate." Randall's voice echoed down the hallway as Jake made his way out of the courthouse annex.

Bringing Kate might seem a damn good idea to Randall, but Jake wasn't so sure. Maybe Scott had been right. Maybe hearing him testify and having to face his past head-on would hurt her. And he didn't want that.

* * * * *

That night Jake slept over. They made love for hours—sweet, tender love unlike the usual fiery sex that left her body sated but her heart unsure.

It seemed to Kate that Jake's feelings for her were growing stronger. And his solicitous attention over the next few days reinforced her happiness.

On the day of the trial, she dressed carefully in the yellow suit she'd had on when he asked her to marry him. She wanted to look her best, so as not to shame him in front of the woman he'd once loved.

"All this mess will be over soon," he told her, holding the car door open for her in front of the courthouse. Strain showed in the lines that bracketed his mouth.

"I hate it that you have to go through this," she told him.

"Not a problem. I've wanted to see Yates put away for a long time." He put his arm around her, and they walked slowly up the courthouse steps.

Kate spied a tall, blond woman surrounded by what looked to be an army of lawyers who were all wearing three-piece suits despite the August heat. Jake's biceps muscle twitched against her back.

"That's Alice holding court over there," he said through clenched teeth.

His bitterness was evident, its edge as sharp as any knife. His expression had hardened, and his arm tightened almost painfully around Kate's waist.

"Do we have to talk to her?" She could barely speak past the knot in her throat.

Not able to fight off envy, she stared resentfully at Alice's blond curls and the white linen suit that set off her slender figure to perfection. No wonder Jake couldn't bring himself to care for anybody else. He'd been married to a goddess.

Oh, no!

The goddess had just detached herself from the contingent of attorneys and was approaching them with a look of desperation on her perfect face.

Jake's grip tightened even more.

"Alice," he said curtly when she stopped directly in their path.

"Won't you please have mercy on us? For old times sake?" she pleaded in a voice so smooth and sweet it reminded Kate of sorghum molasses.

When Kate looked at Jake, she cringed at the pure hatred she saw in his obsidian eyes. Whatever he may have said to Alice was lost to her, because he'd just broken her heart.

Jake might not realize it, but he was still capable of feeling deeply. He'd once loved this gorgeous woman, and now he hated her with a vengeance. It was painfully evident to Kate that Alice still stirred him in a way she had never been able to do.

She couldn't marry Jake. A man of deep passions, he someday would find another woman to inspire his love. Kate couldn't deny him that by shackling him to her with vows he would honor but wouldn't mean.

She had to get away. Twisting her body, Kate eluded Jake's grip and began to run, despite the steep steps and the high-heeled shoes she was wearing.

Blindly, not caring where she went, she stumbled along the sidewalk until her lungs ached. Finally she slumped onto a park bench two blocks from the courthouse. Tears streamed down her cheeks, but she lacked the strength to wipe them away.

* * * * *

Consumed with fury, Jake concentrated it all on Alice. "I'll give you the same mercy you showed my baby when you got rid of it like yesterday's garbage," he ground out from between clenched teeth.

"You must be as crazy as Yates. After all he's done to try and ruin GreenTex over the past few years, I wouldn't lift a finger to save him for you, even if we were still together and madly in love."

"Do you hate me that much, Jake? So much you'll gloat over putting the man I love behind bars for years?"

Her husky voice used to drive him wild. Now it was just a voice. And his cock that used to spring to attention at the sight of her lay docile in his pants.

"Do you hate me so much you'll let your hatred drive your new lover away?" she asked.

Suddenly Jake realized Kate was gone. His throat constricted. He scanned the curious crowd that had gathered on the steps. He glanced toward his car.

She wasn't there, either.

"Jake."

When Alice spoke, he whipped around and looked into big, tearful blue eyes she used to use so well to get her way. Her perfect face that had captivated him for so long was contorted in a mask of regret and fear.

Jake took a deep breath. "Your husband stepped off the deep end a couple of years ago, when he graduated from libel to hiring goons to sabotage GreenTex wells and drilling sites. He needs to be put away, if for no other reason than to keep him from killing more people because of this crazy vendetta. Believe me, I don't care enough about you to be going after Durwood for personal vengeance."

He felt nothing. No anger, no hatred, not even the bitterness that had festered inside him for so long. Fear was what gripped him now—tense, chilling fear that he'd lost Kate by refusing to let go of old hurts and offer her the deep commitment she deserved.

Alice's perfect lips curved into a bittersweet smile. "I had to try. I've known a long time now that Durwood was headed for trouble. He needs help more than prison, but he refuses to plead insanity. I want you to know I'll have him committed to a psychiatric hospital if we manage to get him acquitted."

She paused, her expression softening. "Go after her, Jake. Be happy."

"Why are you so concerned about me now?" he asked, touched by the tears in her expressive eyes but suspicious of her motives.

"I loved you once. I still care about you," she whispered. "One of us, at least, deserves a little happiness, don't you think?" she asked, using a tissue to wipe the moisture from her eyes.

"I don't want you to hate me anymore," she choked out as she looked down at the concrete step where they were standing.

"I don't hate you." When Jake said the words, he knew they were finally true. "They'll need you in the courtroom soon," he told her softly as he bent and brushed his lips across her cheek in a gesture of farewell.

Then he raced for his car.

Kate couldn't have gotten far on foot. At least he didn't think she could. Still sliding his legs inside, he turned on the ignition.

The trial could go on without him. Yates would be convicted on the evidence with or without his testimony.

Driving more nails in the man's figurative coffin didn't make so much difference now. Kate filled Jake's mind and his heart, and he had to let her know.

Slowly he drove around the courthouse in a widening circle. Every minute he searched, he knew that Kate was hurting, sensed her drawing further away from him. He had to find her.

He saw the little park first, with its ancient trees and weathered wooden benches. Then he spied her. Her slumped shoulders and the bereft expression on her face tore at his conscience.

I love her.

Realizing that brought Jake no joy, for he had a sinking feeling that he'd lost Kate. With unsteady hands, he pulled up to the curb and killed the engine. In a few long strides, he reached her. When she saw him, she turned her tear-streaked face away.

"Let me take you home, honey," he said gruffly.

"What about the trial?"

"It can go on without us. Come on." He reached out to touch her, but she pulled away.

"Don't touch me. Please. I can't think straight when you do. Jake, I'm not willing to be window dressing."

She said it quietly, but her voice rang with determination Jake hadn't expected. "All right. Kate, we have to talk," he said as they walked slowly to his car.

"Not now. I won't air dirty laundry for anybody who walks by to hear."

She'd drawn a curtain around herself. Closed him out. But if she wanted time, he owed her that. Owed her much more than being quiet for the few minutes it would take to get them to her house. Silently he opened the door for her and waited for her to get in.

The silence was eerie, punctuated by the drone of the car's engine and occasional soft sobs Kate apparently couldn't suppress. His breath caught in his throat when he watched her twist and tug at the ring he'd given her after she'd agreed to become his wife.

When he stopped in front of Kate's house, he killed the motor quickly and hurried to help her out.

She'd taken off his ring. Still he wasn't prepared when she dropped it gently into the handkerchief pocket of his jacket. For a moment he stared at her, disbelieving, before reaching out to take her in his arms.

She moved away, not stopping until five feet of the gravel driveway separated them. "I'll talk to you. But not now. Don't come after me. Please," she implored before taking off down the path that led to a little pond in the woods.

Her voice was ragged, her eyelids swollen and her cheeks streaked with tears. But to Jake, she was beautiful. Silently he searched for words to tell her she was wrong.

If only she would calm down and give him the chance to say what he should have told her weeks ago.

Finally he went inside and shed his coat and tie, fishing out her ring and jamming it as far as it would go onto the little finger of his left hand. Its facets caught the noonday light, nearly blinding him as he stared at it.

Had he insisted on this gaudy token for Kate's sake? He admitted now that he hadn't. It was part of the window dressing she had accused him of doing to salve his ego with his family and acquaintances.

Ironically, if he were asking her to marry him today, he would be giving her this same ring. But he'd have bought it before proposing, because it was the best, most perfect gift he could afford to express the depth of his love.

He loosened his collar and rolled up his sleeves. For the first time, Jake really looked at this old house that Kate set such store by. As he wandered from room to room, he saw signs of age and hard times in the faded wallpaper and the well-used pieces of furniture Kate had kept here for them to use. Depressed, he went into her bedroom—the place where they'd made hot, sweet love so many times.

She'd decided not to send her bedroom set or the not-quite-antique round table to the ranch. Jake stared at the table where she used to have that picture of the doctor she'd almost married.

She must have put the photo away, or thrown it out, because Jake hadn't seen it since the first time they'd made love. Now, though, he noticed an ancient looking journal resting where the framed photo had been.

The old book drew him. With care bordering on reverence, he lifted it and thumbed through its yellowed pages. Kate's great-great grandfather must have written this, he thought as he scanned entries set down in stilted English that chronicled the end of wandering, the making of a home.

He smiled at the first entry, where the author set forth his purpose of improving his use of the English language. As he read, Jake could almost see the peddler, trying to eke out a living by farming the land he'd bought, then shrugging his shoulders and taking up the trade he knew and loved after proving his inadequacy at the unfamiliar art of growing things.

One entry touched him deeply, gave him insight into Kate's devotion to her home. He read it again, aloud.

"For as far as I can see, this land is mine. In the days, I smile. Never do I let those who come to buy from me know their scorn tears at my soul. In evening, this place brings me peace. It is my home, my refuge, my legacy to my son and his sons for all time."

He set the journal down and stared out toward the woods. Kate had never expressed her feelings about her home in the eloquent way her ancestor had done. Or had she, when he'd been too concerned with guarding his own emotions to listen?

He thought of his own legacy, one of dollars and oil wells, buildings and equipment whose life spans would equal only their utility. While his grandfather had built a dynasty from oil, Kate's ancestors had tied their roots to this piece of Mississippi soil, much more than to the store that had been their livelihood.

Suddenly Jake understood. This place was all Kate had of her family, all she would have of her heritage to give their children.

Children they wouldn't have if he'd killed the love she said she felt for him. Not able to wait any longer, he strode out of the house. She'd be down by the pond, in the spot where she'd once told him she went when she needed to be alone and think.

* * * * *

Kate's heart ached, but she knew she had done the only thing she could. She loved Jake too much to sentence him to a lifetime of living with her without love.

He didn't love her, but someday he'd love some lucky woman. A woman who would touch his soul.

She heard him before she saw him. Pine needles that blanketed the ground crunched rhythmically when he came into the clearing and knelt beside her.

When he looked into her eyes, she saw pain there that matched her own.

"Don't leave me, honey," he said, as if he really cared.

Her hand went involuntarily to his cheek, already scratchy beneath her fingers even though he'd shaved a few hours earlier.

Trying to hold back her tears, she held his gaze. "I have to. For you as much as me. I can't force you to love me, any more than you can make yourself love me."

"You don't have to force me." He covered her hand with his, as if he was afraid to lose that small contact.

"You said you didn't have deep emotions left to give. But Jake, you do. You may hate Alice. But at least you feel something for her. It would break my heart to see you tied to me when I know you'll find another woman someday who can teach you to love again."

"I've found her," he said, and he leaned closer and rested his cheek against her hair. "She's you."

"What?"

"I love you. Really, deep down, love you. And I'm not about to let you go."

He leaned back and focused his dark, compelling eyes on her face at the same time he took both of her hands and anchored them to his hard-muscled chest.

With all her heart, Kate wanted to believe him. She'd dreamed that someday he'd come to love her the way she loved him. Still, the picture of him looking at Alice with absolute hate in his eyes haunted her.

She had to be sure.

Jake cupped her chin in one big callused hand, forcing her to meet his gaze.

"Honey, maybe I wanted everybody to think I'm flat out crazy over you because it's the truth. It was, even though I hadn't come to grips with my feelings, myself. I never meant to hurt you."

The raw, painful timbre of his deep voice touched Kate's gentle heart. "It does hurt, knowing you asked me to marry you to make people believe you were over caring about Alice."

As much as she wanted to believe Jake's belated declaration of love, she couldn't set aside all her doubt.

"Hell! You think I proposed so I'd have someone to rub in Alice's face when she came around trying to get me to help get Yates off the hook, don't you? Well, I didn't.

"What made me do it at the time I did was the Old Man. He's tired and sick, and he gave me an ultimatum. He called me to his hospital bed and gave me the choice between settling down and giving him some grandchildren, or being shoved—like a round peg in a square hole—into the presidency of GreenTex."

Kate's hard-won self-control snapped. "And you think I like knowing you picked me for a convenient broodmare, any more than I enjoyed thinking you wanted a smokescreen to hide your real feelings? Jake, I have some pride." She tried to pull away, but he held her fast.

"Honey, I'd have asked you anyway. Probably today, the minute after I realized I don't want to live without you. The moment I figured out that you mean more to me than Alice ever did." He paused, and the quickened beat of his heart beneath her fingertips matched her own ragged pulse.

"No. I'd have waited, just long enough to go and spend the last cent I could afford, buying you something like this—maybe even bigger. I'd have wanted you and the whole world to know how much you mean to me."

Before she could stop him, he'd worked the ring off his little finger and put it firmly back where it was before she'd given it back to him.

Where Kate wished she could be certain it belonged.

"Come here, Kate," he murmured as his mouth descended on hers.

His kiss was sweet with promise, hot with the incredible chemistry that brought them together from the start.

When he let her go, she looked into his eyes and saw more than desire. For the first time, she thought she saw love.

"I love you so," she whispered, needing to touch him as she began unbuttoning his shirt. "Love me."

"I do. I will." He reached out and touched her, and her throat constricted. She fought back more tears—this time tears of joy.

Every time he'd come to her with mindless passion, they'd ignited a firestorm that had scorched her with its desperate urgency. Now, it was as though his love banked the flames.

A gentle breeze ruffled her hair, and he played for a long time with a wayward strand, his features somehow softened now. No more handsome, no less rugged than before. But he seemed at peace with himself for the first time since she saw him at the derrick in the light of a setting sun.

He warmed her slowly, as though loving her was the only concern in his world. And when she slid off his tie and unbuttoned the starched shirt he'd put on to go to court so she could enjoy touching his supple, deeply tanned skin, he shuddered and moaned as though he'd feared never to have her hands on him again.

"For you, honey. This time it's all for you," he murmured when he stopped her from unfastening his belt and extending her explorations.

Slowly he aroused her with his hands and mouth, and she paid his magnificent body equal homage. Clothing disappeared piece by piece until they lay naked in the shade of towering pine trees, their bed a mossy bank of the small pond. Her place.

Now it was his place, too. Theirs.

When he finally knelt between her legs and slowly filled her with his hot, hard cock, they came in unison. It was as good as always—yet better than before, because their hearts as well as their bodies moved together in perfect harmony.

Afterward they lay together on the bed of velvety moss, breathing in the fragrance of the piney woods. She brushed back the dark curls from his sweaty forehead, letting go of the last of her doubts.

Kate finally believed—in Jake, in their love and their future.

His eyes opened, and his dark gaze locked with hers. His lips curved into a lazy half-smile. "We're gonna be so good together, honey," he whispered as he caught her hand and brought it to his lips. When he untangled their legs and helped her up, she realized he had made love to her this time without protection.

Finally he'd given her his trust.

Epilogue

"Congratulations, Jake!"

Another pair of beefy hands was pummeling him between the shoulder blades. He'd be damn lucky if he could still walk after all his friends got done congratulating him. Turning, he returned a punch to Mel Harrison's unguarded shoulder.

"Thanks. Hey, I wanted to tell you thanks for bringing the band to play tonight. Hours on end of music like that would've driven me insane." Jake gestured toward the staid group that was playing a medley he thought must date back at least to World War II.

"Wouldn't have missed it for the world."

Ordinarily, big shindigs like this bored Jake to death, but he'd enjoyed sharing the spotlight with Kate and romancing her in front of a crowd that ranged from the cream of Houston society to roughnecks who worked with him out in the fields.

Their part in the extravaganza was almost over, would be as soon as Kate got back downstairs from changing into whatever the hell a going-away outfit was. If he hadn't been in such a hurry to get her alone again, he would have encouraged her to stay here longer, just so he could look at her in her wedding gown.

She'd come to him, practically floating in an ivory cloud with touches of a violet sky. And when they'd danced that first dance, her eyes had shone with love.

He was certain she'd been touched when she'd realized it was him singing, "Love, Look at the Two of Us." The look she gave him made his heart constrict in his chest.

"Did I thank you and the band for the extra time you all put in, playing background music for me so I could tape the voice-over?" he asked Mel.

"Your mother did. Besides, the guys loved doing it. It isn't often that small-time folks like us get the chance to record at a grade-A studio."

Jake was glad Kate had thought to have his mother get Mel's band for their reception.

"Was Kate surprised?" Mel asked.

"Yeah. I'm not usually big on romantic gestures, so I think it meant a lot to her."

Jake resisted the urge to loosen the bow tie that was getting more uncomfortable every minute while he glanced around the ballroom again. "When does your band go on again?" He gestured at the combo across the room that had just finished playing some highbrow-sounding waltz.

"Now. Be happy, Jake," Mel said, and then he was gone.

Four hours. Kate had been his bride for four hours now. And they were going to have a baby.

Jake grinned when he saw Shana and Bear dance by, seemingly oblivious to everything except each other. Deb and Scott were dancing, too, her diamonds catching the light and nearly blinding him when he looked their way.

And there was Leah, looking slim after her son's birth last month as she coaxed Ben onto the floor again. His parents and Mama Anna smiled and waved at friends and acquaintances from their seats at the head table.

The entire wedding party had been on the dance floor earlier when Kate had told him their lovemaking down by her pond six weeks ago did more than cement those deep emotions he'd finally unleashed. The radiant look in her aqua eyes had let him know how happy she was to be carrying his child. He hoped she knew how thrilled he was.

Hell! He'd wanted to shout out the news for all Houston to hear. Fortunately he'd caught himself in time. Even he knew a formal wedding was no place to announce the impending parenthood of the bride and groom.

"Jake?"

He loved the way Kate spoke his name. There was nothing he didn't love about his wife.

"Ready?" Kate looked good enough to eat in a new outfit that matched her pretty eyes.

"I'm ready if you are."

"Then let's go." Taking her hands, Jake traced the gold band that anchored Kate's engagement ring while she gently twirled the plain gold band she'd placed on his finger a few hours ago when they said their vows.

She was his fairy princess, the woman who made him twice the man he'd been before. She gave him back his feelings, made him whole again.

Feeling fiercely protective, as if she were made of spun glass instead of flesh and bone, Jake wrapped an arm around Kate and led her through the throng of noisy well wishers.

Pelted with fragrant rose petals, urged on with raucous advice from the men who worked his oil wells, Jake and Kate walked away from their wedding, into a life he trusted would be full of love.

Enjoy this excerpt from
DALLAS HEAT
© Copyright Ann Jacobs 2003

For nearly two weeks Dan had pictured Gayla, imagined what she'd wear and how she'd fix her satiny sable hair for the banquet. The reality of her in shimmering deep red silk that hugged every tantalizing inch of her from shoulder to ankles, except for a side slit that gave glimpses of one long, silky leg, nearly took his breath away when she let him into her apartment.

"I'm almost ready. Let me get my shoes. Would you like a drink or something?"

Her smile faltered a little, as if she were no more used to going to the glitzy kind of banquet Frank had sentenced them to for the evening than he was. "I'm okay," he told her, wishing he could get out of this monkey suit, strip off her dress, pull those glittering pins out of her elegantly upswept hair, and haul her into the small bedroom he could see from her living room.

* * * * *

"Do you do this often?" she asked after they had driven into the city and Dan handed his keys to an attendant at the downtown hotel where the banquet was being held.

He took her hand, as much to reassure himself as to guide her. "No. I'm here because someone bewitched the chief of our group into believing we can reel in enough donations here so we can keep helping patients who can't afford rehabilitative surgery or therapy. Given the choice, I'd be taking you somewhere quiet—private. How about you?"

Dan felt Gayla's almost imperceptible shudder as she glanced around the ballroom. "It's been years since I've gone to an affair like this one."

"Smile, princess. We'll make this fun." In the ballroom now, Dan searched for familiar faces. His hand at Gayla's waist, he maneuvered her through the crush of elegantly clad guests, making his way to the table.

Introductions went quickly, and before long it seemed Gayla was right at home with Dan's colleagues. Her self-deprecating humor, the easy way she fit in with the members of the team—the twinkle in her dark brown eyes when she looked at him—combined to help him have fun and ignore the serious reason he'd come.

Gayla squeezed Dan's hand as they walked onto the dance floor. He made being back among the Dallas medical community seem easy. Resting her cheek against the crisp black wool of his tuxedo jacket, she let herself move with him, in time with the slow, dreamy song the combo was playing. She liked the partners he'd introduced as his family, and felt as if she belonged when they included her in their irreverent, shamelessly self-serving conversation about finding donors to placate the hospital and keep their program alive.

"I like your friends," she murmured as she watched Jim and Kelly showing off with intricate dance patterns. "Especially Michelle. Frank doesn't seem comfortable, though." The striking blond who looked more like a pro football player than a doctor had uttered maybe ten words other than when he was wooing a potential contributor.

"This is even less Frank's kind of party than it is mine. Since his wife left and took their little boy to California, his whole life is our rehab program. Nothing other than the threat of losing hospital backing could drag him to a function like this."

"Then he and Michelle aren't…"

"He more or less ordered Michelle to come with him. Since she's part of the group, she had to be here anyhow. Frank swore off women after Erica walked out." Dan increased the pressure of his hand at Gayla's back, and instinctively she snuggled closer.

He moved with an easy, natural rhythm that made her melt inside. With him she felt beautiful…protected from the spirits of her past that she'd thought would haunt her tonight.

As they walked back toward their table, the most fearsome of those ghosts appeared, and it looked as though he was heading their way. She grasped Dan's hand a little harder.

Maybe, if she concentrated hard enough, she could call on his strength as well as her own.

"It'll be all right, princess." Obviously Dan was as aware of her father as she was. Gayla wasn't sure if the tension that radiated from his hand all the way to her constricted throat was all her own.

She forced a smile and made herself look at the man she'd idolized—the one who had bitterly denounced and disowned her, she reminded herself when she suddenly had the urge to run to her father and throw her arms around him. "Dad," she murmured when they came within arms' length of each other.

"Newman." Her father gruffly acknowledged Dan's presence but not hers. The lump in her throat grew.

Dan squeezed her hand as if he knew she needed the contact to realize she wasn't alone. "Dr. Harris. It's good to see you."

"It would seem that my wayward daughter has surfaced."

Her father looked not at her but straight through her. When had been the first time she'd turned his stern features icy cold like this? Gayla couldn't remember. All she knew was that this encounter was almost more than she could bear. If Dan hadn't been at her side, an anchor in this emotional storm, she'd have turned and run as far and as fast as she could.

Dan cleared his throat. "If you'll excuse us, sir, we'll go back to our table."

"I want to talk to you, Newman. Alone." Her father locked gazes with Dan, making Gayla shudder again as she turned to walk away.

After she sat down at the table beside Michelle and Frank, Gayla watched her father herd Dan into a secluded alcove. Her father's angry gesticulations and Dan's horrified expression gave her a good idea that she was the subject of the tirade. When Dan came back to the table, he seemed shell-shocked.

"I'm sorry about that, princess. I'd have liked to tell your father we'd have to postpone that talk, but with the power he has as chief of surgery, I didn't dare. Shall we dance?" he asked, his expression so earnest she wanted nothing more than to feel his strong arms around her again.

She couldn't, though. She couldn't put him in a position where her father would want to destroy him. "Please get me out of here, Dan." She tried to suck in a breath despite the excruciating tightness in her throat.

About the author:

First published in 1996, Ann Jacobs has sold more than thirty critically acclaimed books which include a Golden Quill winner, a More Than Magic winner, two EPPIES finalists, and two LORIES finalists. A CPA and former hospital financial manager, she now writes full-time. Ann loves writing Romantica--to her it's the perfect blend of sex, sensuality, and happily-ever-after commitment between one man and one woman.

Ann Jacobs welcomes mail from readers. You can write to her c/o Ellora's Cave Publishing at 1337 Commerce Drive, Suite 13, Stow OH 44224.

Why an electronic book?

We live in the Information Age—an exciting time in the history of human civilization in which technology rules supreme and continues to progress in leaps and bounds every minute of every hour of every day. For a multitude of reasons, more and more avid literary fans are opting to purchase e-books instead of paperbacks. The question to those not yet initiated to the world of electronic reading is simply: *why?*

1. *Price.* An electronic title at Ellora's Cave Publishing runs anywhere from 40-75% less than the cover price of the <u>exact same title</u> in paperback format. Why? Cold mathematics. It is less expensive to publish an e-book than it is to publish a paperback, so the savings are passed along to the consumer.

2. *Space.* Running out of room to house your paperback books? That is one worry you will never have with electronic novels. For a low one-time cost, you can purchase a handheld computer designed specifically for e-reading purposes. Many e-readers are larger than the average handheld, giving you plenty of screen room. Better yet, hundreds of titles can be stored within your new library—a single microchip. (Please note that Ellora's Cave does not endorse any specific brands. You can check our website at www.ellorascave.com for customer recommendations we make available to new consumers.)

3. *Mobility.* Because your new library now consists of only a microchip, your entire cache of books can be taken with you wherever you go.

4. *Personal preferences are accounted for.* Are the words you are currently reading too small? Too large? Too...**ANNOYING**? Paperback books cannot be modified according to personal preferences, but e-books can.

5. *Innovation.* The way you read a book is not the only advancement the Information Age has gifted the literary community with. There is also the factor of what you can read. Ellora's Cave Publishing will be introducing a new line of interactive titles that are available in e-book format only.

6. *Instant gratification.* Is it the middle of the night and all the bookstores are closed? Are you tired of waiting days—sometimes weeks—for online and offline bookstores to ship the novels you bought? Ellora's Cave Publishing sells instantaneous downloads 24 hours a day, 7 days a week, 365 days a year. Our e-book delivery system is 100% automated, meaning your order is filled as soon as you pay for it.

Those are a few of the top reasons why electronic novels are displacing paperbacks for many an avid reader. As always, Ellora's Cave Publishing welcomes your questions and comments. We invite you to email us at service@ellorascave.com or write to us directly at: 1337 Commerce Drive, Suite 13, Stow OH 44224.

Discover for yourself why readers can't get enough of the multiple award-winning publisher Ellora's Cave. Whether you prefer e-books or paperbacks, be sure to visit EC on the web at www.ellorascave.com for an erotic reading experience that will leave you breathless.

Printed in the United States
29403LVS00002B/55-690